HÉCT

ETERNITY

IN

KYOTO

A Novel

TUTTLE Publishing

Tokyo │Rutland, Vermont│ Singapore

Contents

PART ONE

Heaven's Gate

HEIAN AND THE
RASHOMON GATE

The city of Heian, Japan's former capital city, was first founded over 1,200 years ago. The literal meaning of "Heian" in Japanese is "peace and tranquility." Emperor Kanmu constructed Heian following the Chinese architectural model, where straight streets align with the four cardinal points, each associated with a creature from Chinese mythology. The city was protected by walls, with a main entrance gate to the south called Rashomon.

Heian developed quickly, and by the late twelfth century, with hundreds of thousands of inhabitants, was one of the most prosperous places on the planet. Today, we know this imperial city by its modern name: Kyoto.

The Rashomon gate was erected as a symbol of power and protection for the city, but it brought nothing but trouble and misfortune. The gate had to be rebuilt several times after falling victim to fires and enemy attacks. Corpses and unwanted babies were abandoned there. Over time, it gained a reputation for being cursed to the point that it was not reconstructed.

Tourists visiting the Rashomon gate today will be disappointed. There is only a small stone monument marking where it once stood. The best way to imagine the gate, and the Kyoto of the past, is to visit Heian Shrine in the east of the city.

The shrine (平安神宮, Heian-Jingu) is one of the most important Shinto complexes in Kyoto. It was built in 1895 to commemorate the 1100th anniversary of the foundation of Heian, in the architectural style of the Heian era.

It is an ideal place to feel transported to the past. It can be visited every day of the year; its gates open at six in the morning and close at five in the afternoon.

1
THE LAST PORTRAIT

The wheel of my destiny began to turn one Sunday when a mysterious energy compelled me to clean the office. I had spent the morning at my computer refining the design of a watch. After several days of putting the finishing touches to the mechanical components, I was proud of the organization of the wheels and pinions, which were visible from the outside.

I was so focused on the task of adjusting the final details, that it wasn't until I heard the first raindrops hitting the window that I realized I had been in absolute silence for hours. For once, the music that usually masked my freelancer solitude wasn't playing. I had a slight headache and a creeping sense of unease.

I stepped away from the screen to contemplate the final result, as if it was a painting in a museum. It was finished, I decided: nothing to add, nothing to remove. I sent the design files to my Swiss client and immersed myself for a moment in the satisfaction that humans feel when finishing something.

But soon a void opened beneath my feet as I wondered, "And now what?" I played the B-side of my favorite vinyl record, a 1999 album by Sakamoto titled *BTTB*, Back To The Basics. I grilled some bacon and ate it with two fried eggs, lettuce and pickles. But neither the music nor the food was able to calm me.

I continued with my usual project closure ritual. Between bites, I threw away the printed proofs of the design I had just sent. I placed the pencils and markers in their correct containers, and even wiped the accumulated dust off the computer monitor with a cloth.

My friends considered it extremely "vintage" of me to still use paper. They said I was trapped in nostalgia for the past, but it helped me in the creative process. It was a habit my father had instilled in me: "If you can't solve it with pencil and paper and just rely on a computer, you won't understand anything. The pencil helps you think, the computer thinks for you."

Next, I made myself a green tea, turned the record over and sat on the sofa with the intention of letting myself be carried away by the music. The sound of the rain had become so intense that it intertwined with the melody of Ryuichi Sakamoto's piano in the track "Energy Flow," turning it into something different. I still felt anxious. I got up again, deciding to continue cleaning. As I went to get the vacuum cleaner, something compelled me to open the built-in closet next to the door of the room. It had been closed since the day I moved into the apartment five years ago.

Inside were three cardboard boxes.

The first one was full of dragon drawings. These had been my escape during my student years. I studied those sheets of paper with fascination. Some had so much detail that it seemed as if the scales were about to come off the page. I wondered if I still drew as well now as I did back then.

In the second box, I found an old collection of photographs, among them snapshots of various girls I had dated, almost forgotten. I found one of my last girlfriend. We were together for a while, but when she turned thirty, she told me we didn't share the same life goals. At first, I thought she was joking. I had been comfortably resigned to spending the rest of my life with her, but the final blow came when I discovered she was already with someone else.

Since that last disappointment, I had been alone and had lost hope of finding someone to share the rest of my life with. With a lingering sense of bitterness, I closed the box and pushed it to the back of the closet.

I opened the last box. It was full of useless things I'd mercilessly stuffed into a garbage bag: postcards from my first trip to New York, a box of candy from my English grandmother, industrial design magazines, books I never finished reading, music I no longer liked . . .

Among all those relics, I came across a picture of Mia and me, a raft for two in the shipwreck of time. I had almost forgotten that faded color photo. We both smiled unabashedly. Her emerald-green eyes, large and slanted, stared at the camera with such intensity that it felt like she was looking at me through a window. Two white earrings sparkled, adding a playful touch to her ears, tiny compared to her round face, larger than you would expect on a slim body like hers.

Her small, almost nonexistent nose hinted at her origins. Of Japanese descent, she had always been the odd one out at school. Perhaps that's why we had become friends. She wore a blue tank top that exposed the fair skin of her shoulders. I wore a black sweater that I still put on sometimes when I don't feel like leaving the house; it has the Schrödinger equation on the front, with a white cat walking along the top of it. The photo showed that I hadn't cut my hair for months. My head was like a pot holding a mass of hair. My arms were still hairless, but bulky biceps were starting to appear, thanks to the serious gym training I had embarked on. But I still looked like a geek.

Mia's cheek rested on my shoulder. Dark strands of her hair fell over my chest, covering the head of the white cat. She looked relaxed as she leaned into me, but I seemed tense, my stiff torso leaning slightly away from her. Looking again into Mia's eyes, they were like two floodgates, releasing the past. I was seventeen again, sitting with her on that dark gray sofa. We'd met in high school. Her family had moved from Japan because her American father had got a job at the same company where my father worked, but in a different department.

As the daughter of a Japanese mother and an American father, she carried an exotic aura. She was an eccentric girl, but being the most beautiful of the misfits, she gradually became the leader of a group of manga-loving geeks. In contrast, during my student days, I was a solitary soul.

At first, it was challenging to befriend her, but when we realized we shared a passion for Japan and retro video games, we ended up talking almost every day. My obsession with her reached such an extreme that there were times she appeared in my dreams at night. But our romance never crossed the boundaries of my fantasies. She was one of those girls you fall in love with when you're young that you don't have the courage to pursue. I spent years on the sidelines while she dated various other boys. I was the "nice guy," the friend who listened to her when she was down. After using me as a shoulder to cry on, she always moved on to the next boyfriend.

Mia and I took that photo one night at my house, when my parents were away on a business trip. She had asked for help studying for a math exam. We usually met at the library, but, seizing the opportunity, I plucked up the courage to invite her over. It was the first time in my life I'd invited a girl home. I guess that's why I remember in detail what happened that day—and also because it was the last time I saw her before she disappeared. We solved problems with matrices and tensors, as I explained every step to her. Soon she began to yawn, and in the end, she wasn't even listening to me.

"Math is killing me with boredom," she said. "I want my life to be an adventure."

I went on about how math is also an adventure, as it helps reveal the secret code underlying the physical laws that govern the universe, but that didn't seem to motivate her in the slightest. She sat there wiggling her nose from left to right, a gesture that momentarily marred her face and one she usually made instinctively when she didn't like something.

She moved from the desk to the sofa. From her bag, she took

out the novel *The Sound of Waves* by Yukio Mishima—the Japanese-language version that I'd lent her—and began reading. The reading absorbed her so much that it seemed like she wasn't there with me anymore.

I continued studying, but eventually I gave up. All I could think about was that I was alone with her. I went to the kitchen, heated up some water, and prepared two Cup Noodles. I left them covered on a small table in front of the sofa, but she didn't look up until she'd finished reading the last page of the novel ten minutes later. Then, we made a start on the noodles and, between mouthfuls, discussed Mishima's book.

"I've fallen in love with Shinji," Mia said. He was the protagonist of the story.

"He's just a fictional character that emerged from Mishima's imagination."

"For me, he's very real. Especially the scene where Shinji kisses Hatsue for the first time in the middle of the storm, next to the warmth of the bonfire, both naked . . ."

Her perfectly round cheeks blushed as she spoke.

"But after the kiss, she rejects him," I countered. "And Hatsue's mother won't allow her daughter to marry Shinji. It's surprising that traditional values and family opinions in Japan at that time had such an influence."

"You haven't understood anything," said Mia, taking the last noodles from the bottom of the cup with her chopsticks. "So her family's opinion weighs on her, but that's not what holds her back. She sees Shinji as a boy, not as a man. She feels insecure with him."

At that moment, I couldn't help but compare the relationship between Shinji and Hatsue with ours. Mia always used me to tell me about her romances with older guys. She asked me what the difference was between them and me, and what drove her to choose guys who ended up leaving her. I wondered if she saw those guys as men and me as a boy?

"Only when Shinji performs a heroic act—when he saves

the ship from shipwreck at the end of the novel—that's when he becomes a true man. That's when he's accepted, not only by his future wife's family but also by Hatsue. She feels that she can finally open her heart to him."

"A heroic act," I thought, mentally reviewing my existence up to that moment. At seventeen years old, the most heroic events in my life so far involved killing pixelated digital monsters in video games.

As I finished my noodles, I stared at the illustration on the cover of the novel—an island with houses, a lighthouse, and a temple peeking through pine trees sculpted by the sea wind.

"Someday I'd like to live in Japan," I said. "On an island, like Shinji and Hatsue."

"Well, the sea terrifies me," Mia replied. "I grew up in a little house in the mountains of Kyoto until I was ten. Every summer, my parents took me to Asamogawa Beach to try to teach me to swim, but as soon as I saw the sea from the car, I panicked." Her voice faltered, and her face paled as she reclined on the sofa, but I didn't really understand her fear of the sea. As I poured her a glass of water, our eyes met, and I realized that our legs were touching.

"Better in the mountains, then," I said to change the subject.

After finishing the water, she sat up, moving her leg away. "In our house in Kyoto, we had a garden with sakura cherry trees surrounded by a bamboo forest," she said, composed now. "The best memories of my childhood are playing under the cherry blossoms at the beginning of spring with Mukku, our dog. He was my best friend. I wanted a brother, but my parents always had other plans." She paused and placed the glass of water next to the empty noodle cups. "I'm going to have two children and a dog." She turned to me with an inquisitive look.

"I think I would be happy with two children, a dog, and a house in the mountains of Japan," I said.

Then I felt the courage to place my hand on her waist. She tilted her head, resting it on my shoulder, and I held up my camera to take the self-portrait I'd found in the box. All of that happened at seventeen. Twenty years later, looking at the photo, absorbed in the memories of that last day together, I smiled at the innocence of our youth, a time when we didn't know what the future held for us. After immortalizing ourselves in that image, she'd leaned in to fix my bangs with her fingers, while looking into my eyes. I returned her gaze for a moment and I knew it was time to kiss.

But I was paralyzed. The kiss that never happened and the things I never told her remained suspended in time. Instead, I left her side and went to plug in the video game console. Seeing that it had gotten late, Mia asked if she could stay overnight and sent a message to her parents saying she was at a friend's house.

We played a video game where we traveled through Asian countries and explored archaeological ruins. After a while, I noticed she had dropped the game controller on top of Mishima's book. She was asleep. I covered her with a blanket and continued wandering through a Buddhist temple in the pixelated world of the video game until I fell asleep on the sofa too.

At some point in the early morning, I opened my eyes. Mia had changed position and was now sleeping on my shoulder. One of her hands rested on mine. I felt a pleasant shiver. I could feel the rhythm of her breathing, the warmth of her body, and the caress of her breath on my neck. With my free hand, I moved a strand of hair that had fallen over her face to confirm that it wasn't a hallucination.

I fell asleep again, feeling that I had fulfilled a dream, albeit in a strange and elusive way. The last memory I have of her is the warm touch of her hand on mine.

2
THE GATE TO HEAVEN

When I opened my eyes, Mia wasn't on the sofa or in the apartment, where her perfume still lingered. That last encounter became an ethereal memory that faded with time but never completely disappeared.

After reminiscing about the first time I'd slept next to a girl, I put the photo on the desk. Looking at it, I felt a warmth in my hand, as if an invisible Mia was there, caressing me. Her green eyes in the snapshot seemed to be looking right into mine. But Mia was gone, and so was everything that could have been. All I had was that photograph and memories stained by the passage of time. I took a sip of the now cold tea and sat by the window, watching the rain fall. Emptiness dug a hole in my heart. For a brief moment, I had the strange certainty that I was alone in the universe. Sakamoto's piano was my only companion. The melancholic melodies, and the sound of the driving rain made me keep reflecting on the past.

After Mia, I met the one who would be my first girlfriend, and after her, there were other girls I fell in love with, some more than others. All my relationships, whether they ended well or badly, had fallen into the pit of oblivion. However, with Mia, a lingering sensation remained in a corner of my being, like a distant star timidly flickering.

She didn't show up for the math exam. In fact, she never showed up at the school again. When we asked the teachers, they told us that her family had returned to Japan. Years later, I found out from Anabel, who had been her best friend, that Mia had committed suicide in Kyoto at the age of twenty-eight. That was the end of my fantasy of meeting her again.

When I received the news almost ten years ago, a heart-breaking sadness mixed with anger overwhelmed me, thinking that the person with whom I had shared so many special moments no longer existed. Perhaps it was the shock, but when Anabel told me, I didn't ask any questions. But on that Sunday of emotional archaeology, I began looking for Mia on the Internet. Why had she committed suicide? I hesitated before going on RealPeople and searching for her profile. Is it morbid to peek into the digital remains of people who have passed away? It's like digging into a grave or reading the diary of a dead person.

I took off the Sakamoto record and put on Chopin. A faint nocturne filled every corner of the house and my soul. Outside, the rain had turned into a storm. When thunder overhead made the window vibrate, I put on a wool sweater and turned up the thermostat a couple of degrees. Then, I pressed the search button, and her profile picture appeared.

Her face was barely visible, in the shadow of a wide-brimmed hat. Surrounded by vegetation, she seemed to be in some kind of Japanese garden. Her full lips hadn't changed; they were just like the ones in the photo resting on my desk.

I began exploring Mia's past through her activity on RealPeople. She had few friends on the platform and had uploaded only about a dozen posts, which were illustrated with photos.

In the first post, Mia talked about moving to Kyoto from Tokyo where she had been living. This, apparently, was her motivation for signing up to RealPeople:

> Since my family moved back to Japan I've been living in bustling Tokyo. Life's been uneventful, jumping from one job to another. But I finally have something interesting to share. I've been granted a scholarship

> to research the history of Heian! That was the name
> of the ancient capital of the country, now known as
> Kyoto. I don't know what this adventure will bring me.
> For now, I'm packing my bags and moving to Kyoto.
> Japanese kisses!

Under this message, she had posted a photo of herself smiling, next to a bullet train. She had become a woman, but her face was just as I remembered: round, with an air of innocence. But there was a hint of mystery in her eyes, as if she wanted to tell the world something but kept it to herself. From the date of the RealPeople post, I worked out she would have been twenty-five, but in the photo, she could pass for twenty. She wore faded jeans and a thin sweater that highlighted prominent breasts.

This first snapshot had the most likes of everything she had posted, although only ten "friends" had deigned to share the adventurer's enthusiasm. In the next post, there were two photos: in one, she was posing with a backpack at the entrance of an old building with peeling walls and rusty beams; in the other, she was in an office. The post read:

> I'm already settled in Kyoto. This is my office for the
> next few months, where I will focus on studying the
> past of this city. The building is ugly, but the view of
> the matsu pine trees from the window is beautiful. The
> office is inside the Heian Kyoto Foundation museum.
> And most importantly of all, I really admire my boss,
> who's a great expert in Japanese history!

The rest of the posts showed photos of her at iconic places in Kyoto and at other locations in the country, with some explanations about their history. Mia always wore the same tight jeans, sometimes with a hat, sometimes without one, and she was always alone. In some photos, she posed in front of a temple, and in others, she was in a restaurant showing what she was eating. In one photo, she was sitting on the floor in front of a lonely table with a steaming bowl of ramen, and in the next one, she was holding a tray with various types of tempura. Almost all the photos had just one or two likes. No one seemed to care about Mia's life.

In the last entry, she was in a deserted park, with a slide and a couple of swings in the background. She was standing in front of a stone totem about six feet high with the inscription 羅生門, Rashomon. She was holding an English-language copy of *National Geographic* magazine. The cover showed a huge wooden gate and the words: "Heaven's Door. A voyage to the unexpected Japan."

> I'm a cover girl! The results of my research in Kyoto on the disappearance of the Rashomon gate is the leading story in the latest edition of *National Geographic*. Now, only this stone pillar where I'm standing remains, but the cover shows a digital reconstruction that I designed to conclude the study. Thanks to everyone who helped me fulfill this dream. Love you all!

There were no likes for this last photo. If the information Anabel had given me when she conveyed the tragic news was correct, that last photo had been taken the year Mia died. But the success of being published in *National Geographic* and her joyful expression in the photo she had shared on RealPeople gave no indication that she was going to end her life. Of course, social media is a space where even those with miserable lives or going through difficult times share brief moments of happiness.

I was glad to see that she had achieved her dream. But that fleeting feeling was swept away by the regret of never having made the effort to stay in touch with her. Could I be the first person to see this last photo? Or had no one dared to click on like, knowing that she had taken her own life? Other RealPeople pages that belonged to someone who died sometimes have messages from family members explaining the circumstances of the death, but in Mia's case, there was no further activity on her account. It had frozen in time.

After exhausting all the information about her, I was so tired I couldn't keep my eyes open. The record-player needle had made its way to the end of Chopin's first five nocturnes.

I dozed off for a moment and woke up again to a flash of lightning tearing through the night sky. Seconds later came a rumble of thunder, traveling at the speed of sound until it collided with my heart. Dazed, on the border between consciousness and the dream world, I clicked like on Mia's last photo, the one where she was holding the *National Geographic*.

Instantly, I finally fell under the spell of Morpheus. I dreamed that I was standing in front of a huge black wooden gate. I knew that this was the gate that used to be in the place in Mia's photo where now only a stone pillar remained, and which she had digitally reconstructed for that *National Geographic* cover. In my dream I had traveled back in time, perhaps many centuries.

The gate was closed, but I wanted to know what was on the other side. Two large bronze rings invited me to open it, but I didn't even try. Something paralyzed me. My whole body had frozen. Somehow, I knew it was locked, and it wasn't worth the effort.

I felt a presence: something or someone was watching me; it could see me through the wood. But I just kept standing there, in front of the ancestral gate. Hanging from it was a wooden plaque with characters in kanji and a note in English:

羅生門 天国への門
RASHOMON: GATEWAY TO HEAVEN

After reading the words, I looked again at the bronze rings: mysterious black dots had appeared on the surface of both; there were exactly twelve on each.

Just like my freckles.

3

OUR SECRET CIRCLE

I was born with twelve equidistant freckles forming a perfect circle about an inch in diameter behind my left ear.
They decided to name me Nathan because they considered
it an international name and easy to pronounce in any language.

My father was an engineer, a key member of the team that
brought the first fusion power plant in history into operation.
My mother worked in the sales department of a multinational
insurance company.

I had a quiet and uneventful childhood but I was very lonely.
I remember my parents always being busy. It was common for
them to be away for a month at a time on business trips, and
to top it off, they worked most weekends. I envied my friends
who spent weekends with their families. Over time, I learned
to manage without anyone, even to enjoy solitude, but perhaps
that abandonment is one of the reasons why I've always had a
void inside me that I've never known how to fill.

Video games and books became the refuge for my heart, my
drug to complete myself. During adolescence, I devoured all the
novels of Frank Herbert, Robert A. Heinlein, Ray Bradbury, and
Philip K. Dick. As with books, my taste in video games always
leaned toward the retro; I loved playing with emulators of old
game consoles. I've always detested the modern. After learning
Japanese, I began devouring classics of Japanese literature and
playing Japanese video games. That's how my obsession with

Japan started. At the age of fifteen, I started practicing martial arts and watching classic Japanese movies.

Another of my coping mechanisms was to try to please others at all times. Even if they didn't ask, if I sensed someone needed something, there I was. Perhaps my subconscious expected something in return: affection, love? As a result, I ended up being the sucker who repaired electronic devices for all my acquaintances. They only talked to me when they needed help, with repairs, with homework or with anything related to science and engineering. But, even though I knew I was a pushover, I couldn't help but respond to the calls of others.

That's how I spoke to Mia for the first time: I offered to help her with a homework assignment on computer history. Our afternoons in the library quickly became a regular thing. But before long, we discovered our shared passion for reading and retro video games. As I gained confidence, I bombarded her with questions about Japan, where she had spent her childhood before her father was transferred overseas.

Neither of us had brothers and sisters and our parents weren't around much. This meant that when she didn't have a date with one of her boyfriends, we spent many hours together reading or playing video games. But there was something more important that we always shared, which would end up defining the destiny of our lives, mysteriously intertwining them. We each had the same twelve freckles that formed a small perfect circle behind our left ear.

It wasn't noticeable unless you paid attention, especially in her case because she always wore her hair over her ears, carefully styling it to hide the freckles. Mine were visible. Everyone in class knew that I was the guy with the circle behind his ear. No one teased me about it because it was cool; the freckles were aligned so perfectly that they looked like a tattoo.

"Now that I trust you, I want to show you something," Mia said to me one day, after we'd known each other a few months.

That day, instead of our usual library, we were in in a café.

The plan was to spend the afternoon reading a novel by Kawabata. The place was almost empty, and we sat in a corner next to a window overlooking the mountains surrounding the city.

Two cups of coffee rested on the table. Before taking the first sip, Mia turned so that her left side was facing me. At the same time, she lifted the strand of hair covering her left ear with her hand. I remember that moment in slow motion: her hair rose in the air like a wave about to break.

When I saw the circle of freckles behind her ear, exactly like mine, my heart skipped a beat. Then I felt mildly betrayed.

"Why have you hidden this from me all this time?"

"It's not something I like to share with people I don't trust."

"But I'm your friend, right?"

"I noticed you from the first day of class. I saw your ear and your twelve freckles. Believe me, my initial impulse was to come and talk to you."

After a short silence, I recovered from the surprise. "Why do you think we both have the same circle of freckles?" I asked.

"What explanation did your parents give you?" said Mia, throwing the ball back.

"My father says it's something good, that it makes me special and different from others. But my mother won't talk about it."

"And they haven't told you anything else?"

I took a sip of coffee, scanning the horizon, before I spoke. "When I was a child, my father told me one day that he had made the decision to add a special gene to my embryo before I was born. He claimed that this would help me in the future, but he didn't say how exactly. Apparently, my mother opposed it, saying it was a bad omen. I never dared to ask them any more questions."

"That's the same story my parents told me . . . And have you never been curious to know what else they might have modified in us, apart from adding freckles?"

"I've never really thought about it," I said. "And anyway, you and I don't look alike, apart from that circle behind the ear."

We both laughed.

"Now do you trust me?" I asked her.

Mia flashed a mischievous smile. "Yes, but there are a still a few things I'm keeping secret until the time is right."

I never shared that conversation with Mia with anyone. But I always suspected that the things we discussed were related to the fact that our fathers worked for the same company.

When I woke up from my dream in front of the Japanese gate with the Rashomon emblem, my studio was flooded with morning light. Last night's storm had gone. I brewed a cup of coffee and went to my desk. The photo I had found the day before was still there, reminding me that Mia had been a part of my life. As I looked at the image, still confused, I touched again the back of my ear, tracing with my finger the circle of the twelve freckles. It was a tic I'd had since I was a child, but it only affected me in the early morning. It helped confirm that I was awake, not in a dream.

When Mia was still alive, it comforted me to know that there was another person in the world with the same circle. Since she'd gone, I wondered if I was now the only one in the world with the circle behind their left ear or if there was someone else.

After spending the weekend finalizing the design of a watch, that Monday, I had nothing to do. I could only wait for the next assignment from my Swiss client, one of the last companies still manufacturing mechanical watches. They had been paying me the same rate for years, but I couldn't complain. I enjoyed the work, and I didn't need more to live. Besides, I knew they couldn't do without my services because there were no longer any traditional designers in the world of watches.

I put on a Bob Dylan vinyl LP that started with *Knocking on Heaven's Door*. As I began to listen, I remembered the dream in front of that imposing door that I hadn't dared to open. With Bob Dylan's raspy voice in the background, I performed my daily routine on the yoga mat: push-ups, squats, and five asanas.

I felt tempted to lie down on the sofa and spend the day reading. I was rereading *Dune*, one of my favorite novels. Frank Herbert's words took me on a therapeutic journey to the planet Arrakis, the source of eternal life. Or, I could play Uncharted, a fascinating series of retro video games from the early 2000s. From the comfort of my home, I could explore, travel, search for treasures, and fight against pirates without sustaining a scratch.

Reading and playing video games is what I would have done on a free Monday, but that morning, I got a message from my martial arts sensei, asking if I would help him paint the walls of his dojo. When I stepped out into the street after so many days indoors, the sun's rays blinded me, glancing off the puddles formed by the previous night's rain.

Since I was a kid, my sensei had been a constant support. He taught me jujutsu from a young age, and we also practiced Japanese together. He was a father figure to me.

We spent the morning painting the walls, an almost meditative activity that we carried out in absolute silence. When it was time for a break, we went to a small office at the back of the dojo. My sensei took two bottled green teas from the fridge.

"What's going on?" he asked.

After so many years, there was no one who understood my emotions better than him. Just by looking at me, he knew how I felt.

"Nothing . . ."

"Are you sure?"

"A friend I lost contact with committed suicide some time ago. Yesterday, I found a photo of when we were seventeen, both smiling."

"Rule number one: you are not responsible for other people's lives, only your own."

"Maybe if I had stayed in touch with her, I could have helped her," I murmured, looking down.

"You don't have to feel guilty about other people's decisions."

I took a sip of the green tea. It was refreshing and delicious after hours of painting walls. "Is there a rule number two?"

"Number two is: never keep photos or memories of your exes. They only serve to reopen scars from the past." He laughed as he said this, but I wasn't in the mood.

"She's not my ex, just a friend."

"Friend, ex, whatever—it's clear that you felt something for her, and you've reopened the wound. True love doesn't understand the passage of time."

"If you don't take care of yourself first," he said, putting his hand on my shoulder, "you won't be able to take care of others. Let's train!"

We took our half-finished bottles of tea to a corner of the room with tatami flooring where the walls were still unpainted, and we began practicing katas. On the wall was the large scroll that had always hung there, showing a giant dragon in black and white, whose eyes seemed to follow us wherever we moved. I wondered if that ancient picture had been responsible for my obsession with drawing dragons during my student years.

After finishing several rounds of katas, we started sparring.

"I feel like my life has derailed," I said, when there was a break between the kicks and punches.

"Stop kicking and aim for the real goal, Nathan."

"What do you mean?"

"Everything is the same: the kick, the punch, your way of living, and your appreciation of beauty. Either you're lost, or you're on the path."

We continued practicing until we were exhausted. The reddish glow of the sunset spilled through the window to illuminate the dragon on the scroll. Last night's storm had cleared the sky of every last cloud. While toweling off our sweat and taking our last sips of tea, we realized that we hadn't eaten. My sensei surprised me by inviting me to dinner at his favorite Japanese restaurant, run by a friend from Kyoto. Over sake, he told me about his life in Japan before he moved overseas. He spoke nostalgically about his old dojo in Kyoto and his two masters.

"Why don't you take a trip to Japan?" he inquired.

"I don't know if I could manage a trip on my own," I replied.

"It's something you've dreamed about since you were a child, and now you're free to fulfill that dream."

"I will, one day, but I'm just not sure if it's the right time yet."

Sensei opened his well-worn leather briefcase, retrieving a business card from an inside pocket. With a slight bow, he handed it to me. It bore the address of the Taira Jujutsu Dojo in Kyoto, home of the preeminent masters of that venerable martial art.

"You won't be alone if you go there, Nathan."

"Thank you, Sensei. So . . ." The idea was beginning to dispel the shadows cloaking my heart. "So if I go to Kyoto, is it OK if I just show up at the dojo?"

"Of course. In the ancient capital of Japan, you'll find a family. You've been studying Taira jujutsu with me for thirty years. They'll welcome you like a son and will give you a place to stay and everything you need."

When I got home after dinner it was already eleven o'clock, but I wasn't sleepy. I started reading Eiji Yoshikawa's *Musashi*, the story of the eponymous warrior who was one of the most admired and feared samurai in Japan. Then, before going to sleep, I took a look at my RealPeople account, where there was an unread notification. It was from Mia's account.

> Thanks for the like on the last photo.
> I miss you, Nathan.

For a moment, I wanted to believe it was Mia, but that feeling quickly turned into anger:

> I know Mia is no longer with us. Who are you? You shouldn't impersonate her and put words in the mouth of a dead person.

4
THE CALL

When I woke up, the first thing I did was check my RealPeople account for a reply from the impostor. Nothing. I made myself a coffee and opened my inbox to see if a new assignment from Switzerland had arrived. I found a brief message:

Dear Nathan

Thank you for the watch design. As always, it has exceeded our expectations. We will transfer the funds to your account at the end of the month. Due to organizational restructuring, it will take some time before we kick off any new projects in the mechanical watch division.
A pleasure working with you.

I had always suspected that a message like that would eventually come. It was a risk I took by specializing in an industry of the past. There were barely two companies left in the world still producing mechanical watches; it was a declining market.

"Your interest in the old is fine, as understanding the past is crucial for creating the future," my father used to tell me. "But remember, both the present and the future are digital."

During adolescence, I was too lost to think about the future. Contemplating what I would do as an adult overwhelmed me.

The accident at the fusion power plant that claimed my father's life happened a few months before I began my university studies. Still affected by his absence, I studied quantum computing because it was what my father had wanted me to do. When I graduated, I got a job with a multinational corporation, but I loathed the corporate world. Although it was a company that specialized in quantum computing, everything I had learned at university was of little use. The job did not enhance my creativity; I always ended up entangled in political intrigues between departments and trapped in endless meetings.

"My father would be proud," I thought to console myself every day when I finished working on something I didn't like. Then I would start thinking over and over about the moment he left us. It was just a regular day. I had gone to school, and I spent the afternoon studying for university entrance exams. That night, my mother and I had dinner alone. It wasn't unusual for Dad to come home late, but he usually sent a message to let us know. That night, he didn't.

"He must be caught up with some emergency," my mother said, downplaying it. After dinner, I opened a book, and she turned on the TV. There was a sense of unease in the air.

"What time are you coming back today?" was the last message I sent to my father when it was already very late. He never replied. The director of the fusion power plant, close to midnight, sent us a message from the company that I will never forget:

Notice to family members (IMPORTANT)

We regret to inform you that six of our employees (names listed at the end of this message) have died of asphyxiation this afternoon in an accident that was beyond our control. We deeply regret the incident and will maintain ongoing communication with those affected in the coming days.

My heart skipped a beat as I read my father's name among the list of the six deceased. That night of waiting, and the moment we received the fateful message, etched itself into me. It was so traumatic that it took me months, even years, to come to terms with it. That night, I slept as best as I could, and next morning we had another message with more details of what had happened, written in a cold and corporate language:

Analysis of the accident - Notice to family members (IMPORTANT)

A flaw in the design of our automated systems caused a chain reaction of failures and exceptions in the code controlling one of the fusion reactors, creating instability in the ionized plasma. To minimize the probability of a major catastrophe, the Central Artificial Intelligence system made the decision to depressurize several gas chambers.

Unfortunately, at that moment, six of our employees were conducting a routine inspection in a room affected by this depressurization. The door to the room was also locked by the Central Artificial Intelligence system, to mitigate the risk of gas escape to other sectors. None of the six employees managed to open the door and they died from asphyxiation.

We have initiated an improvement process to reassess the value assigned to human lives within the code of the Central Artificial Intelligence system to mitigate similar events in the future.

We appreciate the efforts of our employees and thank them for their services, as well as their families. In the coming days, we will provide financial compensation to the affected families.

I visualized my father trying to open the door until he suffocated. The horrifying image was etched in my mind forever, as if I had been in that fateful room. His funeral is blurred in my memory, like a dark cloud of disconnected fragments. His death created a void within me that I have never known how to fill. Sometimes, I wonder how my life would have been if that disaster hadn't happened.

But although his death weighed heavily on my decisions when it came to studying and starting to work for a multinational company, I soon realized that my happiness could not depend on what my father would have wished if he were alive.

After a year of working for the quantum computing company, I resigned. I began sending the watch designs I had been creating in my free time to different companies, until I received a response from Switzerland. I ended up specializing in mechanical watches.

It wasn't intentional but rather an instinctive rebellion against the distress that working for a multinational caused me. My mother wasn't happy when she found out about my decision.

"What would your father say if he saw how you're wasting your potential?" she said.

My relationship with her had cooled over time, especially after I left home, and she moved in with a boyfriend I never liked. However, we continued to see each other occasionally until she died of a heart attack.

What would my parents say if they knew that, at the age of thirty-seven, I had failed in all my relationships and was without stable employment? But still, I had enough money saved to live comfortably for a while without commissions. So I didn't respond to that message from my only faithful client. Or rather, my once faithful client.

After half an hour of yoga on the mat and a shower, I returned to the adventures of Miyamoto Musashi that I had left the night before. Suddenly, a voice call on RealPeople interrupted my reading. When I saw that it was from "Mia," I couldn't believe my eyes. Instinctively, I brought my hand behind my left ear to make sure I wasn't dreaming. My touch detected the twelve freckles.

"Hello?" My voice trembled as I spoke.

No one answered, but there were people speaking in the background in Japanese. Male laughter sailed over the formless and mysterious sea of voices.

"Who are you? How did you get Mia's account?"

After a few seconds, during which only the distant murmur of voices could be heard, the laughter fell silent, and a deep male voice said, "You shouldn't have clicked like on the last photo."

"So you think clicking like on a photo is worse than stealing the account of a dead person?"

"You've got it wrong, Nathan," came the emphatic voice, louder now, deep and cold.

"Do you know what an *oni* is?" the voice said.

"No."

"Since you like to snoop around on social media, pay attention." The owner of the voice seemed to be breathing with difficulty. "A too-curious child once followed his mother into the forest. She always told him she was going to pick mushrooms, but her trips became longer, and the child felt lonely at home. One day, he followed her into the forest and saw a strange creature appear. The boy hid behind a bush. The creature was an oni—a Japanese demon. When these demons decide to interact with mortals, they take on human form. You can recognize them because they are larger than us. They are strong and powerful, with muscles that no human being could possess."

There was a moment's silence before the voice continued. "Oni are cruel and can destroy entire towns and cities, but they can also steal the hearts of women. Like the mother of that kid—the kid who was forced to watch as his naked mother cried out with pleasure from beneath the demon."

The voice stopped again. Ten seconds went by. Filled with confusion, I thought they'd been cut off, but then the voice came back.

"The story has several endings. In one version, the oni realizes that the child is watching and captures him to devour him in front of his mother in ecstasy. In another, the little one manages to run to the village and tell his father, who fights the oni and ends up dying. Whatever the version, curiosity ends up destroying the child's life."

"What are you trying to tell me? Who are you?"

"You've seen what you shouldn't have seen."

"I haven't seen anything!"

"You've seen the gate."

Confused, I wondered what was wrong with seeing a photo of Mia showing the Rashomon gate on the cover of a magazine. But the voice surprised me again.

"Sooner or later, you were going to dream about the gate; it was inevitable. The moment of truth has come, Nathan. Soon, you'll know why you were born."

"I don't know what you're talking about," I said, feeling a chill. "Who are you? How is it possible that—"

"Do you really want to know?" interrupted the voice. "Do you want to see what's on the other side of the gate? For that, you'll have to come to Kyoto."

After a few moments of silence, the voice added, "Don't be the kid who hid behind the bush, Nathan."

And then the line went dead.

5
MOUNT FUJI

As I looked out the window, I sensed a certain lightness within me. Away from my usual routine, I felt like a fish leaping into a rushing river, letting myself be carried along by the current, after a life confined to a lake.

This time yesterday, I had received a call from a stranger using Mia's account on RealPeople. Now, I was in Japan. It was my first time in Asia, and the current that was carrying me was the maglev train bound for Kyoto.

Undoubtedly, it had been a hasty decision. No matter how much I thought about it, I couldn't understand why I was in this part of the world following an anonymous call. I wondered what would have happened if I hadn't decided to clean the office that Sunday, if I hadn't opened the box with Mia's photo, if I hadn't pressed the "like" button on her last post. Probably, I would have continued to swim down the same old river that had been my life for years.

There were so many questions in my mind. How did that stranger from Kyoto know I had dreamed about the Rashomon gate? Did he know Mia? How had he taken control of her account? Had she given him the password before committing suicide? These questions had me heading straight for the airport.

As the plane accelerated down the runway, I felt like a detective setting out to solve a mystery in a faraway place. However, when we landed in Japan, I realized that I didn't have a plan.

My only clue was that call lingering in my memory like a hallucination. I suspected that there was a hidden agenda for me on this trip.

Getting to Tokyo Narita Airport and boarding the maglev train had been too easy. As emphasized by the author of *A Geek in Japan*, a book that had been gathering dust on my shelf for years, rule number one was, "Don't worry, Japan is easier than it seems." The book said it was one of the safest countries in the world, and it was hard to get lost since there was always a train to board and a Japanese person willing to help.

Here was the paradox: it was impossible to get lost in Japan, yet I felt completely disoriented.

While I was lost in thought, an attendant entered the car with a trolley of food and drink. She smiled as she moved down the aisle, maintaining a regular pace. She announced something in a high-pitched and monotonous tone that sounded like a chant amid the silence of the car. The passengers seemed to ignore her presence. I was the only one watching, fascinated by her smooth, robotic presence. I was hungry, but I didn't dare to stop her to ask for something. I feared being reprimanded if I interrupted that ritualistic dance along the aisle.

When she reached the end of the car, the attendant turned to face the aisle she had just walked along. She looked up and placed the palms of her hands on her abdomen. She paused for a couple of seconds and then executed a bow, tilting her torso forty-five degrees. She left the car, taking a step back without turning at all until the door closed automatically.

As soon as she disappeared, I turned my gaze back to the window. The Tokyo suburbs were gradually fading away, transforming into rugged mountains. After going through a tunnel, the landscape turned into clusters of houses. They all had identical shapes and dull colors, as if they had come out of the same factory, or had been arranged by an indifferent player of a city-building simulation video game.

The train was swallowed by the darkness of another tunnel

as we plowed our way through a mountain. Silence had fallen since the attendant had left the car. I could hear the tapping of a computer keyboard in the row behind me. In front of me, someone was leisurely flipping through the pages of a newspaper. It was refreshing to see how Japanese people combined the old with the new, that some still read on paper, like me.

Shortly after exiting the tunnel, the silence was unexpectedly broken by excited voices. Several passengers had risen from their seats to look out the window. Some raised their phones and took photos. Others took no notice, absorbed by their phone screens.

The man in suit and tie sitting next to me—some kind of executive businessman, perhaps—was eating a rice ball without taking any notice of the excitement, sipping from what seemed to be a beer can. The rice ball looked somewhat bland, but the executive seemed to be enjoying it as if it was a delicacy.

Intrigued, I decided to join the passengers who seemed fascinated by what was happening. I stepped into the aisle to look out of a window on the opposite side. That's when I glimpsed the majestic silhouette for the first time. A triangle with a conical peak and slightly curved sides was outlined on the transparent surface of the window. The snow-covered summit was gleaming.

Childlike excitement took hold of me, and all my embarrassment and shyness disappeared for a moment. I asked two young girls sitting at the window on that side if they would let me come closer to photograph Mount Fuji. Blushing, one covered her mouth with her hand and shrank into her seat, the other nodded at me shyly.

The first one stood up next to me, making slight bows while indicating with her hand that I could sit in her place. After thanking her, I knelt in her seat and leaned over the other girl to look through the window.

In the foreground was a city, full of low, whitish buildings and prefabricated houses. It felt as though we were rocketing above it. Electrical cables, streetlights, and industrial chimneys dirtied the landscape. I had read that Japan was one of the few places in the world where cables were still above ground; I had seen this kind of wiring in photos, but it was startling to see it with my own eyes.

Beyond the tangle of cables, where the city ended, that man-made chaos gave way to the majestic Mount Fuji. Awestruck by the image of the mythical volcano, I took several photos. We were moving so fast that it soon disappeared into the distance. I returned to my seat, feeling a sense of wonder and gratitude for the unexpected spectacle I had just witnessed.

I needed to share that moment with someone, so I sent a message to my martial arts instructor.

> The day after our dinner, something happened that inevitably led me to the airport. I'm going to use the Taira Jujutsu Dojo card you gave me! I'm on my way to Kyoto and just saw Mount Fuji. I've attached several photos.

After sending the message, I searched in my book about Japan for the chapter on Mount Fuji. Although it was considered an active volcano, the last eruption was in 1707. This sacred mountain had been a source of inspiration for poets and artists from time immemorial. I imagined travelers centuries ago passing by on horseback. For people in those days, the mountain was a god who, if angered, could spew fire, flames, and magma from within.

I closed the book and my eyes. I was exhausted from the long journey. As the train pulled in to Kyoto, the warm rays of the setting sun poured through the glass roof of the station, casting shadows of passengers along the pristine platform. I made my way through the station and out into the street, where I was hit by the oppressive heat and humidity that engulfed the city in the month of August. I stopped, and looked around, noticing a communication tower reminiscent of Soviet Russia. From my pocket, I took out my phone, and entered the address on the card my sensei had given me.

I hopped into a robotaxi. The car door opened smoothly, and once I was seated, it closed again. I noticed the crocheted covers on the seats, fascinated that the Japanese took the trouble to decorate the interior of a driverless taxi with artisanal details. I told the car my destination, and it started immediately.

Inside the robotaxi, the noise of the city faded away, and Beethoven's Ninth Symphony took center stage. Through the window, traditional temples rubbed shoulders with modern office blocks. After reading and dreaming about the old capital so much as a child, I could finally see it. It felt strange to come face to face with this world that was both familiar and unknown. I had a constant sensation of déjà vu.

Checking my messages, I saw that my sensei had responded. He said he'd told the Taira Jujutsu Dojo that one of their students needed accommodation.

The robotaxi proceeded along a broad avenue and then turned right, crossing the Kamogawa River. Wide and shallow, the river was bordered with trees and grassy areas. People strolled in groups and couples along its banks. A group of children sat on the grass next to their bikes, playing with their handheld consoles.

The low-rise buildings on each side of the river revealed that the city was watched over by wooded mountains. As we headed toward the mountains in the east, my robotaxi entered an alley that snaked up between trees and small houses until it reached a building illuminated by a single streetlamp. Night had quickly fallen, and a gentle rain mixed with the humid air, forming an atmospheric mist. Beethoven's Ninth Symphony was nearing its end, and I was reluctant to move until I heard the last note. Through the rain-spattered window, I read on the entrance door: Taira Jujutsu Dojo. As soon as I got out, a skinny little man emerged from the shadows and greeted me with a silent bow and a smile as he took my luggage.

The robotaxi disappeared into the darkness in search of its next passenger, and the song of crickets took a strange prominence, along with the faint rustling of trees swayed by the wind.

We entered the lobby, and the man introduced himself as the building's concierge. He was middle-aged, with slouched shoulders and glasses held together with tape. He told me that his boss, the founder of the dojo and a friend of my sensei, had been unable to come and meet me and had asked him to come instead. After this brief introduction, we walked down a hallway, and as we passed an open double door, I caught a glimpse of a large tatami-covered room where three men were practicing jujutsu under the light of two lanterns.

In the rest of the building—which had around thirty rooms, the man told me—the silence was so profound that it felt completely deserted.

At the end of the hallway was my room. The concierge gave me the key and explained how to take out the futon from the closet. When he closed the door, I lay down and immediately closed my eyes.

With the time difference, I couldn't even work out what day it was. In the limbo between sleep and wakefulness, I thought once again that none of this would have happened if I hadn't started cleaning my apartment on Sunday. By opening my Pandora's box, the wheel of my destiny had begun to move in a strange, new direction. My past was stranded far behind me, and this was a new beginning. For a moment, a mysterious nostalgia overwhelmed me, not for the past but for what was yet to come.

Soon after, I succumbed to fatigue. On that first night in Japan, I slept for twelve uninterrupted hours.

6
THE DOJO

Confused by jet lag, I woke up thinking I was still in my studio. My body was already in Japan, but my mind wasn't quite there yet. The unfamiliar feel of the futon on the tatami flooring helped me readjust my awareness to the fact that I had arrived in Kyoto.

I looked around. I was in a six-tatami-mat room. Through the window I could see a shadowy forest. A strange and unfamiliar aroma filled the air: it was the scent of tatami mixed with humidity. I left the room, which didn't even have a bathroom.

I found a bathroom in the hallway, but no showers. I headed to where I had seen three figures training the night before. Peering through the doorway, I saw thirty men sitting in meditation, lined up in rows of ten, silently facing the windows, which overlooked a garden with a pond.

I shifted my gaze from the meditators and spotted the emaciated figure of the concierge at the end of the hallway. He was gesturing at me. I didn't understand what he was trying to convey, but from his serious expression, I gathered that he didn't appreciate my intrusion into the room where the men were meditating. As I approached him, his gestures became increasingly abrupt. He crossed his arms with fury as if he didn't want me to come closer. Finally, when I was standing next him, he gave up and stopped gesturing. I asked him in Japanese where the showers were, but he didn't reply. He simply took his phone out of his pocket and wrote in Japanese characters on the screen:

> Strict rule of our dojo: absolute silence throughout
> the building before seven thirty.

In response, I grabbed his phone and wrote:

> Okay, but where are the showers?

> You can't use the showers before seven thirty.

I looked at my phone; it was six fifteen. Resigned to this Kafkaesque situation, I headed for my room, the concierge's eyes boring into my back. I passed the thirty men still meditating. The aura of serenity emanating from the room gave me a sudden feeling of calm, so I decided to go in, and sat in the last row.

The first thing I observed was a gigantic wall hanging decorated with the same dragon that adorned the dojo where I had trained my entire life. Its eyes seemed to sweep the room, as if supervising every movement. Next to the dragon hung another smaller scroll with traditional Japanese calligraphy:

世々の道をそむく事なし

I knew that the words meant "You will not act contrary to the great future that awaits," and I reflected on them for a moment as I sat down in the same position as the others, closed my eyes, and focused on my breathing. The first few minutes felt long and tiresome until, subconsciously, I entered a state of relaxation, forgetting about time until the gong sounded at seven.

The thirty meditators stood up in unison. I noticed looks of discomfort, although one of them bowed to me before pointing to a cabinet at the back of the room. There I found a uniform for practicing martial arts. I assumed that meant we would now practice Taira jujutsu.

For the next hour, I practiced the same katas I had learned as a child with my sensei. But now I was in Japan, at the founding school of my style. I performed well in that environment. In fact, I was concentrating so deeply on the perfect execution of each movement that I forgot I was in the Land of the Rising Sun. Between kata and kata, my stomach began to growl with hunger, and sweat started to soak my uniform.

After the solo kata practice, we paired up. Suddenly, the largest and most muscular of all my companions stood in front of me. I noticed his left eye was bionic: a black cover surrounded the center, where a small screen displayed an artificial eye. His right eye was slanted, but a dark blue. From the electronic eye, a long scar traversed his cheek to end near his powerful jaw. He had a shaved head, but a bushy beard.

"My name is Kamyu. *Yoroshiku onegaishimasu,*" he said in a low, deep voice, bowing. I responded by stating my name and echoing "yoroshiku onegaishimasu." Seconds later, he launched a kick that I instinctively blocked. But I could barely keep up with the pace of the rest of his movements. His skill surpassed mine and that of my sensei, with whom I had been learning all my life. I practiced with Kamyu until, finally, the eight o'clock gong sounded. I wasn't used to training with such intensity.

"You're good," said Kamyu.

"Thank you, but you're better," I replied, bowing with my hands pressed to my legs.

"I hope this doesn't scare you," he said, pointing to his electronic eye. "I lost my eye in the Battle of Mongolia."

I smiled, unsure whether I should look at his electronic eye or his biological blue eye. "I need a shower," I said, feeling the sweat running down my body.

"Now, everyone goes to the *ofuro.*"

I knew that *ofuro* meant "bath" but I had never experienced a traditional Japanese bath. I followed the others down the hallway, toward a translucent door. We undressed in a changing room and tossed our sweaty uniforms into a huge bucket, which was picked up by a woman who didn't seem the least bit embarrassed about seeing us naked. We went into the shower room, were we sat on plastic stools and washed ourselves. Finally, we went outside to the open-air bathing area. A huge ofuro was filled with steaming water, surrounded by a beautiful garden. We immersed ourselves in a tub so large that we could all fit in at once and I found myself surrounded by thirty naked Japanese men. Bathing in those dark, sulfurous, volcanic waters after meditating and practicing jujutsu was so enjoyable that I forgot I was hungry. As I relaxed, I took in the view of the garden, with its trimmed pines extending to a forested mountain slope.

"You must be the newcomer, welcome!" said some of my companions, wearing on their heads the small towels they'd used to cover their modesty. I bowed my head and thanked them. Kamyu sat in a corner of the bath, separated from the rest of us, his back against a rock. His bionic eye was switched off, and his biological eye was closed. The muscles of his shoulders and chest could be seen through the steam of the water.

After our bath, we went to the dining room, where the concierge and the woman who had taken away dirty laundry served us each a breakfast tray with a grilled sardine, a bowl of rice, a bowl of miso soup, and a plate of fermented natto beans. A dried sardine with pitiful eyes accompanied by fermented soybeans wasn't something I craved early in the morning, but the rumbling of my stomach forced me to devour it. Everyone ate voraciously without exchanging a word. When I finished eating, I dared to break the silence by asking, "Where is the founding master of the dojo?"

Everyone laughed in unison, except Kamyu, as they gave me incredulous looks, as if I had just asked something stupid. Finally, one said, "He hasn't been around for years. Now, he has more important matters to attend to."

"I just wanted to thank him for the hospitality. Isn't there anyone who runs this place?"

"Not really, but the dojo belongs to Taira Corporation."

"The same Japanese corporation that controls half the Internet, including the site RealPeople, whose founder and CEO hasn't been seen in public for decades?"

"Yes, that's right," another replied. "Japanese companies tend to diversify. Mitsubishi, for example, makes everything from pencils and chopsticks, to nuclear fusion reactors."

A chubby young man sitting at our table chimed in. "Did you know that Nintendo started by selling playing cards? They even ran love hotels in Kyoto and had a taxi service in Osaka. Japanese companies spread like cockroaches—they'll do any type of business. Taira Corporation is the same; it controls the world's largest social networks, has robotaxi companies all over Asia, and much more, but the business started with the foundation of this dojo." He thumped the table with his fist to emphasize his next words with certainty and pride: "Our martial art, Taira jujutsu, was the spark that changed the entire world."

Kamyu stood up and gestured for me to follow. We walked in silence down the hallway. When we got to the reception, Kamyu bowed to the concierge.

"The envelope," he said.

The small and scrawny concierge looked like a dwarf next to Kamyu. He opened a drawer and handed me an envelope. "Before opening it, you have to sign here," said the concierge, pointing to a kind of receipt.

I signed my name and wrote the date, and then I opened the envelope. Inside was a handwritten note.

Dear Nathan
  We're glad you arrived safely in Kyoto. I'll be expecting you at Smart Coffee at 10:00.

"Who sent me this?" I asked, surprised.

The concierge shrugged. Kamyu gave a grimace that made his neck muscles stand out. He swung open the front door, a silent prompt for me to embark on the journey to Smart Coffee.

7
SMART COFFEE

The shop was filled with the aroma of roasted coffee beans. At the entrance, an old coffee roasting machine was on display with metal levers and huge buttons that gave it a steampunk air. The place had about a dozen tables with leather chairs. Floral-themed paintings hung on the walls. Most of the customers were middle-aged, except for two boys in school uniform who were looking at their phones.

An extraordinarily beautiful young woman was reading a book at a table at the back of the room. Her sky-blue dress hugged her curvy body. Black hair framed a face that emanated purity and harmony. I stared, hypnotized by the delicate way she turned the book's pages, by her long legs visible under the table. I managed to turn away to survey the clientele of Smart Coffee, but I didn't see anyone who looked like the person who had written the note, although of course I had no idea who that person was. Amid these musings, the girl in the blue dress stood up—she was taller than me—and walked toward me.

"Nathan?"

I couldn't believe she had really said my name.

"Yes," I said, taking a step forward.

"Nice to meet you. My name's Reiko," she said, with a bow.

As we sat down, our gazes met. Her eyes were large and dark, and each iris seemed to contain kaleidoscopic patterns that hinted at otherworldly secrets.

"The pineapple cake they bake in the mornings is delicious," she said, breaking the uncomfortable silence.

Her voice had a sweet yet firm tone. I didn't particularly like pineapple, but I didn't want to go against her.

"Pineapple cake and coffee," I said.

"Do you want white coffee or blend?"

"Just black coffee."

"I think you mean blend coffee," she said, smiling.

"I just want black coffee, no sugar or anything."

"Here, we call coffee without anything blend."

"One of those, then," I said, realizing that although I'd mastered the Japanese language, I was lost with cultural details. Reiko spoke to the waitress, then turned to face me again.

"I thought I was going to see the man who suggested I come to Kyoto," I said, trying to sound more confident than I felt.

"You mean Masa. I work for him. I'm his trusted person for simple tasks like this."

"Then you can explain why I'm here. How does your boss have the password to my old friend's account?" I said, getting straight to the point. I didn't care that she had just labeled me a "simple task." I didn't mention that her boss magically knew I had dreamed of the Rashomon gate. Maybe she knew too and had answers?

She looked at me with surprise and disappointment. "Don't you know it's bad taste to ask a woman about another woman?"

I was speechless. Reiko shifted in her seat, and crossed her legs. I couldn't help but trace those long legs with my gaze. I knew she was aware of my boldness. But her expression remained completely relaxed. I, on the other hand, was tense, my clenched fists resting on my legs under the table.

"Also, in Japan, it's considered impolite to talk directly about business before both parties get to know each other," she added.

The waitress, dressed in a white shirt and black waistcoat, brought the order. I took a first bite of the pineapple cake, unsure of what else to say.

"What's wrong? Don't you want to know who I am?"

"Yes . . . Of course."

She took a sip of her coffee and tucked a strand of hair behind her ear. I caught sight of something on her neck, just behind her ear, but her hair quickly fell back to its natural position and it disappeared before I could figure out what it was.

"I was lucky to be born here, in the best city in the world," she said, after taking her first bite of cake. "I've never wanted to live anywhere else, and when I travel, after a few days, I find myself thinking about how nice it would be to go home and take a walk along the banks of the Kamogawa River. Have you seen it?"

"I crossed it when I came; it's wider than I imagined."

"Crossing it is not enough to feel it. You have walk along the banks, following its course. It's even better at night when its waters are darker than the starry sky."

"I'll add it to my list of things to do," I replied, feeling as though I was having a conversation with a travel guide. "What makes you think Kyoto is the best place in the world?"

"I guess many of us tend to think that what is ours is the best."

"Not necessarily. I've always wanted to escape the place that I'm from, but I never succeeded."

"You've succeeded now. You're here with me in Japan."

"Yeah, but it's just a short trip."

"Well, you can't be sure about that," she said.

Reiko smiled, with a touch of arrogance, as if she knew something I didn't and was hiding it. A few moments of silence passed between us, filled with the murmurs of customers and the sounds of plates and cutlery.

"Where was I?" she asked.

"You were born in Kyoto . . . You've always been here."

"Oh, yes! I went to school, and college here. I recently did my PhD in philosophy at Kyoto University," she said proudly.

I nodded to indicate that I was listening, but my gaze still didn't know where to rest. I felt that if I looked into her eyes I would fall into a bottomless pit.

"Masa told me you're a brainiac."

I felt uneasy that she knew this. Perhaps her boss had obtained that information from my RealPeople page, where I showcased each of the watches I designed.

"I'm more of a failure who wanted to follow in my father's footsteps but couldn't. I left my career in quantum computing to design everyday objects, like the watch you're wearing."

I felt my ego inflating enough to be able to converse with this extraordinary woman.

"Wow!" she exclaimed, looking at her wrist as if she had never seen the watch before.

"You're fashionable; it's a model I designed a year ago."

"You're a multitalented genius—Masa is right."

"About what?" I asked nervously.

"Masa is convinced that your brain is unique."

Amazed, I took another bite of the pineapple cake and a sip of the bitter coffee. I've always liked the abrupt change from sweet to bitter—it's just like life. Reiko continued to fix me with her gaze, and I had the strange certainty that this extraordinary woman understood things about me that I didn't even know.

"You must be intelligent too," I said. "A PhD in Philosophy doesn't seem easy."

"It was very easy! The hard part is earning enough money to live in Kyoto."

"Is that why you work for Masa?"

"Yes, he pays me generously, and he's always treated my family well. And also because I admire him. He's an important man, you know."

"I don't know anything about him. The only contact I've had with him was when he hacked into Mia's RealPeople account, and we had a strange conversation that included him telling me a Japanese fable about oni demons. Honestly, I didn't like him."

Reiko brought the hand with the watch to her mouth and laughed, covering lips that seemed drawn by the strokes of a painting genius.

"Don't judge him by that one conversation. Masa may seem cold and somewhat strange at first. According to him, dramatic stories serve to activate parts of our subconscious that are asleep. He likes to play pranks and tell stories to test the personality of his future friends or enemies." For a moment, another smile that was difficult to interpret appeared on her lips. "You're fortunate to have been able to talk to him," she continued. "Masa is a hard-to-reach man. There are people who have spent their whole lives waiting to meet him and will never succeed. He owns more than a hundred companies in Kyoto, grouped under the Taira Corporation holding. The social networking site he developed, Real People, is one of the most popular globally."

I leaned back in my seat to digest what she had just said. Connecting the dots in my mind, I realized that Masa was the abbreviated name of the legendary Masahiko, one of the richest men in the world. He had disappeared from public view for over a decade, amid rumors suggesting illness.

This piece of the puzzle revealed by Reiko, along with what my dojo companions had explained to me at breakfast, led me to another unsettling conclusion: Masahiko, or Masa as Reiko called him, was the founder of the Taira Jujutsu Dojo.

Why had my sensei hidden the business success of the founder of the school of jujutsu we had been practicing for so many years? I hadn't known it, but Masa had been in my life, at least indirectly, for a long time.

Coincidence?

"Being the owner of RealPeople doesn't give him permission to use users' private accounts," I said.

"How innocent you are. Privacy doesn't exist! Masa can know everything."

"Everything? Even what I dream?"

She flashed another sarcastic smile, with a air of superiority, while narrowing her seductive eyes.

"Exactly." She spoke with great emphasis. "Thanks to your circle of twelve freckles, we can read your dreams."

8

TAIRA CORPORATION

Don't look at me like that—there's an explanation," she said, seeing my bewildered expression. "The cards of your destiny were shuffled before you and I were born. Masa will tell you more. I'm just the messenger."

"And why would someone so powerful want to see me?"

"Masa needs you. He'll explain everything."

Reiko excused herself for a moment to go to the bathroom. Meanwhile, I took the opportunity to send a message to my sensei.

> Why did you never tell me how important the founder of our dojo is now in the business world?

Forgive me, Nathan. I promised your father not to say anything, to protect you. Not knowing certain things helps you live.

> I'm not a child anymore. I don't need anyone to protect me. I thought you taught me jujutsu so that I could handle any situation in life.

You'll understand soon. I'm leaving this in the hands of our founder, Masa.

When she came out of the bathroom, Reiko went straight to one of the waiters and paid the bill. Then she said, "Let's go. Masa is waiting for us."

The pedestrian street ended in a cobbled square, surrounded by traditional wooden houses. The determined clack clack of Reiko's heels echoed above the murmur of a stream and the rustle of weeping willow branches. We passed a group of girls dressed in floral yukata kimonos. I wanted to stop and take pictures of that scene reminiscent of another time, but Reiko quickened her pace. As I fell behind, I was captivated by the graceful way she moved, almost seeming to float.

We crossed a wooden bridge, and Reiko stopped in front of a garage nestled next to a traditional house. Inside was a silver Porsche 911.

"It's not mine," Reiko said, inviting me to get in. "We only use this company car for important clients."

It was the first time I'd ever been in such an old sports car. I felt like my seat was almost at ground level. When the car started, the strong vibration of the motor made me tremble. I felt my pulse quickening.

Despite the car's power, Reiko drove slowly along the cobbled street. Among the wooden houses appeared a Shinto shrine. The entrance was marked by a *torii* gate, formed of two orange columns, with two fox statues on each side. One of the foxes carried a kind of scroll in its mouth. As we drove past in the Porsche, I had the feeling that the foxes were watching me.

Soon we reached a street with low commercial buildings and wide sidewalks crowded with pedestrians. Reiko shifted gears, and I felt the acceleration in my stomach, as if the car, the asphalt, and my body were one. As we gained speed, a female voice began to sing a nostalgic melody.

"What did you put on?"

"It's Namie Amuro, a famous Japanese pop star who retired in 2018. Do you want to know what the song says?"

I nodded.

Reiko slowed down to a stop at a traffic light. A stream of pedestrians flowed in front of us, most of them looking at their phones.

Just when I thought she wasn't going to say anything more on the subject, she suddenly started quietly singing a song in an improvised translation:

> *We all have a spark, we shine in the darkness,*
> *we can light up the sky.*
> *Even on rainy mornings, darling, don't cry.*
> *Even when love disappears, darling, don't cry.*
> *I remember when I saw you waiting at the crossing.*
> *Your smile hasn't changed,*
> *even though three years have passed.*
> *Time flies.*
> *When I was going to call you,*
> *someone appeared by your side and I looked away.*
> *But the sky reflected in my eyes is still the same.*
> *Someday, I'll gather all the tears I've cried*
> *and make them shine in the sun.*

With Reiko's velvety voice, the purring of the Porsche engine, and the streets of Kyoto, I felt like I was living a dream.

We arrived in a high-rise district of the city. When we stopped in front of one of the skyscrapers, a security guard scanned Reiko's face by pointing a wristwatch at her for a few seconds. After the scan, he looked at her and let us pass.

"These are our offices," said Reiko. "This is the second tallest building in Kyoto after the communications tower in front of the station."

The glass-clad skyscraper reflected the blue noon sky and a couple of solitary clouds.

We left the car in an underground parking lot and got into the elevator. A small screen showed Reiko's identity data after she was scanned by the elevator cameras, and the door closed.

I noticed that there were no buttons, just a small screen indicating the floor we were on.

Sunlight flooded the glass elevator as it emerged from the basement to the first floor. Squinting in the light as the lift continued to ascend, I watched Kyoto spread out beneath our feet. I focused on the mountains in the east that sheltered the city. Among the greenery of the forests stood a stunning temple with a multitiered pagoda, which I couldn't take my eyes off until suddenly I heard a tinkling sound and the door opened on the twenty-seventh floor.

Reiko's heels echoed on the white marble tiles of the reception area. The walls here were also glass, letting in the radiant light. A receptionist greeted us with a bow. I wrote my name and phone number on a slip of paper to get a temporary security card, which allowed me to pass through to an endless hallway with a high ceiling. Along the way, we crossed paths with a couple of employees dressed in lab coats, and then we reached a massive mahogany door. Reiko touched the sensor with her security card, and it silently opened.

On the other side was a majestic room, so large that, if divided by walls, it could have accommodated a six-bedroom house. The outer walls were glass, and in the center was a stylish oval table surrounded by leather chairs.

On an inner wall hung a solitary painting of sunflowers, in the style of Van Gogh. I approached to contemplate those vivid colors.

"It's one of the originals," said a quiet voice behind me.

9
A WORK OF ART

Masa left his place behind a cluttered black desk stacked with piles of books. I noticed that he was in a wheelchair.

"It wasn't cheap, but it was worth it."

"It's beautiful," I exclaimed, amazed.

Masa wasn't how I imagined him from his voice. He must have been around sixty, wearing an elegant suit, the shirt casually open at the neck. His head tilted slightly to the right, as if it was difficult for him to keep it straight. Undoubtedly, in the past, he must have been a handsome man, but now he looked worn out by the illness that prevented him from walking.

After crossing the room, Masa's wheelchair stopped a few feet away from us. Reiko stood to the side. She'd become serious all of a sudden. She bowed in Masa's direction. I imitated her, giving my best bow.

"Welcome to Taira Corporation," he said. "Thank you."

After a subtle gesture from her boss, Reiko left. The automatic door closed behind her. Once the clacking of her heels had faded, Masa and I were surrounded by silence. I looked beyond the glass walls at the Kyoto cityscape below, stretching either side of the Kamogawa River toward the mountains, where I could see the temple in the forest that I had spotted when riding the elevator. Masa invited me to sit in an armchair under the sunflower painting.

"Do you like art?"

"Yes . . ."

I felt self-conscious, as if I was in a job interview.

"Do you understand it?"

"I think so," I replied, uncertainly.

"Those who claim to understand art are lying."

Realizing it was a trick question, I corrected myself, "I suppose it's not about understanding but feeling."

"Exactly, Nathan, art is emotion. Emotions appear and disappear like magic." He contemplated the sunflowers for a moment. "Artists are magicians."

I listened to this business tycoon without fully understanding why he was talking to me in this way. Perhaps it was the beginning of another of his stories or jokes to test my personality.

"I got this painting at an auction—one of the last in his sunflower series," he continued, "The initial ones he painted showed withered flowers. One of them was bought by a Japanese compatriot but was destroyed in the Allied bombings during the war. The one you see here is the only one from the series preserved in Japan."

A young man entered through a door camouflaged in a mahogany wall, carrying a tray with a white porcelain teapot and two cups. After two bows, one to Masa and one to me, he served green tea and left the room with a backward step, avoiding turning his back.

"All that interests me is magic and good stories, Nathan," said Masa, taking a sip of tea. "I think of my life and the lives of others as works of art that we can create at will." He paused dramatically, holding the teacup in his hand. "The problem with you is that you've had such a boring life it's a story not worth telling. But we'll fix that, my boy; soon you'll be a magician too. Do you still have feelings for Mia?"

I was taken aback at the abrupt change of subject. "You must have felt lonely to dig into the past. Am I wrong?"

"I suppose you're right."

"The solitude of each man is a personal matter; I won't inquire. In reality, I brought you to Kyoto because I need you for—"

He fell silent, as if struggling to breathe. He placed a hand on his side in pain, hunching over in the wheelchair. But a few seconds later, he managed to sit up straight again.

"As you can see, I don't have much time left. I'm suffering from a terminal degenerative disease. My days, hours and seconds in this world—or rather, in this reality—are numbered."

Even though he was a rich and powerful man, I felt sorry for that soul facing such a close and certain death.

"All animals on this planet are condemned to die," he continued. "What sets us, *Homo sapiens*, apart from other living beings? We are the only ones with the awareness that we will die in the future. Dogs and cats don't worry about their death—ignorance makes them happy."

I considered his hypothesis and nodded.

"This fear of death that binds us all, rich, poor, fortunate, or unfortunate, has led us, from the beginning of time, to create myths about the possibility of achieving immortality. Do you know the poem, *The Epic of Gilgamesh*?"

"I know it's one of the oldest stories ever preserved."

Masa's eyes sparkled as he activated the wheelchair to move to a display case behind his desk. From the display case he took out a stone tablet bearing inscriptions, and then made his way back to me.

"Be careful," he said, as he handed me the piece of stone. "You are holding tablet number nine from *The Epic of Gilgamesh*. It's over four thousand years old, written in Akkadian."

"Another original—like Van Gogh's *Sunflowers*."

Masa nodded proudly. "This tablet tells how King Gilgamesh, grieving the death of his companion Enkidu, embarks on a journey in search of Utnapishtim, one of the few individuals granted eternal life by the gods. Gilgamesh travels halfway around the world until he reaches Mount Mashu. When he gets

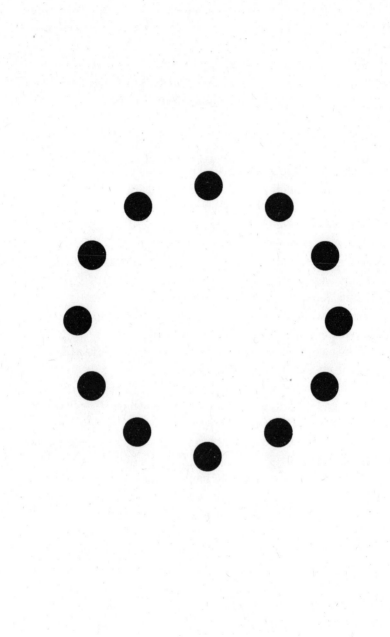

there, he stands before the entrance to a tunnel that no human has ever gone through. It is guarded by two giant scorpions that won't let him pass. After negotiating with them, Gilgamesh manages to go through the tunnel to the other side, where he continues walking for twelve 'double hours.'"

"Double hours?"

"You are the expert in measuring time. Why do we divide the day into twenty-four hours and not twelve double hours?"

"I suppose it's easier to divide the day into equal parts."

"Exactly. The Egyptians tried dividing the day into ten parts with sundials, but to measure time at night, they had to invent more complicated methods based on the position of the stars. Also, if you try to divide a circle into ten equal parts, you end up with ugly and inconvenient angles of thirty-six degrees," he said, warming to his subject. "Later, the Babylonians and the Sumerians invented the sexagesimal system. They were the first to propose a more elegant division of time, into the twelve equal parts we still use today. It was also the Babylonians who wrote the adventures of Gilgamesh on tablets, one of which you hold in your hand. It contains one of the first historical references to the passage of time in multiples of twelve, in beautiful angles of thirty degrees, just like any clock or the twelve freckles behind your ear."

I visualized the twelve freckles in my mind. As they were behind my ear, I'd only seen them in mirrors or photos. But yes, they were spaced at thirty-degree angles, just like the hours on a clock. I traced the freckles with my finger, confirmation that I was awake, although that first day in Japan was turning surreal. Besides, jet lag was weighing on me like a burden.

"Both you and Reiko have only seen me from the front. How do you know about my freckles?" I asked.

"Without your circle, we would never have been able to remotely read your dream of the Rashomon gate. The circle is an interface that, with the right equipment, allows us to access certain parts of your interior."

"Don't worry," he said, seeing my horrified expression. "We can't see everything you think; we only have access to certain key dreams that we encoded when you were born, with your parents' permission. I know a lot about you, Nathan, from before you were born. In fact, I need you because of that twelve-hour circle."

Resigned, I accepted that Masa could read my dreams and almost knew more about me than I did.

I carefully placed tablet number nine of *The Epic of Gilgamesh* on the glass table that separated us and finally mustered the courage to look into the man's eyes for a few seconds without feeling intimidated by his wealth or power. Those eyes were small, but there was something in them that betrayed a knowledge difficult to fathom. I leaned back in my seat and crossed my arms, waiting for him to tell me more. I remembered my father's words when I asked about my freckles: "They will help you in the future," and also my mother's words: "They're a bad omen, but your father insisted."

"Don't blame your parents; they made the right decision, and if they didn't give you details, it was to protect you. They did it because they loved you," he said, as if he could read my thoughts.

Masa seemed to be trying to lift himself from the wheelchair, leaning his body toward me. "Before you were born, I took a business trip to visit the fusion power plant where your father worked. I wanted to invest in it. We quickly became friends, and he told me that your mother had just become pregnant. Then I offered him the opportunity to participate in the launch of my Kyoto Mythos program. It took some convincing, partly because your mother opposed the idea of genetically modifying your embryo. But it was inevitable: you had the ideal characteristics, extremely difficult to find, to be part of the project. You're fortunate, Nathan. We analyzed the genetic code of thousands of candidate embryos before finding you."

"And Mia was another chosen one?"

"Exactly! You're connecting the dots. You share the freckle circle and also your fate."

"I have no intention of committing suicide."

Masa's smile was reminiscent of Reiko's smug grimaces during our conversation at Smart Coffee, as if he too was disclosing only the information that suited him at the moment.

"Mia had the courage to choose her destiny. We don't choose our birth, but we have the power to decide how we want to die. If you've read the classic works of Yukio Mishima," he said, pointing at the pile of books on his desk, "you'll understand that many Japanese see suicide as a work of art, something we can sculpt at will. Mishima spent over ten years planning his suicide down to the smallest detail."

"I prefer nature to choose my death," I replied. "In reality, I disagree with Mishima and with you. Like Gilgamesh, I've always rebelled against the idea of death."

He let his gaze rest on the stone tablet with the Akkadian inscriptions and, after taking a sip of his tea, managed to straighten his neck with some effort. "There are twelve tablets in total, but I have only the ninth, which ends with Gilgamesh walking the twelve 'double hours.' The last three tablets tell how Gilgamesh continues his journey until he reaches the island where Utnapishtim lives. There, Utnapishtim offers him eternal life under one condition: 'To conquer death, you must first conquer sleep. If you manage to stay awake for six days and seven nights straight, you will live forever.' Gilgamesh accepts the challenge but fails. He falls asleep before the week ends and remains a mortal like us."

A look of sadness filled Masa's face. "In my case, you are the one who can save me. There's not much time left."

The man who had brought us tea came into the room again, carrying a black folder embossed with a golden symbol, which he placed on the table. Masa opened it, took out a document and put it in front of me. It was written in English, in two parts. The first was a confidentiality agreement, and the second was an employment contract that included accommodation in Kyo-to and an annual salary with many digits.

"I want you to work for me."

As I mentally converted the yen, I wanted to sign at once.

"Take your time, Nathan . . ."

"What would my job entail?"

"It has to do with quantum computing and 3D design for a virtual world," said Masa. "But I can't give you more details. It's a strictly confidential project. When you sign, you'll be able to learn everything about our technology, and I can also reveal more details about the functionality of the special gene you have inside you, which manifests in the circle behind your ear. It serves for much more than allowing us to observe your dreams."

"I studied quantum computing because that was what my father wanted, but I barely lasted a year before I started to hate working in a company. Since then, I've specialized in designing mechanical watches. I don't think I'm suitable for other types of job."

"You are more than qualified for the mission. Don't worry. I won't make you deal with corporate politics."

"Thank you . . ." I replied, overwhelmed by this stranger's offer, and confused by how much he knew about me.

"By the way, they probably already told you that the dojo is mine. It's part of Taira Corporation, like the school where you practiced jujutsu with your dear sensei. We've been friends since childhood, but he decided to leave Japan. Without you knowing, Nathan, your destiny has been linked to mine for a long time, through martial arts and your parents' decision to genetically modify you."

A strange smile lingered on his lips, as if there was still some-thing he couldn't tell me. He reached into his pocket, moving his arm with difficulty, and took out a key.

"For some things, we like to be traditional," he said, observ-ing the key for a moment before handing it to me. His deter-mination and enthusiasm made it easy to forget he was in a wheelchair. He accompanied me to the door. "Let's create a work of art more beautiful than Van Gogh's *Sunflowers* and *The Epic of Gilgamesh*. You and I are going to create a new story. Let's make it extraordinary." He sneezed, and his head wobbled. He regained his voice before the door closed: "I don't have much time so we need to act fast. You have twenty-four hours to sign. Otherwise, you will force me to take other measures."

I walked down the hallway with the black folder under my arm and the key in my pocket. I didn't know what to make of Masa. On one hand, he had welcomed me into his office and offered me the highest-paying job I had ever had. On the other hand, he had the audacity to violate my privacy and he knew things about my family that no one had ever told me before. In the end, he even threatened me.

But I was beginning to resign myself to the surreal twist that my destiny was taking, seemingly controlled by that puppet master named Masa.

10

THE DANCE OF THE ELEMENTS

Reiko was waiting for me at the reception. She smiled as I went through the security turnstiles holding the contract under my arm. Seeing her, I felt relieved. I realized that I was comfortable with her, and all the time I had been with Masa, I had felt tense and nervous.

I had the feeling that what was happening was all too easy. Their kindness toward me seemed excessive. In any case, she and her boss confirmed what I had read in my book about Japanese culture about *omotenashi*, the art of making outsiders feel at home.

We took the elevator. The view of the temple pagoda protruding through the foliage, like an ornament in a geisha's hairstyle, gave way to darkness as we descended into the underground parking lot.

"You're lucky, Nathan," Reiko said as she started the Porsche again. "Many Japanese dream of working for Taira Corporation, but they will never achieve it. Besides, Masa has offered you extras, like the house, that only senior members of the company receive."

"I don't usually sign anything without being sure of what it implies, and no one has clarified what my job will entail. If you could provide more details . . ."

"I'm sorry. I'm not allowed to really talk about anything until you sign. If you want to know, you'll have to sign. Why are you so afraid of making a mistake? Life is what happens between decisions."

We both fell silent. As we drove through the old streets of Kyoto, I tried to make sense of what was happening. I had traveled to the old capital in search of answers, but the questions had multiplied.

After crossing a bridge over the sun-dappled Kamogawa River, Reiko pulled into a parking lot. "Let's have something to eat," she said, "and then I'll take you to your new home."

The restaurant was inside a simple wooden house, with no signage, overlooking the river. Reiko greeted the chef behind the counter with familiarity. Apart from us, the place was empty. We took off our shoes before going through sliding doors into a private room, where we sat on the floor on cushions.

A woman in a kimono came in. She was young, but her formal movements and the makeup covering her face made her look older. She knelt on the tatami and greeted us with a bow. Then she placed two teacups on the table alongside steaming rolled-up towels.

Reiko ordered without looking at a menu. The kimono-clad woman left the room with a slight bow and closed the sliding doors behind her.

Reiko took one of the towels to clean her hands. I followed suit; it was warm and damp. I took a sip of the tea, which had a different flavor than I was used to.

"It's genmaicha," she said, noticing my expression. "It's tea mixed with toasted Chinese rice."

She sat outlined against the window, a view of the bridge over the Kamogawa River beyond her. Her dark, straight hair shone with an almost unreal aura. This was one of her favorite sushi restaurants, she told me, and she preferred coming for lunch rather than dinner, when the place was crowded.

"In silence, food tastes better," said Reiko.

The kimono-clad woman entered with the first dish, thin slices of white fish so translucent that the pink color of the plate showed through. Each piece was carefully arranged, forming a circular pattern around the center. We poured soy sauce into our dipping bowls, mixed it with a little wasabi, and then began to eat.

"I see you're good at using chopsticks."

"Yes, of course, I've eaten sushi many times. But this is sashimi, right?"

"It's better to start with sashimi. Only people with empty hearts have sushi as a starter."

"Ah . . ." I said, thinking of all the times I had started a Japanese meal devouring tuna and salmon sushi.

"Tuna comes last because it's ecstasy. You have to save it for the end, like the punchline in a good story."

"Then, tuna is dessert."

"Exactly. Sushi is more than eating raw fish, as you Westerners believe. The order and rhythm in which each fish arrives at the table matter, as well as the colors, the arrangement on the plate, and the decoration of the room. Even the conversation while eating is important." She put down her chopsticks and continued as if she was talking about a crucial part of her life. "It all begins when the fisherman ventures into the sea. There's a struggle between man and nature until the fisherman manages to catch his prey. By the way, the chef of this restaurant is a fisherman. He brought the *hirame* flounder we're eating from the depths of the Sea of Japan to our table."

I picked up a piece of that almost transparent fish, dipped it in soy sauce, and brought it to my mouth. It was delicious. "It melts on the tongue."

"And explodes on the palate," added Reiko, taking a bite of hirame and closing her eyes.

The courses arrived at spaced-out intervals, and it felt like time in that room was passing more slowly than in the outside world. No matter how much I ate, it didn't seem to fill me up, and I was in a constant state of anticipation for the next dish. Finally, the red fish—salmon and tuna—arrived.

"This is *chutoro*, and that's *otoro*," said Reiko, pointing to two varieties of tuna on the plate. "My favorite is chutoro."

I tried the otoro, but it seemed too fatty. But the flavor explosion of the chutoro had me closing my eyes with pleasure. When I opened them, Reiko was also eating with an expression of ecstasy, eyes half-closed. I let my gaze rest on her neck and then on the legs stretched over the tatami. When I looked back at her face, her cheeks were flushed.

Eating that delicious meal with Reiko, I almost forgot everything that had happened in the last few days. A feeling of lightness finally filled my heart.

And as we arrived at the end of our culinary journey, Reiko locked her eyes with mine and said, "Sex is much better after eating sushi."

11
RAPTURE

I didn't know what to say to that, so I muttered an excuse about going to the bathroom. That morning, I'd left the dojo in a hurry, and I hadn't had time to look in the mirror. Jet lag was taking its toll. There were dark circles under my eyes, and the two-day-old stubble was starting to enter the realm of the unpresentable. I washed my face before returning to our private room, where a small but strong-looking man with hard features was sitting next to Reiko. That wasn't the only surprise. She was gagged and the man was tying her arms behind her back with a rope with a calm expression.

"Please, have a seat," he said.

Under her disheveled hair, Reiko's eyes still emitted a beauty from another world, even immersed in fear. Her silent gaze begged me to do as the man said.

"What do you want from us?" I asked.

"Masa has made you a good offer," he said. He was holding the black folder that Masa had given me. "But we recommend that you don't work for him. It's not a good idea, Nathan."

"Why?" I asked, bewildered.

"Masa uses his influence in the media and his wealth to create a reputation that is nothing but a facade. Those who do business with him find out he's a shark, a predator who ends up devouring others." He spoke very slowly, as if he thought I wouldn't understand. "First, he attracts you, seduces you, like a siren in the sea. Once he's caught his prey, he'll finish you off."

"Excuse me, who are you?" I asked.

He just smiled indulgently. I was aware of Reiko's breasts straining against her dress, and I felt ashamed that I could be so easily distracted.

"My name is not important. I work for a company that was revived after Taira Corporation made us bankrupt. I'm here to ask you to work for us. We'll give you twice the money Masa has offered."

"I am not a commodity sold to the highest bidder."

"What you carry inside is very valuable, Nathan."

"Do you mean my special gene, my freckle circle?"

"Of course. It would be a shame if you ended up serving old Masa. Either you come with us willingly, or we'll have to use other methods."

This mobster-like character took the chopsticks Reiko had been using and picked up the last piece of salmon. He put it in his mouth and chewed it with relish.

"Look out the window, Nathan," he said. Do you see that black van parked on the bridge?"

I could see it.

"If you don't sign our contract, we'll put both of you in the van. You will come to our laboratories, and Reiko, whom we don't need at all, will end up at the bottom of the river with a weight tied to her swanlike neck."

"Oh no you won't," I said without hesitation.

Ignoring my words, he dropped Masa's contract folder on the table and pulled a white folder from his bag. He opened it in front of me.

"These are the conditions we offer you. What do you want to do?"

To show that he was serious, he twisted Reiko's arm. She moaned in terror.

"We also offer you residence in Kyoto, but with double the salary. You have to sign, Nathan. Otherwise . . ."

He pointed the chopsticks at the van. With the other hand, he grabbed one of Reiko's wrists, reddened by the force of the knot. She whimpered as she struggled to pull away from him. I jumped up, but just as I was about to grab the man, a sushi plate hit me in the face. Then he lunged at me across the table. The rest of the plates fell onto the tatami, spilling the leftover soy sauce. Before I could recover, a punch in the stomach left me breathless. In an instant, I was pinned against the wall, with one of his hands squeezing my throat. The man was small but tremendously strong.

"Don't act tough," he snarled, his face so close to me that I could smell his foul breath. "Besides, I'm not alone. My colleagues are waiting for me in the van. It's better if we settle this amicably, don't you think?"

Reiko let out a muffled scream through the gag. Realizing that he had let his guard down for a moment, I punched him in the side with all my strength, followed by a low kick to a calf to make him lose his balance. His small and sturdy body collapsed onto the table.

Before he could get up, I kicked him in the head, and he fell unconscious. Looking out the window, I saw two men in suits getting out of the van.

I quickly removed the gag from Reiko.

"Where did you learn to kick like that?" she said.

"Many years of jujutsu," I thought, but I was panting so hard that I didn't manage to speak the words.

Through the window, I saw a third man in front of the van taking out binoculars to watch us from a distance. The other two suited men were walking quickly toward the restaurant. Ignoring the white folder from the thug, I grabbed the black folder with Masa's contract, and we headed for the door. The restaurant was completely empty now, even the staff had fled, but as we were about to step outside, the two suited men, tall and powerful-looking, blocked us.

Behind them emerged a figure I recognized immediately:

Kamyu. He fixed his bionic eye on one of the suited men and, with a quick, silent movement from behind, strangled him until he fell unconscious to the floor. When the other man realized what had happened, he threw a punch that Kamyu dodged.

"Through the window!" Kamyu shouted as he kicked to defend himself.

While Kamyu tried to subdue the second man, Reiko and I escaped through a back window onto a rooftop. I took Reiko's hand and we jumped from the roof to an adjacent balcony. From there, we ran down the emergency stairs to a fairly crowded pedestrian alley. But we hadn't shaken off our pursuers. The person watching us through binoculars from the van had seen us escape through the window. Another group of men in suits emerged from the van and started running toward us.

We turned the first corner intending to blend in with the crowd. Reiko held onto my wrist and guided me. She seemed to know these cobblestoned shop-lined alleys by heart.

She walked as fast as she could barefoot, with her heels in her hand. Looking back, I realized that the van's henchmen were getting closer. They weren't running anymore to avoid drawing attention, but they were advancing with long strides, and were getting closer and closer.

"You stand out more than Kyoto Tower. Lower your head!" Reiko shouted as she pulled me to enter the *shotengai* shopping street where Smart Coffee was.

I never would have thought that being six feet tall was going to be a problem. I bent over to the height of the pedestrians around us and continued to dodge my way through the crowd with Reiko's guidance. After passing by Smart Coffee, whose aroma perfumed the early-evening street, we made a ninety-degree turn and entered the garden of a tiny Buddhist temple. The light of a stone lantern glowed gently in the encroaching twilight.

Reiko guided me to some bushes. We crouched down behind them, and through the leaves, we saw the thugs briskly making their way past the temple. We waited in silence, the only sound the beating of our hearts, until we were sure the men had gone.

The danger seemed to have passed.

"Let's go this way," said Reiko, pointing to a gap in the back of the fence surrounding the temple.

"And Kamyu?" I asked, concerned.

"Don't worry about him, he can take care of himself. Today's stuff is a piece of cake compared to his adventures in Mongolia."

Soon, we reached a main road and went into a 7-Eleven where we bought some bottles of water. Reiko cleaned her feet with a tissue and put on her shoes. Then we got into a robotaxi to which Reiko gave an address. After passing through several steep streets, we arrived at an area of large houses with gardens. The moonlight tinted the nearby forest trees with slivery hues.

The robotaxi stopped in front of one of the houses. Reiko said, "This is where you'll be living. You'll be safe here. Only Masa and his closest collaborators know this place."

We got out of the robotaxi, and I opened the door with the key Masa had given me. Reiko seemed strangely calm after everything that had happened.

"Their ways are unorthodox, but there's no need to fear them. They're the minions of our competitor, Genji Corporation," she said. "If we had ended up in the black van, Masa wouldn't have taken long to rescue us."

"Do you really believe that? Anyway, I don't understand why everyone suddenly wants me," I said.

Instead of answering, Reiko said, "The powerful have powerful enemies; the weak have none." She lifted her chin, bringing her face close to mine. "Soon, you'll be powerful too."

She guided me to a room overlooking the nighttime cityscape. On a wall next to the bed hung a scroll with a poem signed by Matsuo Basho. The fluid lines of the Japanese characters seemed to have been created with a single brushstroke.

Reiko read it aloud: "Every moment of life is the last, every poem is a poem about death."

Then she kissed me. At first slowly and gently, tentatively exploring with her small and restless tongue. Then she closed her eyes with abandon and grasped my neck with her delicate hands. As I embraced her and caressed her back, Reiko's legs began to tremble.

My body also experienced a tremor at the prospect of discovering what lay beneath the blue dress that had hypnotized me since early that morning. I unzipped the dress, and she took care of removing her lingerie. Unable to believe what was happening, I lifted her up and carried her to bed.

The silver light of the moon illuminated her naked body, which radiated a beauty I had never seen before. Her skin seemed to glow against the bedsheets, like a mermaid with silver scales dancing in the sea.

I had never desired a woman so strongly, but I forced myself to take my time caressing the tender skin of her breasts and letting my fingers trace the warmth of her belly and hips.

Then I parted her legs with my hands intending to kiss her deeply, starting from those feet as white as snow. As my lips traveled along her legs the warmth turned into heat. I tentatively touched her with the tip of my tongue ,while holding her trembling legs with my hands, and she sighed with pleasure.

Her back arched, and her hands clung to the sheets as if she was trying to stop herself from falling off a cliff. As she vibrated with pleasure, she squeezed her thighs against my head as if she didn't want to let me go.

Her interior was a warm home. In that moment, the past and the future ceased to exist, and the present stretched like a rubber band traversing the universe from end to end. I stopped kissing her to look into her eyes for a moment. It seemed to me that those eyes could see into my heart. As my own eyes closed in ecstasy, I suddenly remembered Mia's smile in her last RealPeople photo. Mysteriously, that snapshot had ignited the spark that had brought me to Japan. I had the strange sensation that Mia, from somewhere, was watching us.

After, exhausted, Reiko and I lay beneath the Kyoto moon, which watched us through the window, the sole witness to our passion. Reiko rested her head on my chest and uttered a word I didn't understand, but just the sound of her voice made me feel dizzy. Then she fell asleep.

With adrenaline still coursing through me, I was wide awake. I stared at the moon, and reflected on that second day in Japan. I was exhausted, yet I felt a certain lightness of spirit. It was as if new opportunities were opening up to me and I could let go of old baggage and escape from my boring and routine life of the past few years.

But I still didn't know who I was associating with. I didn't entirely trust Masa. Why were thugs from a company called Genji Corporation willing to do whatever it took to prevent me from signing with Taira Corporation?

All I knew was that it all started when my parents agreed to introduce genetic changes into my embryo. Did they intend for me to end up working with Masa? Why did they never want to explain the details to me? Were they trying to protect me from something?

I stopped gazing at the moon and focused on Reiko's long neck. The rest of her face was hidden in the shadows. As I looked at her nape, I thought of Mia again. Reiko and Mia only resembled each other in one thing: the part of the neck near the ears had the same delicate and fragile appearance. I traced the skin, barely touching it with my finger, hoping to feel the mark I had glimpsed there this morning at Smart Coffee, but I felt nothing.

As I closed my eyes, trying to fall asleep, memories of my teenage afternoons reading novels with Mia flooded back.

12
THE INFINITE KNOT

I was woken by the first rays of the morning sun. Reiko was still asleep, her naked body bathed in a kind of aura from the timid early-morning light.

Finally, I could see what was hidden behind her ear. When I saw that it wasn't a circle of freckles, I felt a mixture of relief and disappointment. It was just a simple tattoo, a kind of knot with no beginning or end.

Fascinated, I wondered why Reiko would have chosen that symbol to mark her body. Beyond the curves of the profile of her sleeping face, I admired the green hills of Kyoto. Among the branches swaying in the gentle breeze stood a solitary temple pagoda. It was the same one that had caught my attention the day before from the elevator of Taira Corporation.

I opened the window to let in the morning air and to gaze at the six-story pagoda that rose above the tall and slender Japanese cedars that surrounded it. Beyond that sacred place stretched a garden with pine trees pruned like giant bonsai and a pond with lotus flowers. Against the clear sky, I noticed a solitary cloud had paused over the roof of the pagoda.

I headed to the living room, which was so spacious that the Steinway & Sons grand piano in the middle of it barely seemed to take up any space. In front of the sofa was a window overlooking the garden. Beyond the landscaped area, the dojo building could be glimpsed and I could see the tiny figures of my jujutsu classmates performing their morning training. I could see Kamyu, huge among them. I wondered how he saw the world through his bionic eye.

I stood next to the window to exercise with my own stretches, push-ups, squats, and katas, enough to break a sweat before showering. When I had showered, I prepared breakfast with what I found in the well-stocked refrigerator of what was now my new home. After beating eggs with butter and cinnamon, I dipped several slices of bread in the mixture and put them in a pan. I put the kettle on, and while the water was heating up, I checked the messages on my phone. I had received one from Mia's account:

> How happy I am to see that you're in Japan!
> Sign the contract that Masa offered you and
> we can meet again. Kisses from Kyoto Mythos.

I glanced at the black folder containing the contract that had been left on the kitchen counter the night before.

> I know you like to joke around, Masa.
> I haven't decided yet if I want to sign
> your contract.

> I'm not Masa, I'm Mia. Don't be fooled by
> appearances, I didn't commit suicide in the
> traditional sense of the word. I just decided
> to start a new life elsewhere. Don't you regret
> never confessing your love for me?

> I respect all the success you've achieved,
> dear Masa, but your jokes are starting to
> tire me.

Do you remember the afternoon at the café,
the first time I showed you my freckles?

> I thought the genetic modifications you
> introduced into me only allowed you
> to read some of my dreams, but I see
> you have access to my memories . . .

Intuitively, I brought my hand behind my ear to count my twelve little bumps and make sure I was awake.

A final message came that concluded the conversation:

I'll be waiting for you on the
other side of the gate, Nathan.

I didn't respond. Nervously, I ground the coffee beans and placed them in the filter. I slowly poured water over the fresh grounds. From the slightly spicy aroma that filled the room, I recognized it as an Indonesian variety.

At that moment, Reiko came in with a sleepy expression.

"How embarrassing," she said, walking toward the living room sofa. "I don't want you to see me without makeup."

I smiled as I watched her cover her face. She made no attempt to kiss me, nor did she show me any affectionate gestures. It was as if nothing had happened between us the night before. She sat on the carpet to apply her makeup, with a small mirror balanced on her knees, while I set breakfast on the table in front of the sofa.

"Your boss, Masa, is sending me messages from Mia's RealPeople account," I mentioned.

"Even though I like to play around, I'm jealous. I already told you not to talk to me about other girls," she replied.

"But I'm talking to you about Masa," I insisted.

"You're talking to me about Mia, and—" she began, as if she was about to reveal something, but she stopped.

To change the subject, I asked her, "And that tattoo you have behind your ear? It reminds me of an engraving by Escher—I really love his work."

"It's a Buddhist symbol. I got it when my father died."

"I'm sorry."

"You don't have to be sorry. My mother and I were glad when he died. The bastard used to hit us."

I was speechless. She kept putting on makeup, as if she was telling me something trivial. "Every morning, before going to school, I went to Nanzen-ji temple. I'd sit in front of a Buddha statue and pray for my father to die."

I set the last breakfast plate on the table while Reiko put away her makeup. "My father was a popular man in Kyoto," she said, after a few bites of toast. "No one could have suspected how violent he was when he was alone with us. One night, he beat my mother so badly that I thought he would kill her. I had just turned fifteen, and I escaped from the house by climbing out of my bedroom window. That night, I snuck into Nanzen-ji temple to wish for my father's death again. I fell asleep on the tatami under the Buddha statue."

"And what happened?" I asked breathlessly.

"When I got home in the morning, my mother was just coming back from the hospital, where she'd spent the night. But she acted as though she'd only had some kind of little accident. My father had gone on a business trip to Mongolia. He never came back. That evening, it was reported on the news that a private jet full of businessmen had crashed in the Gobi Desert."

"Your wish came true."

"Yes, but then something unexpected happened. When I found out that my father had died, I started having a nightmare about him every night. In the dream I loved and missed him. But when he approached me, the love turned into repulsion and I ended up strangling him. That's why I kept going to Nanzen-ji temple every morning to ask for the nightmares to disappear, for my father's ghost to leave me alone." She swallowed hard, as if that memory was still alive inside her. "One morning, a monk who had noticed that I'd been going there every day asked me why I kept coming. When he heard my story, he told me that my father's death was not my fault, and that Buddhism is not meant for making wishes but to teach us to accept life. Then, he pointed to a metal candlestick with the Buddhist infinite knot."

"Is that what your tattoo is?"

"Yes. After talking to the monk, I went to get the knot tattooed on my neck and the nightmares disappeared," she said, brushing her hair aside so I could see it. "The infinite knot represents acceptance that all existence is subject to the passage of time and change. The infinite cycle of samsara is the only truth of the universe. Everything else is an invention of the human mind."

Having said that, she took a sip of her still steaming coffee and gazed into its dark depths for a moment.

"How did you and your mother manage on your own?"

"My father worked for Masa—"

"Everyone works or worked for Masa," I muttered resignedly.

"He was one of the executives of Taira Corporation. He had been setting up the Mongolian operation for years. When the accident happened, Masa employed my mother as manager of one of their geisha houses in Pontocho, here in Kyoto. They also paid for my philosophy studies in exchange for me working part-time for them. Later, they offered me the permanent job I have now. Somehow, the corporation became our new father, but better than the previous one. This new father pampered us instead of mistreating us."

I glanced toward the pagoda, radiant under the morning sun.

I had only spent a day with Reiko, but I felt as though I'd known her forever. I remembered what Albert Camus said in his novel *The Stranger*—that someone who had lived for only one day would have enough memories to keep them from being bored during a one-hundred year prison sentence. Reiko took the last sip of her coffee and pointed to the black folder containing the contract.

"Masa jokes sometimes, but when he gives orders, they must be followed to the letter," she said, her tone colder now. "Yesterday he told you that you had twenty-four hours to sign. You've hardly any time left. With each passing minute, Masa is closer to death, and only you can save him."

After hearing the story of how Masa had helped Reiko's family in difficult times, I felt a strange affection for him, mixed with pity. Despite his power, he seemed like a man with a good heart. I set the coffee cup aside, opened the black folder, and signed the contract with Taira Corporation without further thought. Reiko flashed her characteristic smirk, a mix of a smile and something more.

"Now you too are part of our infinite cycle," she said. "Come on, Masa is waiting for us."

13

THE DREAM OF THE RASHOMON GATE

When I opened the front door of what was now my house in Kyoto, a huge car with giant wheels was parked in the driveway. Its rectangular lines gave an almost military appearance. The windows were tinted such a dark black it was hard to distinguish them from the body of the car. Next to it stood Kamyu and the dojo caretaker, waiting silently. Both smiled and bowed as we came out of the house.

"Welcome to Taira Corporation," they said in unison. "Welcome to our family."

"I see news travels fast," I said, surprised, glancing sideways at Reiko. It had only been a few minutes since I signed the contract, which Reiko was now carrying in her handbag.

Kamyu was holding my suitcase, which he had brought from my room at the dojo. He handed it to the caretaker, who, after asking permission, took it into the house. The four of us got into the car. Kamyu's bionic eye blinked, emitting red lights that activated the automatic driving system. After a while, we arrived at the parking lot of the Taira Corporation skyscraper.

Back in the buttonless glass elevator, I gazed again at the temple pagoda protruding from the forest. I could also see my new home, right next to the temple. It was barely discernible, half hidden among the trees.

When we got out of the elevator, Kamyu and the caretaker disappeared. Masa greeted me and Reiko with a wide smile and invited us to sit beneath Van Gogh's *Sunflowers*. Instead of retreating, as she had done the previous day, Reiko took a seat beside his wheelchair.

"I apologize for the inconvenience caused by Genji's men at the restaurant," he said.

"They were about to—"

"They want you, and they want our technology," he interrupted, "and we need certain things from them. But don't worry, I'll do my best to protect you. You're one of us now."

He paused to sit up straighter, struggling to keep his neck upright, and exclaimed cheerfully, "Let's forget about all that Genji nonsense. Today we have something important to celebrate. Thank you for signing, Nathan! We've been waiting for this moment for a long time. Your father would be pleased, if he was here."

I merely nodded.

Then, the door camouflaged in the wall opened, and the same suited employee from the day before entered with a tray in one hand and a black briefcase in the other. After bowing ninety degrees, reminiscent of the greeting my sensei had taught me, he served green tea for the three of us. The aroma of the infusion filled the air.

Next, the employee opened the briefcase and took out a golden card, which he placed on the table. It bore my RealPeople profile picture and my first name translated into Japanese:

Taira Corporation
Nathan
ネーサン
Employee ID: 293901

He also took out a retina scanner and proceeded to scan my eyes. Then, Reiko pulled the signed contract from her handbag and gave it to him. He placed it carefully into the briefcase and withdrew after another bow.

"The card is a commemorative detail. To access any place in this building, your eyes are enough. You'll also be able to enter any of our subsidiary facilities. You just need to open your eyes wide so the sensors can read your retinas. Now you're part of the family—"

I noticed Masa stroking Reiko's leg. She didn't seem to mind.

"—and we can share our secrets with you."

I tried to ignore the groping of the leg that I had kissed hours before.

"As you can imagine," Masa continued, "a large corporation like this has all kinds of business interests. I've always liked making investments that support traditional Japanese culture— helping martial arts dojos or geisha houses from falling into oblivion, while also betting on the most modern social networks like Real People, fusion power plants, quantum computing . . ."

Reiko was looking at her phone screen, ignoring our conversation. He continued to openly stroke her leg.

"Although these are businesses that are working well for us, I'm always thinking about how to innovate. Our survival as a company depends on our ability to create the future. Six months ago, one of our subsidiaries dedicated to quantum computer development, Taira Quantum, achieved a breakthrough that puts us a hundred years ahead of the competition." His neck had started to droop to one side. With effort, Masa grasped the armrest of the wheelchair. He took a breath. "Until now, the most powerful quantum computer only has two thousand qubits. Our prototype reaches ten million qubits."

"Impressive . . ."

"If such computing power fell into the wrong hands, it would pose a serious danger. It allows decryption of any encrypted message transmitted over the Internet."

When he mentioned "wrong hands," doubt crept over me. With things unfolding as they were, with the contract already signed, was I sure I had allied myself with the "good guys"?

"Factoring in polynomial time, with that computing power, you could even decrypt 4096-bit RSA encryption," I said, boasting of what I remembered from my time as a specialist in the quantum computing company.

"That's a piece of cake for our quantum computer! In fact, using Shor's algorithm with a ten-thousand-qubit computer would be enough to crack the encryption used by governments and military agencies. If we wanted to, we could uncover the biggest secrets of any country and sell that information. But we have other intentions."

He took a sip of his tea and squinted, as if thinking about how to proceed.

"For now, we don't want anyone to know about the existence of our quantum computer," he said. "This instrument can change the fate of humanity. That's why you've just signed a contract that includes a confidentiality clause."

"I can keep secrets. What do you plan to do with that immense computing power?"

Gathering his thoughts, he raised the hand that had been stroking Reiko's leg. She remained absorbed in her phone screen.

"Our purpose is more playful and harmless. We're developing a next-generation video game that uses the quantum computer to simulate a virtual world. The early tests are spectacular. The immersion is total!"

"Like in the classic *Matrix* movies? A kind of metaverse?"

"Even better. Once you're inside, it's hard to tell if you're in reality or in a video game. It's like entering a parallel dimension. One of the most challenging tasks is to generate that virtual world. For that, we have nearly ten thousand designers creating 3D objects. You'll join that team."

"Wow . . ."

"We've named our virtual world Kyoto Mythos."

Instinctively, I flipped over my employee card:

Taira Corporation
Chief Architect of Kyoto Mythos

I was relieved to know that I could handle that job without any issues. Designing objects, real or virtual, was my specialty.

"Everything will go smoothly, Nathan. I know we'll get along."

Reiko stood up, visibly bored with our conversation. She opened a drawer in Masa's desk and took out a small box. From it, she extracted several pills one by one and placed them next to Masa's teacup. Then, without a word, she turned her back on us and strode out of the room.

"She's as rude as she is beautiful," said Masa with a wry smile.

I had a sudden flashback of the night I had just spent with Reiko: her endless legs, her face in the dim light, her eyes . . .

Masa tapped the touchscreen on the armrest of his wheelchair, and the backrest tilted forward. This helped him straighten his head, which was flopping backward under the strain of fighting with his sick body. He grabbed the handful of pills and swallowed them in one gulp with a sip of tea. The morning sun streamed in through the window, casting strange reflections on the walls. The Van Gogh flowers, partially illuminated, seemed to watch over us.

"Soon you'll learn more details about my true intentions," Masa announced solemnly. "But before that, I'll reveal something about your father that we've kept hidden from you until now, for your safety. You need to know so you won't feel betrayed in the future."

"My father . . ." I murmured, head bowed.

"But let me start with a story. Have you ever heard of the Fermi Paradox?"

I shook my head, anticipating another one of those stories that he enjoyed telling and that I was starting to get used to, even enjoying.

"According to calculations by the international scientific community, there should be thousands of civilizations in our galaxy, many of them capable of finding planet Earth and communicating with us. The Fermi Paradox raises the question of why we haven't been visited by extraterrestrials. At the same time, it questions why we haven't communicated with them, if theoretically we have thousands of neighbors. Tell me, why do you think we haven't had extraterrestrial contact?"

"I suppose we're not a species advanced enough to pique their interest," I responded. "Perhaps it's like when humans see an anthill out of curiosity, but nothing more."

"That's a valid explanation," said Masa. "Another explanation is that more advanced civilizations eventually lose interest in the physical world and prefer to live in simulated realities. Human beings or any type of extraterrestrial life are limited by their biology. It's more efficient to transfer consciousness into virtual worlds. If extraterrestrials from advanced civilizations live within virtual worlds, that would explain why they haven't communicated with us. Once they exist within a simulation, they lose interest in exploring any other reality."

"I see. And is that what you aim to achieve with Kyoto Mythos?" I didn't understand where he was going with this.

"I want to save humanity, Nathan. If a civilization fails to master the technology to take refuge in a virtual world, it's most likely to end up invading every corner of its planet and its solar system until it exhausts all resources and becomes extinct."

"Or self-destruct through war or accident," I added, completing his argument.

"Exactly! Removing the constraints of our biological bodies will solve all these problems. As you can see, Kyoto Mythos will be more than just a realistic video game. It will represent an unprecedented leap in human evolution."

As he spoke, Masa had been sitting up in his wheelchair, his back becoming increasingly straight and leaning forward. It was as if explaining his grand plan was giving him back some of the life consumed by his terminal illness. His eyes sparkled with excitement.

"And why choose me to work on something so important?"

"I owe you another explanation as to why."

"I'm all ears."

"As I told you yesterday, before you were born, I traveled to Europe to visit the company where your father worked. That trip marked the beginning of negotiations that resulted in a substantial investment initially and later in a complete acquisition of the company, which we kept as a subsidiary."

I blinked, not quite believing it, before saying, "I knew the company where my father worked was Japanese, but I never knew it was Taira Corporation."

"The acquisition was carried out through a ghost investment fund to hide the movement from the public. Around that time, I fell ill. Doctors gave me a year to live, something I naturally refused to accept. Thanks to various intravenous chemical cocktails and pills, I've managed to delay the fatal moment. But I know it's a temporary solution; the drugs aren't going to save me. Drawing inspiration from classics like *The Epic of Gilgamesh*, I began the search for a permanent solution. And that's why I created the Kyoto Mythos program."

I took a sip of my tea and glanced at the Gilgamesh tablet I had held the day before. It was back on display in the cabinet behind the desk.

"When I started studying the problem of eternal life, I went back to the original ideas of pioneers like Ray Kurzweil from the late twentieth century," he continued. "His fundamental thesis was we would reach a point where technology would be so advanced that the line between machines and humans would blur as we uploaded our consciousness into cyberspace. But that moment never came due to two major limitations: the lack of processing power to generate virtual worlds equivalent to physical reality, and the incompatibility between our biological bodies and organic silicon-based computing systems. To overcome the first limitation, we started a research line in the Kyoto Mythos program. This led us to develop our quantum computer, capable of simulating entire worlds. At the same time, to overcome the second, we created a department to genetically modify humans so they could connect to the simulation. Do you follow?"

I nodded without saying anything, awaiting the final revelation. Though I felt bewildered by everything he was telling me, I could already sense what was coming.

"I focused on solving the second limitation, and for that, I studied genetic engineering. The culmination of my work, perhaps the greatest achievement of my life, was the design of what I called the samsara gene. In Sanskrit, the word *samsara* means 'eternal return' or 'the endless cycle of life.'" His voice gave special emphasis to the word "samsara."

"By introducing this gene into a human being, it was theoretically possible to upload their consciousness into the virtual world our quantum computing team was developing. But unfortunately, we faced a new obstacle. The samsara gene could only be introduced into people who had not yet been born. Additionally, they had to possess certain characteristics in their genetic code that made them suitable for assimilating it. So we asked for help from employees who were about to become parents. Among all the embryos of employees and employees' wives whose DNA we analyzed, we found several perfect candidates into whom we could introduce the samsara gene . . ."

"Me and Mia among them?" I asked, trying to digest what I was hearing.

Masa simply smiled. "Thanks to the samsara gene we introduced into you and Mia with the consent of your parents," he emphasized, "both of you were born with that characteristic circle of freckles. It's an interface to connect to Kyoto Mythos."

Despite how strange that story was, I felt some relief at finally having a complete explanation for something I had wondered about since childhood.

"I still don't understand why my parents and Mia's, or my sensei never explained this to us. What were you trying to protect us from?"

"From many things, including our competitor, Genji Corporation. They are developing a virtual world similar to ours, but they lack the samsara gene. That's why they attacked you at the restaurant yesterday. Until recently, they were unaware of your existence, but your arrival in Kyoto has been impossible to conceal. Their methods are less orthodox than ours, and my intention has always been to protect you, as well as your family. You are more valuable to me than a son."

I was tempted to ask about the accident in which my father had died, but I refrained. I was listening to the story of my life from someone who until a few days ago I didn't even know existed. I was beginning to see Masa as some kind of puppeteer weaving the threads of my destiny from before my birth.

"And aren't there more people with the samsara gene who can work within the virtual world?"

"There were other children in whom we inserted samsara before they were born, but almost all the carriers died in strange circumstances . . ." He paused and looked at Van Gogh's *Sunflowers* for a moment, as if he was evaluating whether he should explain more about those circumstances. I was beginning to realize that I had just signed a contract to offer myself as a guinea pig in an experiment with no guarantee of success.

"Forget about those who didn't make it," said Masa, as if he could sense my concern. "Luckily, four of you survived: Mia, Akira, Murakami, and you. Mia doesn't need an introduction. You'll meet Murakami and Akira soon. They'll be your guides during the first hours in Kyoto Mythos." He paused again before continuing. "When we manage to eliminate the last technical obstacles, we will be able to introduce the samsara gene into adult people." He had an increasingly intense gleam in his eyes. "It will be the final step to save me, and to save the rest of humanity. It will be the beginning of the era of eternity. Human beings will be able to connect to Kyoto Mythos, and those who can afford our services theoretically will be immortal as long as the quantum computers keep working."

Masa stared at his bony hands trembling on the armrests.

"As you can see, I'm not hiding anything from you." His smile contained hope but also bitterness. "I admit that part of this plan is selfish. I need to edit my DNA to introduce the samsara gene into my old and worn-out body, and thus connect to Kyoto Mythos before this disease that has been destroying my biology for decades kills me. But to achieve this, we need to capture the complete expression of the samsara gene in combination with other genes you carry within you, which form a cluster of genes that function together. That's why we need you to enter Kyo-to Mythos, to see how it reacts with your body. We still don't know how to introduce it into adult humans without adverse reactions. I'm sure we can decode this final secret if we see how the samsara is activated at a 100 percent level combined with the rest of the gene cluster."

"I still don't understand . . ."

"You need to understand some of the technicalities of bio-technology and what gene expression means. Imagine the gene cluster as if it were a hundred or more needles scattered throughout the solar system. Mysteriously, they connect with an invisible thread called samsara. Finding them would take eons, but if you had an immensely powerful magnet with which you could attract the needles, you would manage to collect them all in a moment. You are the magnet that can help us find them."

It all started to make sense. I understood my mission. "Then, what do I have to do to fully activate the samsara gene?" I asked.

"After studying many historical figures, I've come to the con-clusion that only true heroes manage to express their full poten-tial in life. To fully activate samsara, you will have to become a hero. You must free your mind from Western Cartesian think-ing, limited by beliefs about cause-and-effect, and trapped in the clutches of time. Inside the simulation, you will understand. When the time comes, your body will free itself from the fears accumulated throughout your life, and our computers will be able to capture the interactions of samsara with the rest of the gene cluster. In short: you will become a true hero when you fight and manage to kill the dragon that dwells within you. Any more questions before we begin?"

"Mia . . . Is she inside Kyoto Mythos?"

"Of course. She's been living there since she decided to leave her biological body. She will tell you the details of her transition," he said, as if it was obvious. "Unfortunately, neither she nor the other chosen ones have managed to express the samsara gene fully. You are my last hope."

So the messages I received this morning from Mia's account on RealPeople were really from her. At this point I couldn't fathom the consequences that the return from the dead of my old unrequited love would bring.

I took a sip of tea. "If you'll allow me one last—"

"Of course, my child."

"What does 'the gate' mean?"

"All who possess the samsara gene carry the dream of the Rashomon gate within them. It's encoded in a special memory located beneath the skin of your twelve freckles. When one of you dreams about the gate, it sends a signal to our Taira Quantum computers, notifying us that the carrier is ready to enter Kyoto Mythos. Depending on the person, the dream manifests sooner or later. For the samsara gene to be fully activated, one needs to be in an ideal emotional situation, that is, without attachments."

I remembered the night I had dreamed of the gate. Indeed, at that moment, I was without any attachments.

"Mia was premature; she dreamed of the gate when she was young. We just needed you to do it. We almost have all the pieces of the puzzle!"

"So, you created the dream . . ."

"As I've explained, I'm the creator of the gene you carry within you. I wrote every DNA base pair of the samsara gene, one by one. In a way, I am also your father."

14

ENTERING
KYOTO MYTHOS

Masa guided me to the end of a hallway that ended in a dark door with a plaque hanging from it reading:

Kyoto Mythos - Entry Bathtub

"I'm putting my faith in you, my son." Those were his last words to me before he left. As the whirring of the wheelchair faded away, the door opened automatically. I found myself in a square room with back walls, a black ceiling, and a black floor. I felt as though I was in a bank vault. At the far end of the room, a mysterious halo of white light emanated from a huge, circular bathtub. This was the only source of light in the room.

In the center of the vault-like chamber, there were two Eames lounge chairs. I recognized them immediately because an Eames chair was one of those things I had always wanted but couldn't afford. There were no other furnishings in the room.

Sitting in one of those wood and leather chairs was a man in a black short-sleeved shirt and black jeans, his figure blurring into the darkness as if he was a ghost. He was engrossed in reading a book. When he became aware of my presence, he closed it, and I could see the cover: *The Castle* by Franz Kafka. Then I looked at his face. It seemed familiar, but I couldn't place it.

"My name is Murakami," he said, rising to shake my hand while bowing his head. "It will be a pleasure to work together."

"Pleased to meet you, I'm Nathan," I replied, astonished to realize I was facing the famous writer. I couldn't understand how it was possible for that novelist, who had passed away years ago, to be there. "I thought you—"

"I'm like the characters in my novels," he interrupted me. "Always alive and dead at the same time."

"I don't understand," I said.

"Human beings perish, but fictional characters are immune to the passage of time. When a reader opens a novel, it doesn't matter if hundreds of years have passed since it was written. As soon as they start reading, the characters come to life."

"But you're not a fictional character. Or are you?"

Murakami smirked. The ghostly shadows projected by the aura of the tub made his expression hard to interpret. And then, as if he had changed his personality, he said in a jovial tone, "I was joking!"

"Joking?"

"I don't want Murakami to be forgotten. That's why I take advantage of our physical resemblance to dress and style myself like him—and to borrow his name. I do it in his honor!"

"Then, you don't write novels?"

"I write stories in Kyoto Mythos. Without my narratives, this virtual world would be a boring desert where no one would want to live." Seeing my confused expression, Murakami pointed to the bathtub. "It's better if you see for yourself," he said.

He pulled out a small box marked with the company logo from his pocket. From it, he extracted two pairs of earphones, and we put them in.

As a carrier of samsara, he must have had the freckle circle too. I glanced over and saw that he had it in the same place as Mia and I, but instead of forming a complete circle of twelve points, he had a semicircle of seven.

Then he gave me a case containing two contact lenses. As I

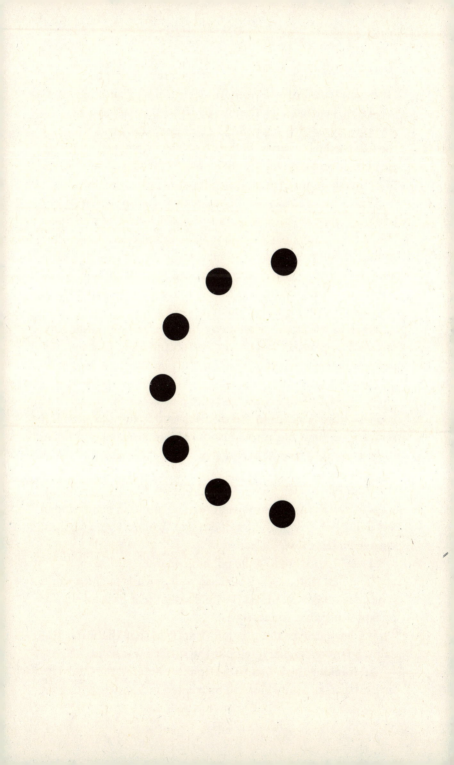

put them in, I saw that they had circuits printed on their interior. He began to undress in front of me as if it was nothing. I imitated him, fascinated by the idea of accessing that virtual world. As I put my clothes on one of the Eames chairs, I was struck by the extraordinary nature of the situation. Two naked men with earphones and electronic contact lenses in a dark room, about to immerse themselves in a backlit pool.

"The water temperature is regulated to mimic that of our bodies. It also contains Epsom salts, which will help us float. When you enter, float with your arms extended looking at the ceiling. If you feel tension in your neck, try to release it. It's not good to be tense when your consciousness leaves reality and jumps into Kyoto Mythos. If you do it right, at some point you will stop feeling the water touching your skin."

Next, Murakami took out two pills from the box and gave me one. "You need to be floating in the tub and looking at the ceiling within thirty seconds of taking the pill. We must be quick."

"What is it?"

"It's 5-MeO-DMT combined with a patented formula so that it doesn't break down in the stomach and is fully absorbed. It serves to expand the consciousness of human beings and help them enter into something greater."

"A drug . . ."

"Your pineal gland naturally produces 5-MeO-DMT, but always in low doses. This molecule can be found in plants and in any living being. It's a matter of dosage. To enter Kyoto Mythos, we need a large dose."

"I see," I said, holding the pill in my hand.

"The first time is scary because your spirit is facing a world it has never been in. In fact, I would say it's fear of yourself, fear of exploring what you really are."

We leaned over the tub, and I noticed that the water was calm. So much so that it felt like the surface was solid.

After taking the 5-MeO-DMT pill, we entered the fluid. I lay on my back, as Murakami had instructed me, and extended my arms and legs. My shadow was projected on the ceiling, as if I was the Vitruvian Man.

Suddenly, the light in the tub went out. I still had my eyes open, but the darkness was so deep that I didn't know what was going on.

I heard Murakami's voice saying, "There's always the possibility that you or I may not return to this world."

I felt my heart pounding, but there was no turning back. The last thing I noticed was a multiple pricking sensation, right on my twelve freckles, below my ear, as if I had been struck with a cactus.

In that absolute darkness, I couldn't see or smell. I had stopped feeling the water around me. A strange lethargy indicated that I was losing consciousness, but at the same time, I felt more awake than ever before. Around us, the silence was so profound that I could feel it. "There's no space, time or matter," I told myself as I dissolved into an endless present. "The universe is consciousness. My consciousness is everything, or nothing."

I had the strange sensation that I was returning home, a remote place I hadn't visited in a long time, but which felt familiar. An entire universe made of blackness, and I, its only spectator. It was as if a strange force had ripped my consciousness from my body and thrown it into outer space, to a distant place nothing could reach, not even the light from the stars.

"You're at the edge of the universe. What are you now?" my consciousness asked me.

I tried to look around, but I had no eyes to see with.

"You're just consciousness. I am you, and you are me," my consciousness responded.

It was impossible to tell if seconds or days were passing. In the end, I concluded that even time had ceased to exist.

Then I felt a flickering of my eyes, the first part of my body to return to existence. I forced my eyelids to open and searched for some point of reference in the darkness. The blackness gave way to two-dimensional geometric shapes of colors that gradually took on volume. In the distance, fluorescent lines appeared, forming rectangular patterns. They danced back and forth, creating a kind of corridor through which I sped. They began to organize into kaleidoscopic patterns, combined with lines and vertices that formed a three-dimensional mesh. At the end of this corridor of geometric shapes emerged an iridescent ball that reminded me of the sun.

Looking down, I noticed that I didn't have legs. Beneath me, there was only water, a dark, colorless sea that seemed to have no end. I flew like a bird, witnessing the formation of oceans.

Suddenly, I realized I had a body again. In that instant, I fell from the sky into the dark water, which now moved like a giant whirlpool ready to engulf me. Panic, unlike any I had ever experienced, tore through me. As I fell, the sensation of vertigo grew more powerful, and the eye of the vortex grew larger and larger.

I began to retch and convulse, as if my intestines were exploding. The pain was so intense that there was no room for fear. I could do nothing but surrender to the elements and let the marine whirlpool engulf me. In that moment of desperation, time took shape again, and I felt it starting to run ahead of me.

Blinking, I found myself in an elevator with no familiar buttons. It seemed to be moving, but I wasn't sure if it was going up or down. Had I returned to reality? Had I left the bathtub and the building?

I was naked, so this wasn't the best way to return to the world. Feeling embarrassed, I could hear the beating of my heart in the elevator-like box. I felt along the walls for some sensor to open the doors. As I crouched on the floor, I saw something shining in a corner. It was a golden medal on a metal chain. I picked it up and realized that the same infinite knot that Reiko had tattooed behind her ear was engraved on that amulet. I put on the pendant and felt its cold touch on my bare chest.

Suddenly the elevator stopped. Through the elevator walls, which I realized were made of clear glass, I could see that we were above ground, as though the capsule had pushed its way up through the soil, like a shoot emerging from a plowed field.

On the other side of the glass, it was night and raining heavily. The elevator door opened, and I felt I had no choice but to step out into the open. Not knowing where I was, I began to walk on the muddy ground, among bushes. A strong wind whipped the driving rain.

I walked naked through that storm-ravaged place until I came to a huge gate. Although visibility was poor, I immediately knew it was the one I had dreamed of the night I saw Mia's photo. The structure, supported by wooden posts, emerged in the eerie landscape, spectral and majestic. It was too big to be the entrance to a city; it was more like a building of ten stories or more—exactly like the one I had seen in my dreams.

Without a doubt, I was in front of the Rashomon gate.

It was standing on an elevated wooden platform, and a roof protected the area around it. I started ascending the steps to the wooden platform to shield myself from the rain. As I reached the top of the stairs I noticed two statues standing on each side of the gate. They watched me with threatening faces. One demon had its mouth open, and the other clenched its lips. I had the impression that the first one was staring at me fixedly, while holding up the palm of its hand as though to block my path. Paradoxically, with the other hand, it seemed to be beckoning me to step through the gate.

Once I reached the top of the stairs I took a step forward, and the giant hand that appeared to be blocking my path started to move. My heart skipped a beat, but after my psychedelic journey, the fact that the demonic statue was apparently alive seemed almost normal to me.

"It's a video game," I said, to calm myself down.

"You cannot pass," said the demon with a deep voice that seemed to emanate from its entire body. "Only those who know what they fear most in life can go through Rashomon gate and enter the city of Heian."

"What do you mean?"

"What do you fear most in life?"

"Well . . . suffering from a painful illness, ending up homeless, being thrown into jail . . ." My response seemed to displease it. It moved its hand toward me as if to squash a fly. Reflexively, I jumped back to avoid the deadly swipe.

"Those are mere fantasies, Nathan! There's something you fear much more."

As I searched for another answer, the demon took a step toward me and crouched down to observe me closely.

"Dying alone, without family or friends," I said, still trying.

"You're wrong again! Until you get it right, you can't pass."

Since childhood, I had played video games and had often found myself facing an enemy blocking my path. But this had taken on such a real dimension that fear had me paralyzed.

Trembling, my thoughts raced, as I tried to think of what it was that I feared most. What if it was a riddle? Perhaps the solution lay in what would calm the demon enough to let me access the city.

Summoning my courage, I said, "I'm afraid of never surpassing my father's achievements."

The demon shook its head and snorted; its infernal breath engulfed me like lethal gas. I felt like trapped prey. Any movement of its hand would crush me instantly.

"If you don't know what you fear the most, you don't know yourself."

I glanced sideways at the other demon. Unlike the one that had come to life, this one emanated calmness and silent wisdom. At this statue's base, I saw the symbol of the infinite knot. Following an inspiration from my experience playing video games, I removed the amulet I had found in the elevator and held it up. A glow emanated from it, like a light bulb shining from my hand. The glare seemed to blind the threatening demon, but brought the other to life. With slow movements, as if awakening from a long slumber, it leaned over me and extended its enormous hand.

"Give me the amulet of the infinite knot," it said.

And as I handed over the amulet, the answer to the first demon's question emerged within me: "What I fear the most is that, after a long existence, when the time comes to die, I will realize that I have never fully lived."

Upon hearing this, both demons stepped aside, leaving me a clear path, but I felt an ominous foreboding. A chill ran down my spine as I realized that the Rashomon gate was opening. Through it, under the relentless storm, I could see a muddy avenue. A lightning bolt struck the surrounding mountains, illuminating the wooden houses that lined both sides of the avenue.

In a state of wonder, I went through the gate with a sideways glance at the demons, who had returned to statue form. On the other side of the gate, my bare feet sank into the mud of the avenue, and a putrid, nauseating smell filled the air.

Looking down, I realized that I was standing in a puddle of blood. I lifted my head. All around me were samurai corpses, katanas and helmets.

My strength abandoned me, my legs buckled, and I fell to my knees in the bloody mud. Before losing consciousness, I saw the shadow of a girl walking toward me.

PART TWO

Kyoto Mythos

The chapters set in the universe of Kyoto Mythos are headed by the symbol Ψ, honoring the Schrödinger equation.

THE GENJI AND
THE TAIRA

As well as establishing Japan's capital city of Heian, Emperor Kanmu initiated a tradition that would change the course of Japanese history. As his family grew significantly, he created an independent branch for his distant relatives called the Taira.

Initially, the Taira lived in Heian and acted under the command of the imperial house, but over time they gained political and military power, eventually becoming one of the largest samurai clans in Japan.

The emperors who succeeded Kanmu imitated him and created their own clans to protect their extensive families. Thus, the Genji clan was born, and it grew to the point where conflict with the Taira became inevitable.[1] In the year 1180, to the south of the capital, a war erupted between the samurai of the Taira and those of the Genji. The conflict ended five years later with the defeat of the imperial court, and the loss of absolute imperial power in Japan. This marked the beginning of the first shogunate, a military government organized into feudal domains, where the Genji held power. Up until that point, the

---

1 To be historically accurate, Genji is the alternative name for the Minamoto clan, and Taira for the Heike clan. In this novel, I decided to use Genji and Taira, as these are the simplest names to remember for a non-Japanese speaker.

emperor had been an all-powerful being descended from the gods, but now the Genji controlled Japan.

Although the emperor continued to live in Heian, the military government of the shogunate and the capital of Japan were moved to Kamakura.

Heian, which literally means "peace," had ironically become a place engulfed in conflicts, wars and death.

Over the centuries, the threads of the Genji and Taira have not been broken, and their descendants continue to control the destiny of Japan, and the entire world, under the guise of a democratic government that is merely a facade. Today, the emperor's only activity is to stroll through the gardens of his palace in the center of Tokyo.

Taira Corporation and Genji Corporation are two of the largest companies in the world, and their leaders no longer fight for control of Japan but for the future of humanity. They do not want to weaken the connection between humans and the gods, as happened when humans used to fight in wars. They aspire to the opposite.

Both Taira Corporation and Genji Corporation want to restore our union with the gods. They have come to the conclusion that this union is the only way for human beings, threatened by the destruction of their planet, to continue living in this world forever.

15
A NEW AWAKENING
Ψ

Upon hearing her voice after such a long time, I had the sensation that an angel had come to rescue me. Her first words were:

"Have you missed me?"

I was so exhausted that I couldn't speak. I could barely muster the strength to open my eyelids halfway. As I turned my head with difficulty, I still felt dizzy and my vision was blurry but I could see that I was lying in a tatami room with wooden walls. On one side of the room, what seemed to be panes of translucent washi paper allowed daylight to filter through.

She was dressed in a simple yukata cotton kimono with pink tones; the sleeves revealed her delicate wrists. Her hair was tied in a ponytail, except for two strands tucked behind her ears.

Next to the futon where I had woken up was a tray with green tea, a bowl of white rice and a bowl of miso soup.

"Are you real?" I managed to ask, still dazed.

"It depends on your definition of reality," Mia responded.

I reached behind my ear and couldn't feel the twelve bumps of my circle. If I was dreaming, it was the most realistic dream I had ever had.

"It's not a dream," she said, as if she knew what I was thinking. "Welcome to Kyoto Mythos."

"You don't have freckles in this world either?"

"No. Here our avatar is similar but not exactly the same as our biological body."

At that moment, I realized I was dressed in a navy blue yukata. I blushed at the thought that I had been found naked in the rain.

I sat up on the futon, and she placed the tray of food on a wooden stand. My stomach growled. Mia knelt on the tatami in formal *seiza* position, resting her hands on her knees.

The first bite of white rice tasted heavenly. Then I took a sip of the soup, which warmed my body.

"How long have I been asleep?" I asked.

"Two days and two nights."

I took a deep breath, trying to piece together my last memories before entering the bath in the dark room.

"Where is Murakami?"

"Writing upstairs."

With a gentle movement, Mia changed position: she moved her legs to the side and crossed her hands over her thighs. As she moved, strands of hair escaped from behind her ears. Fascinated by the sight, I recognized the Mia of my adolescence, but at the same time, she was different. Her gestures and her sweet, distant expression were those of an adult woman. The light coming through the washi briefly bathed her white complexion in warm tones. She had neatly plucked eyebrows, like lines drawn with a fine brush. Then I noticed her eyes. Her tender and innocent gaze was just as I remembered it, but with one difference . . .

"Your eyes were emerald green."

"I asked Masa to change the eye color of my avatar. That's why they are black now." She lowered her neck, and the two strands of hair fell in front of her face. "I always wanted to be completely Japanese, but the green eyes I inherited from my American father gave me away. Since I was a child, I prayed to wake up the next day with dark eyes like my mother—a native of Kyoto—but in the real world, there are things you can't change."

"Here in Mythos, you can choose who you want to be," she said, tucking the strands of hair behind her ears. "Everything is negotiable."

I wondered if this black-eyed girl was the same Mia I shared my adolescence with. And was I even still myself in this simulation where we were talking?

"You look more handsome and muscular. You've got a lovely strong jawline now."

"When you returned to Japan, I started taking jujutsu training seriously. With age, my teenage features changed—I guess that's natural."

"I always wanted to learn martial arts . . . Will you teach me?"

As we talked, I gulped down the bowl of rice and finished the soup. Little by little, I was regaining my strength.

"I still can't believe it," I said.

"What?"

"I never thought I'd see you again. It's not every day you come across the dead."

"Do I look like a ghost?"

We both smiled, and those unfamiliar black eyes sparkled.

She leaned close. I was aware of the bare skin of her arm beneath the sleeve of her yukata. Her pupils were dilated, as if she was trying to cast a spell over me. I was flooded with a mix of happiness and bitterness.

Twenty years had passed since the last time we saw each other. All that time wasted in oblivion. Hypnotized, I set the chopsticks down next to the rice bowl. She reached out and touched my hand. Suddenly, the distance in time vanished. Twenty years turned into a second as the invisible threads of our joint destiny came together once again.

In that moment, all my doubts disappeared. The touch of her fingers ignited the embers of the fire I had been carrying inside me for years.

This was the unmistakable touch of my first love.

16

A MEETING AT THE PINNACLE

Masa had called a meeting of the board of directors at his office with its magnificent view of Kyoto. Van Gogh's *Sunflowers* looked down on the scene, indifferent to what was happening around the conference table. Sitting under the painting, Reiko was busy making notes of what was being discussed.

The first agenda item was the announcement that Taira Corporation had become the largest company in the world for the first time in its history, surpassing Tesla Inc., which had been the largest for decades.

Although this was cause for celebration, Masa seemed exhausted and pained, his head bowed, as if he barely had any strength left.

"Congratulations to all! Today we gather to celebrate this great triumph, but you all know that my ambitions go beyond this," Masa began.

The board members listened attentively.

Masa stroked his chin, lowered his gaze, and continued with his speech.

"I am proud of our financial results, but if we don't continue innovating, if we don't make sure that every human being, regardless of age and genetics, can access Kyoto Mythos, sooner or later investors will lose confidence in us, and our stock price will fall . . ."

Masa paused, a hesitant expression on his face. He knew that the words coming out of his mouth were mere corporate jargon, a kind of dishonesty.

"I need to enter Kyoto Mythos as soon as possible!" he said, decisively, clenching his fists on the table, and turning to the director of biotechnology with a threatening look.

"We are doing everything possible to find the biological key," she replied, nervously. "But we struggle to make progress if every time we conduct a test the subject dies."

"Excuses, excuses," said Masa.

"Dear President Masa, this month three volunteers have died in our facilities in Mongolia, and another seven have died here. If we continue at this rate, we are going to raise suspicions," warned the scientist. "The high percentage of deaths we declare as workplace accidents is putting us in danger. If the government opens a criminal investigation about these cases, our dream will be over."

"Forget about the government!" Masa shouted, beside himself. "We are above them. The sacrifices will not be in vain. Remember that we do this for the advancement of our species. If a few have to die so that we can finally live in a happy world without suffering, it will have been worth it."

"Yes, but with no samsara—" said the director of biotechnology, trying to interrupt.

Masa cut her off. "Now you have Nathan in Kyoto Mythos. I want your team to focus all their efforts on monitoring his progress with the mission until 100 percent of the samsara manifests within him. We cannot afford to lose Nathan under any circumstances!"

"But you know it's impossible to guarantee his survival," said Reiko.

Frustrated, Masa grunted and began to sneeze uncontrollably. Reiko got up from her chair and handed him a handful of pills. Between sneezes, he managed to swallow them all at once. Instantly, the attack began to subside.

"Don't you think we're risking too much by putting all our eggs in Nathan's basket?" said the director of the quantum computing section, a middle-aged man with gray hair. "We need a plan B."

"I just explained that we lost ten carriers of the samsara gene before it fully manifested in them," said the director of biotechnology angrily. "Now all we have is Nathan. Of course, we're working with new embryos, but they won't be born in time to save our CEO . . ."

"The iteration speed of experiments in your biotechnology section has never been adequate," countered the director of computing, adjusting his tie, "Plus, your root cause analysis of the carriers' deaths is still a mystery."

"Mind your own business!" shouted the director of biotechnology, offended. "You only have one quantum computer capable of running the Kyoto Mythos simulation. If the only quantum computer we have fails—"

Masa had now recovered from his sneezing fit, and was able to respond more calmly. "This is not a time for division; we are a team. We've tried hundreds of plans and strategies, and they've all failed in one way or another. But that has always been the nature of scientific experimentation. Through trial and error, we've learned along the way. The end result is the only thing that matters. It's time to work with more unity than ever. We are in the final stretch."

When the meeting had finished, Reiko, Masa, and the director of biotechnology left the iconic Taira Corporation skyscraper, walking across a garden with several ponds where colorful koi carp were swimming.

After going over a wooden bridge, they reached the entrance of a modern structure with elegant curves that contrasted with Taira Corporation's glass tower. This building housed a gigantic facility with an interior structure of beams and metal walls of dull gray, where hundreds of employees in white lab coats rushed around.

A technician guided them down some stairs leading to a basement. Masa slid down a ramp in his wheelchair. As they descended, the temperature dropped.

The four of them donned spacesuits before entering a sealed and refrigerated room. Inside the room were vertical glass tanks the size of a human body filled with bubbling greenish liquid. Through the upper part of the glass, the features of human faces could be detected.

"We have no room for these latest bodies in our facility," said the technician who was guiding them.

"We could discard them," suggested the head of biotechnology. "The contract that was signed has a clause that allows us to dispose of the body. None of these bodies have families who will miss them."

"Having bodies and brains in culture capsules is good," said Masa. "We never know when they will come in useful for conducting experiments. Besides, remember they were heroes. They managed to live within a simulation, even if it was only for a short length of time. When the time comes to make our research public, this is something that will be written about in history books."

"We'll prepare extra capsules just in case," said the director.

Masa's face darkened. "We cannot allow Nathan to end up in one of those capsules before extracting the samsara. The next twelve months are crucial. If we don't succeed, I will die—I will disappear forever."

Reiko, who hadn't stopped taking notes until then, looked up at Masa. "Shouldn't we have told Nathan that after his entry into Kyoto Mythos, he only has twelve months to fulfill his mission?" she asked.

"All the risks are detailed in the fine print of the contract he signed, but of course, nobody ever reads a contract properly" Masa replied.

With that, he set off in his wheelchair, and as he went up the ramp to leave the laboratory, he stopped and turned.

"I know that very soon the samsara will be ours!" he shouted. "Nathan will be able to choose his destiny when his last freckle is about to disappear . . ."

Reiko and the director of biotechnology walked behind Masa. They looked at each other and exchanged knowing smiles. They had been with him for years, and they knew his obsessions and sudden mood changes.

Back in his office, Masa's weary gaze was a sharp contrast to the radiant color of Van Gogh's flowers.

"I'm exhausted," he said.

"You haven't even allowed yourself to celebrate our global leadership," said Reiko.

"You know I won't do that until we achieve a complete victory," Masa replied.

He glanced at the touchscreen installed in his wheelchair. A percentage in red marked the probability of dying in the next year, based on his health condition. Since he had started monitoring his health with the best available technology, the percentage was gradually becoming higher.

"72 percent . . . Worse than ever." Masa sighed dejectedly. "Give me my injection."

Reiko took a syringe from a case and knelt beside him to inject the liquid into his arm. Seconds later, Masa's eyes regained their usual sparkle. Even the skin on his face seemed smoother and brighter.

"These injections won't keep me alive much longer. I need to enter Kyoto Mythos, whatever the cost," said Masa, extending his hand to touch Reiko's thigh, but she ignored him, moving away toward the desk, which was cluttered with books as always, and activating a screen installed there. Instantly, Nathan and Mia appeared in Kyoto Mythos. They were in a tatami room. Mia was holding Nathan's hand while he looked into her eyes. Catching her breath, Reiko switched off the display. She bit her lip and cast a bitter look at Masa, who had fallen asleep, and poured herself a glass of wine.

As she drank, gazing out over Kyoto, a warmth in her groin reminded her of the moments she'd shared in bed with Nathan, and her heart filled with joy. She poured herself a second glass.

17
MEMORIES OF PARADISE
Ψ

When Mia withdrew her hand, the warmth of her touch lingered for a while until I fell asleep again. She wasn't by my side when I woke up again in this new world. But I noticed that strength had returned to my limbs and my headache and dizziness were gone. I could see my surroundings clearly. From the futon where I lay, I saw that the wall of washi paper panels was open, revealing a Japanese garden, as though it was a picture in a frame.

I gathered my strength and got up. As I stepped out of the tatami room where I'd been sleeping and walked to the edge of the wooden veranda, which was slightly raised above the grass, I felt as if I was on a boat sailing across a green sea.

Fascinated, I gazed at the scene, from the wooded hill on the far side of a stream, to the leaves of a bush growing next to the veranda where I stood. I studied the leaves of the bush, trying to find defects or detect the pixels that had generated such a realistic graphic, but in vain. This virtual world was generated with such perfection it was impossible to differentiate it from reality. And not only visually—the aroma of the tatami mingled with the scent of fresh air, and birds chirped in the cherry blossoms lining the stream that divided the garden in two. A small vermilion bridge connected both parts of the garden.

A black butterfly with white spots fluttered by and I watched it land on the bush. I still couldn't wrap my head around the fact that I was living in a simulation—everything felt so real.

I wondered where Mia was and what would happen to me if I ended up trapped and alone in this virtual world. Would I be able to get out?

For a moment, I regretted signing Masa's contract without knowing what I had agreed to. My breathing quickened, and I had the feeling you get when you are having a bad dream but no matter how hard you try, you can't wake yourself up.

Then suddenly, I remembered something Mia had said last night: "Murakami is writing on the second floor."

I turned to look from the veranda to the interior of the tatami room. At the back was a small door. It opened onto a wooden staircase. As I climbed, my legs still felt weak.

Upstairs, a narrow hallway ended in two doors: one to the left with a sign that said "Mia" and another to the right that said "Murakami." I knocked on Mia's door, but there was no answer. On Murakami's door was another wooden sign beneath his name:

I am writing.
Do not disturb.

I hesitated for a moment, but, anxious about being trapped and alone in that place, I knocked a couple of times.

Murakami opened the door.

"Can't you read?" he grumbled.

"I apologize for interrupting," I said, bowing.

He stepped aside and beckoned for me to enter. It was a spartan room with only a low table by the window overlooking the garden, and some cushions scattered on the tatami. In the presence of another human being I felt my anxiety start to lift.

Piles of papers and scrolls were stacked on the table next to a bronze candelabra holding some unlit candles. What caught my attention the most was the antique quill pen resting next to an inkwell.

"Wow, the oldest thing I've used is a fountain pen," I said.

"I acquired this quill in the gardens of the Imperial Palace," Murakami said as he knelt on the tatami, facing the desk.

"How do you take care of it?"

"Just sharpen the tip occasionally."

I sat next to him, and he handed the quill to me. The base was white, then it turned orange, and at the tip, golden tones sparkled.

"It's from a phoenix," he said.

"I thought that was a mythical bird that doesn't exist . . ."

"We're inside Kyoto Mythos, where myths are reality."

"A virtual world created by Masa," I said.

"I dislike the word virtual. Do you think the quill you hold in your hands doesn't exist?"

"It's real to me, here, now."

I ran my index finger over the quill's tip, and my skin became stained with black ink.

"Everything we can imagine has a certain quality of reality," Murakami said. "Imagination can create worlds."

"But technically, we're inside a quantum simulation."

He took the quill from my hands with a grunt, and put it back on his desk. "I loathe technicalities," he said.

"Upon reflection, the real universe is also a quantum world."

"Exactly. Being in a different layer of the onion doesn't imply greater or lesser truth."

"And only God can see the whole onion?" I asked.

"Each layer has its own gods. Do you believe in a single all-powerful God?"

"I only believe in what I can see."

"When you read a story, you don't see the characters with your eyes, but with your imagination. Does that mean you believe nothing of what you read? Imagine for a moment that we're characters in a novel that an author is writing in another world. Does that make us less real? Do we cease to exist just because we're part of a story or myth imagined by someone else?"

Murakami pointed to the piles of manuscripts on his desk. Then I noticed the title written at the top of a scroll. The characters were large enough for me to read from where I stood:

Kyoto Mythos - Nathan's story

"You still can't read it, it's only half-finished," Murakami said, when he saw where I was looking. "In fact, I won't be able to finish it if you don't start moving and making decisions."

Without understanding anything, I simply nodded. Making decisions. That was something I hadn't been doing for a long time; I had simply let my life be carried along by external forces. Had I chosen to come to Japan or was I simply following the breadcrumbs that Masa was putting in front of me?

Murakami moved several piles of scrolls onto the tatami and, after rummaging through them, he pulled one out and handed it to me. It was bound with string. I could make out the title of the manuscript:

Kyoto Mythos - User Manual for
Taira Corporation Samsara Carriers

"Start here. It will help you understand your purpose in this layer of the onion," Murakami said, standing up and turning his back on me. He dipped the phoenix feather pen into the inkwell as I got up with the manuscript under my arm. When I reached the door, I stopped.

"Where is Mia?" I asked, turning to face Murakami.

"At the Imperial Palace, with her fiancé," he replied.

18

THE SWORD

The monitor on Masa's desk displayed images of Nathan and Murakami in Kyoto Mythos, as if they were characters in a historical movie. Masa looked away from the screen and turned to the window that overlooked Kyoto. He gazed at the Higashiyama mountains, at temples peeking through the trees, at the cluster of buildings in the city center divided by the Kamogawa River. The splendid blue sky was adorned with tiny clouds that seemed to float like balloons escaped from a birthday party.

Although his mood could change from one minute to the next, at that moment he felt optimistic. He was certain that, finally, his grand plan was going to work. The monitor calculating the probability of dying in the next year had increased 10 percent since the last time he checked it and was now at 82 percent.

He realized that his longed-for dream of living in the past was soon to become a reality. He felt a pang of sadness at the thought of having to leave the real Kyoto forever. He felt nostalgia in advance for the life he was about to leave behind as soon as he could introduce the samsara gene into his body.

He pressed a couple of buttons on the desk, and Reiko, the biotechnology director, and the quantum computing director came into the room.

"Everything seems to be going well in Kyoto Mythos. Now we have to take care of what's happening here, in the real world," said Masa. Reiko and the two directors exchanged knowing glances. They sensed that Masa was in a good mood.

"My department has started building a second quantum computer in case the one we have in operation fails," announced the quantum computing director.

"Good, thank you for taking the initiative, but that's not what I'm referring to," Masa replied.

"You mean Roku, right?" said Reiko. "And Genji Corporation . . ." As she was the one who knew Masa best, she could sense what was worrying him at any given moment. And she knew that Roku's Genji Corporation, one of the most successful companies of the last few years, always focusing on building technologies and products rivaling those of Masa's Taira Corporation, was never far from his thoughts.

"Exactly, we need the Kusanagi sword," said Masa.

The director of biotechnology looked down, shaking her head. "One of your absurd beliefs," she muttered.

"Absurd?" Masa smiled in a way that said he expected nothing more than this kind of response from the director. He had hired her for her rebellious nature. She was one of the few employees who didn't let him intimidate her, and wasn't scared of challenging him.

"Our work here is based on scientific principles—" the woman began.

"You know I don't fully trust science," Masa interrupted.

"But—"

"*The Epic of Gilgamesh*, which has nothing to do with science," he said, pointing to the showcase where tablet number nine was displayed, "was my inspiration for making Kyoto Mythos a reality. This is what will save me, not doctors."

"Science only advances when a pioneer's imagination believes in something impossible," said the director of quantum computing, as he adjusted his tie, words that he maybe hoped would please Masa.

"Beliefs only cease to be beliefs when they are ruled out by science," countered the biotechnology director. "Furthermore, they must be falsifiable for us to consider them, or have you never read Popper?"

The quantum computing director adjusted his glasses.

"I'm so tired of all this mental masturbation," said Reiko.

"Enough of the arguing—we are a team!" said Masa.

"But we're talking about a damn rusty sword!" shouted the director of biotechnology.

"Do not disrespect history," said Masa. "You know how important the Kusanagi sword is for us. When the time comes, it will be a key element to activate the samsara to 100 percent inside Nathan. In any case, I want the sword that Roku has stolen from us. It belongs to us!"

Both directors looked away, out at the blue sky of Kyoto, where white clouds moved slowly, carried by the wind.

"Someone will have to go negotiate with Roku," said Masa. His eyes came to rest on Reiko.

19

CHERRY BLOSSOM VILLA

Ψ

Back on the ground floor, I sat at the edge of the veranda and unfurled the scroll Murakami had just given me.

Welcome to Kyoto Mythos!

Congratulations on your successful entry into the virtual world created by Taira Corporation! You have the honor of being one of the pioneering carriers of samsara. If you are reading this, it means you have survived the entry process. We apologize for any inconveniences caused to you during the first few days. We are still adjusting parameters to reduce the suffering and pain experienced by the user upon entry.

You now live in a world that meticulously emulates the city of Heian, the Kyoto of the late twelfth century. This was always the vision of our CEO, Masa, a lover of Japan's past.

As stipulated in the contract you signed with Taira Corporation, you have not come here to enjoy a second life, as future users of our services will do. As an employee of our corporation, you will have to assume certain duties that will be explained to you in due course.

There are three other employees of Taira Corporation alongside you in Kyoto Mythos:

- *Mia: a historian who specializes in twelfth-century Japan. She is responsible for ensuring that this world closely resembles ancient Japan.*
- *Murakami: a writer specializing in mythology. He is responsible for crafting the possible scenarios that our users can experience within Kyoto Mythos. Without his imagination, life here would be dull, like a paradise where nothing happens.*
- *Akira: a hacker, and expert in quantum computing. His cabin in Kyoto Mythos is the only place whose appearance does not emulate the past. This cabin allows us to communicate with the real world and download your consciousness back into your biological body (see footnotes).*

When I saw Akira's name, I understood that I would have to speak with him if I wanted to leave the simulation. Wondering about the procedure for exiting Kyoto Mythos, I searched for the footnotes at the end of the scroll, but I couldn't find them. I continued reading:

As for the rules of this place, they are still in the beta testing phase, and any help from you and the other members of our team will be welcome. We need your expertise in watch design to address certain inconsistencies that are occurring in the synchronization between the Kyoto Mythos simulation and the real world.

We assume that these discrepancies are due to time not being a real dimension within the framework of quantum mechanics, as it is in the real universe governed by the laws of relativity formulated by Albert Einstein. For now, we only have hypotheses. We have not been able to discern a theory that explains these discrepancies.

Our quantum computing department has not been able to solve this problem in the real world. It is necessary for you to intervene by working from the virtual world. We believe that constructing a clock within Kyoto Mythos will help synchronize the space-time dimensions of the virtual world with the real world.

I looked up from the manuscript. Among the trees, on the other side of the stream, I caught sight of Mia walking toward me. After crossing the vermilion bridge, she greeted me with a smile. She was wearing a yukata in shades of orange and carried a basket on her arm. She sat down beside me and took out a lacquered box.

"I brought you palace food," she said as she began to unpack plates and smaller boxes. I helped her open them and arrange them on a tray. There were vegetables, fish, and balls of different colors and sizes that resembled meatballs, but I couldn't identify them. The smell of food mingled with the spring fragrances. Several birds, attracted by the aromas, fluttered down from the treetops to perch nearby.

Finally, from the bottom of the basket, Mia took out two bowls of rice, and we began to eat. Even though I was aware that all of this was a simulation, being there with Mia, looking out over that idyllic landscape, was a dream come true.

"Do you remember our last day together?" she asked.

"I have this strange feeling that it was yesterday. I remember your boredom with math, that look of concentration on your face while you were reading the Mishima novel, your excitement about having two children and a dog, the way you fell asleep on the sofa . . ."

"I remember the kiss you didn't give me."

"Why did you leave without telling me?"

After taking a bite of a pink ball of fish, Mia shook her head sharply from side to side, screwing up her nose, just the way I remembered. It was her typical expression of boredom, marring her face for a moment, before her angelic expression returned.

"I didn't make the decision to leave," Mia said, her gaze sinking into her rice bowl. "My father had to move to Tokyo for work."

"Yeah, but . . . that doesn't explain why I never heard from you again until—"

"I'm sorry, I cut off all communication. Not just with you, but with my past life. It wasn't an easy time. I was never happy in Tokyo as an adult; it's a place where everyone seems to have a personal agenda that doesn't include anyone else."

"I missed you," I confessed. "You were always on my dream agenda for the future."

"I guess that ended when you found out about my suicide," Mia said, a strange smile on her lips, as if this was something she was proud of. "It wasn't easy, but it's probably the best decision I've ever made in my life."

Without saying anything, I put a shiitake mushroom in my mouth. Mia tossed some grains of rice to the birds. A gust of wind swept through the cherry trees, and the blossoms fluttered down to settle at our feet.

"During my study of the Rashomon gate, I began to imagine what my life would be like in Japan's past. There came a point where it became such an obsession that I wished I could vanish from the present, disappear. Then I dreamed of the gate and met Masa, my savior. When I learned what was possible in Kyoto Mythos, I gave up my biological body and declared my death a suicide. My parents don't know that I still exist here, in the Kyoto of the past . . ."

"Wouldn't they be happy to know that you are still alive in this dimension?"

"I don't think so," she said with a sudden change in tone.

I never knew what kind of relationship Mia had with her family, so I didn't inquire further. She continued to feed the birds rice grains, and I took a bite of a fish that looked like sardine, and turned my gaze to the cherry trees.

"I couldn't say if those petals are white or pink," I said.

"Sakura cherry blossom is a symbol of Japan, as well as of this house—it's called Cherry Blossom Villa," she said.

A gentle breeze blew, and some sakura petals escaped to land on the surface of the stream, like tiny, delicate rafts. Others flew farther, fading into the distance.

"It's always spring here."

"Are the cherry blossoms always in bloom?"

"Every week, after the previous week's petals have fallen, the flowers bloom again. Deep down, Masa is a romantic: he designed Kyoto Mythos so that we can enjoy an eternal spring."

"I still don't quite understand about the passage of time," I said, pointing to the scroll I had left on the tatami.

"Time passes, but the seasons don't. In any case, for technical questions, ask Akira."

With that, she stood up, hopping from the tatami to the garden. The birds fluttered away and disappeared into the branches of the sakura trees.

"It's time for you to get moving. Let's go see Akira."

20
THE GAZE OF VENUS

W hy do I have to talk to that jerk?" asked Reiko.

"You're the most suitable person. You know Roku and I have been enemies since we executed the hostile takeover of those six companies from his financial group. He hasn't picked up my phone calls in years."

"They're gangsters," added Reiko. "You saw what they did to me at the restaurant."

"They wanted Nathan, not you, which is why you're the ideal person to negotiate with them. They won't harm you again."

"I don't trust them. People from Genji Corporation are capable of killing without blinking."

"I beg you, Reiko, I'm running out of time!"

"Do I have to sleep with Roku?"

"No!" said Masa, with a look of repulsion. "You know our rule as a polyamorous couple: only with our friends, never with the enemy."

Reiko caressed his hand. "Don't assign me just any bodyguard. I want Kamyu."

Masa began to sneeze, holding his side. Reiko ignored his gesture of pain and left without looking back or saying goodbye.

Kamyu was waiting for her in the garage. He was a man of few words, but Reiko liked being with him because she felt both safe and free; she was the one who decided how to act and when to break the silence.

They got into the Porsche that Reiko liked driving most, and headed for Osaka. As they joined the fifth elevated level of the highway, reserved for manual cars, Reiko asked, "Don't you get bored with your job? Most of the time, you have nothing to do."

"I'm busy every second, visualizing worst-case scenarios."

"Even now?"

"Of course."

"What could go wrong now?"

"Like in life in general, most of the time nothing bad happens. But when things do go sideways, the ones who have prepared for the worst are more resilient. At the moment, I'm visualizing our arrival at Genji Corporation. There's a possibility they might detain us to extort Masa, but don't worry: they have more to lose than to gain if they capture us."

On the horizon, the skyline of Osaka began to emerge, with interconnected skyscrapers that seemed to defy gravity.

"It must be tiring and depressing to always be thinking about the worst that could happen." Reiko said, biting her lip.

"Once you've seen the horrors of war, you stop being afraid of anything. The eye I lost in combat witnessed horrors that are hard to believe. I've already seen the worst."

Silence fell. Reiko realized she was missing Nathan and wondered what he would be doing in Kyoto Mythos with Mia.

After twenty minutes of driving on a highway that cut through the interior of several skyscrapers, they arrived at the headquarters of Genji Corporation, located on the outskirts of Osaka.

Unlike Kyoto, where conservation laws limited the height of any construction to less than 330 feet, in Osaka, the headquarters building rose more than a mile high, disappearing into the sky. A car elevator took them to the 110th floor, where a robot took the Porsche to the parking lot for manual cars.

They stepped out into a wooded park full of thick clouds, where solitary executives ate from their bento boxes. As Reiko and Kamyu headed toward the reception area, they passed by crowded restaurants among the groves. An android was waiting for them by the entrance arch to the building. After a deep bow, it granted them access to the office of Roku, the CEO of Genji Corporation, guiding them down a corridor to a tubular elevator, which took them to the executive dome on the 250th floor. The building's artificial intelligence system scanned their faces to ensure they were authorized to change levels in the skyscraper. The android accompanied them with the kind of unwavering smile a human would have been unable to maintain.

At the door of Roku's office, two human guards in black uniforms and augmented reality glasses stepped forward. Without a pause or a word, they inspected Reiko and Kamyu's bodies. One removed his glasses and, on tiptoes, closely examined Kamyu's artificial eye. The inspection done, they stepped aside, and the entrance to the CEO's room opened automatically. There stood Roku, with the movie-star good looks that were often portrayed on the covers of business magazines. His seductively dimpled smile was a topic of conversation among women across the country.

After greeting them politely, Roku bowed to Reiko, ignoring the presence of the bodyguard.

"I'm glad to see you, beautiful," he said.

Kamyu's mouth dropped open at his overly familiar tone. Reiko gave Roku a cold look and didn't return the bow. Nor did she wait for him to give her permission to sit herself down on a chair in the center of the office, which resembled Masa's. Completely unperturbed, he sat opposite her.

"I apologize for what happened at the sushi restaurant, darling," he said.

"Don't call me darling!" Reiko replied, her face tense.

"You know that sometimes we have to use force," he said. "As I grow older, I stop believing in peaceful methods."

"You're a bastard, that's what you are," Reiko said.

"If you're too peaceful, you become the fool of the playground. That's what always happens in Japan."

Kamyu, who had remained motionless until then, lowered his hand to the grip of his rail gun.

"Now, tell me, why are you here?" said Roku.

"To say hello and have tea, for God's sake."

Impassive, Roku smiled and signaled to another android. With great precision, it served them each a cup of green tea. Genji Corporation's most successful product was the android, a field in which Taira Corporation had failed to advance.

The android returned to its place by a window above the clouds, as if on an airplane. Roku crossed his legs, leaned back, and waited.

Reiko took a slow first sip of tea. "We want the Kusanagi sword," she said, placing her cup on the table.

Roku looked at her with curiosity. "If that's why you came, you may as well leave now," he said calmly.

"You know it belongs to us," Reiko insisted.

"It all depends on how we interpret history," he said with a soft smile. "Let's say that the sword was yours before and now it's ours, but that doesn't mean it belongs to you. The same goes for our quantum computer company, which you took over against my will."

"Don't change the subject. I've come to talk about the sword," said Reiko.

Roku leaned forward in his seat, with a seductive expression. "And what do you have to offer in exchange for the sword?"

"We would be willing to negotiate. We know you've redeveloped quantum technology and already have a simulation up and running, but you haven't managed to get anyone to connect to the system . . ."

"You're preaching to the choir. You know we want Nathan."

"That's the only thing we can't give you," Reiko replied firmly. "You know that."

"Then you'd better leave. Forget about that sword."

Reiko tried to relax by shifting her gaze to the Renaissance artworks in the office. In the center, Botticelli's Venus seemed to stare fixedly at them and at the sea of clouds that floated outside the windows.

Then, in a subtle and practiced movement, Reiko let one of her high-heeled shoes slip from her foot and fall to the floor. With a bare toe, she gently caressed her ankle on the other leg—a move she knew was irresistible to men. Roku couldn't help but lower his gaze to her legs.

She stood up. "We offer you Van Gogh's *Sunflowers* in exchange for the sword."

The president of Genji Corporation took a step toward her. "Get out," he snapped. "Your tricks won't work with me."

21

AKIRA, THE FOURTH CHOSEN ONE

Ψ

I followed Mia through the garden. I was wearing wooden clogs with rope thongs that I was still getting used to. We crossed the small bridge to the other side of the garden. From there, I turned to contemplate the facade of the house for the first time, after three days dozing on the futon in Cherry Blossom Villa.

On the second floor, there were at least ten windows. It was a huge house, big enough for several families. The roof was made of dark tiles, decorated with crests bearing a round symbol.

"What does that symbol mean?"

"It's called a *tomoe*," said Mia. Nobody knows its exact meaning, but the samurai clans associate it with Hachiman, the god of war. Some believe that the three comma-like circles represent Humanity, Earth, and Heaven."

As I lowered my gaze from the roof, I noticed Murakami, sitting at one of the windows, writing.

We walked along a path made from a mosaic of stones. That side of the garden was so thickly forested that we couldn't see the sky. As we walked, I realized that since the night of the storm on my arrival, every day had had a springlike blue sky.

Finally, we arrived at a clearing in the forest where there was a small cabin. As if our presence had been sensed, the door swung open and a tiny man stepped out.

"Thank goodness you've arrived," he said excitedly. "Welcome!" He was no more than five feet tall and wore a long-sleeved jacket and a skirt tied with a white belt. He had a dark complexion and dark glasses that hid his eyes. His small mouth was adorned with a thin, elongated mustache. Despite his diminutive body, an aura of strength radiated from him.

"You must be Nathan," he said.

I nodded and bowed.

"My name is Akira."

We removed our shoes and entered a room where daylight barely entered. Suddenly, the spell of living in a place set in the past was broken. The walls were covered with cables, and shelves full of books. In the center of the room were several plastic tables with computers, tablets, virtual reality headsets, and all kinds of electronic equipment. I realized that this was the place mentioned in the scroll that Murakami gave me this morning.

I plucked up all my courage. "What is the procedure to return to reality?" I asked.

"What? You've just met me and already you want to leave? Do you dislike me that much?" He gave me a playful punch on the shoulder, as if we were lifelong buddies.

"I just wanted to know . . ."

"My house is the only place in Kyoto Mythos where there's modern technology," Akira said proudly as he pointed to a monitor. "Look, see this terminal? It's a direct interface with the quantum computer that simulates this entire world, including your bodies."

Akira took a seat and began typing rapidly, continuing his technical babble. "Interesting, isn't it? This device is a simulated computer within Taira's quantum computer. With it, I can communicate with the computer that's simulating it all. It's like having a way to communicate with an almighty god who generates the material world."

I glanced at one of the screens, where Mia's RealPeople account was open. I understood that she had sent me those messages herself, from here, when I thought it was Masa pretending to be her.

Akira typed into the terminal:

```
Nathan.current_mission();
```

And on the screen appeared:

> MISSION: build the Clock Tower. It should be the most precise clock humanity has ever known.
> CURRENT STATUS: meet with Su Song.

"The current status indicates the next step you should take. As you can see, it's easier to know what you have to do here than in real life."

"Where can I find Su Song?" I asked, bewildered. "And who is that?"

"That's the fun part, Nathan. It's good to have some clues so you don't feel lost, but if everything is handed to you on a silver platter, it loses its charm. If you always knew what was going to happen, you'd end up doing nothing." He got up and put his hand on my shoulder. "I'll help you, but don't get used to it," he said.

He looked at me with a stern expression, and I was close enough now to see tiny eyes behind the dark glasses he wore.

Mia, Akira and I walked back to the vermilion bridge that led to the other side of the garden. Mia crossed it to go back home, leaving me alone with Akira. We followed a stone path that led to the streets of Kyoto. I felt a pang of unease as I realized I was without Mia. The idyllic tranquility suddenly vanished. The street we were walking down was bustling with people and with oxen carrying goods. The people wore geta clogs and kimonos in subdued colors. Some wore wide pants with the legs rolled up. Merchants were selling their wares from carts at the side of the road. Their goods were displayed with care, a contrast with the chaos of the street.

We passed by a stall selling spices that were arranged by color, from intense red to darker tones. Their pleasant aromas gave way to a foul smell coming from a nearby fishmonger. There, an entire family, including children, were going about their business beneath the day's catch that hung from the ceiling of their house.

Although there were crowds of people, there was no loud noise, just a soft murmur of voices and the clatter of passing carriages.

"This is Suzaku Avenue," said Akira. "To the south is the Rashomon gate; to the north, the Imperial Palace, the city's nerve center."

I kept close to my guide, afraid of getting lost in the crowd. I bumped into a man carrying vegetables in a large basket, and he shouted at me to get out of the way. As we continued to walk, the outlines of tall buildings—much taller than the merchant houses we were passing—started to appear on the horizon. To my left, I could see hills, where a multistory pagoda divided the sky in two.

At the end of Suzaku Avenue, we could see the building that marked the entrance to the Imperial Palace. Smaller than the Rashomon gate, its walls were orange-red. A pair of golden horns crowned the roof, whose emerald blue blended with the blue of the sky.

Four porters passed us, shouldering a carriage with a small window. Through it, I glimpsed a woman with white makeup and hair arranged like a geisha's. They were escorted by a retinue of men wearing tunics with broad shoulder pads. Two of them sported katanas hanging from their obi sashes.

"They're samurai serving the imperial court," said Akira.

"Like the rest of the people you see around you, they're virtual entities controlled by an advanced artificial intelligence."

For a while, I had forgotten that everything around me was created by artificial intelligence. With renewed awareness, I studied the apparent chaos around me. I observed fixed patterns in the way people walked, in their way of gesturing, in their expressions. I noticed the roofs of the houses were all exactly the same. Everything was so well done—as though directed by the conductor of a virtual orchestra—that I really had to focus hard to spot these strange regularities.

We left Suzaku Avenue, lost sight of the Imperial Palace, and ventured into alleys filled with inns where people were eating and drinking. Suddenly, Akira slowed down and drew close to me, as if he wanted to hide his tiny presence in my shadow. Ahead of us was a group of samurai, dressed in simpler clothes than those on the avenue, but also with katanas tied to their obi sashes. They were standing in a circle and chatting animatedly.

Akira grabbed my sleeve and whispered, "We'll go down this alley. They're samurai from the Genji clan. A bunch of rogues—better to avoid them!"

We bumped into a group of drunks coming out of a tavern. One was so drunk that his companions had to help him walk.

"Let's have some sake!" Akira suggested, pointing to the place they'd just come out of.

"But don't we have to start building the clock? And what about finding this Su Song I need to talk to?"

"Don't be so impatient. Let's have a couple of drinks first, and then we'll get down to business."

22

THE OIRAN HOUSE
Ψ

The tavern consisted of a huge tatami-matted room, where three groups of men were eating and drinking around their respective *irori* fire pits. The high ceiling was crowned by a chimney that absorbed some of the smoke that filled the place.

We sat down next to a fire pit with a sandy base. A ragged old man brought us a basket of raw fish and a pot full of vegetable soup. He hung the pot from a hook over the fire and dumped the fish disdainfully onto a tray.

Akira took one of the fish. "You have to put the fish on this iron skewer and then plant it in the sand," he said. "The fire is at just the right distance to cook it slowly . . ."

As I skewered one of the fish, I remembered the moment I had gone through the Rashomon gate and had passed out next to the bloody bodies of the samurai.

"Do you see those guys by the fire over there?" said Akira, pointing to four strongly built men, all with beards and hair tied in a ponytail. "They're the samurai serving the Genji family. We're in the year 1178 now. Next year there will be a coup d'état, and the Genpei War will begin." He picked up a fish and skewered it. "To try to take control of Japan, the Taira will fight against the Genji, who are always around this neighborhood looking for trouble. They mocked me in public a few days ago, but I didn't give in to their provocation."

Akira noticed my confused expression.

"The Genji are snobs who do nothing but kiss up to the imperial court. They're favorites of both the prince and the emperor. As for the Taira, we're the rebels loved by the people, and we have many connections with powerful Buddhist monks."

"It's fascinating how many resources Masa has put into replicating this era," I said as I nibbled on one of the fish.

"Masa's ancestors were the Taira; hence the name of his company. The simulation is designed to be an experience close to the historical events of the late Heian era, which culminated in the clash between the Taira and the Genji, but we've incorporated other elements to add excitement."

"What are they?"

"The virtual characters in this simulation are programmed to create conflicts, so that everything becomes an adventure. If it was a faithful simulation of the era, you would come here and spend your life planting rice to feed your virtual family. But of course that would be boring! If that's all you're doing, you might as well stay in the real world. If you think about it, it's ironic: people will pay to come here, not only to achieve eternal life, but also to seek trouble, because they're bored with their monotonous lives."

A sour-sweet aroma permeated the place. Looking at the walls blackened by smoke, I still found it hard to believe that all of this was a simulation, not a journey to the past in a time machine.

The man dressed in rags brought a small barrel and placed it next to the tray of fish. Then he lifted the lid and from the smell, I knew it was sake. He dropped a couple of square wooden cups into the barrel, and they floated in the liquor like little boats.

Akira took one of the floating cups and dipped it to let it fill. I copied him.

"Kanpai!" he said, raising the cup in a toast. "Cheers!"

"Kanpai!" I responded.

As I drank the sake, I felt the alcohol warming my body.

"What's your talent, Nathan?"

"I don't know . . ."

"Since childhood, mine has been programming computers."

Akira downed another sake in one gulp, then eagerly served us more fish and soup.

"I was never really sure," I said, after thinking for a while. "I ended up becoming a watch designer, and over time, I could say it has become my passion. But it wasn't something I was determined to do from the beginning . . ."

"It's hard to know what comes first, the passion or the ambition to pursue it," said Akira as he submerged the wooden cup back into the barrel. "Is passion the thing that seeks you out, or are you the one who finds it? It's a snake eating its own tail. Sometimes it takes a while to awaken, but we all carry an *ikigai*—a reason to live—within us. I knew what mine was from when I was a child. The first memory I have is pressing the buttons on a video game controller, furious because Bowser had eliminated me for the umpteenth time."

"And that's how your passion started?"

"I would get really angry when I didn't win. But at the same time, I started to develop the ambition to control the intelligence of that monster. I began to wonder who created those clever creatures that I struggled so much to beat. At the age of four, I asked my father to buy me a computer and programming books and I started learning how to program video games."

"You're a genius . . ."

"I am, but I avoid being a nerd. My second passion is women. I want to be the best programmer in the world, but also the greatest ladies' man of all time."

With that, he burst into a roar of laughter that caught the attention of the drunken samurai gathered around the fire pits. He refilled his cup with sake and took a gulp that nearly emptied it in one go.

"After graduating, I started working at Nintendo," he continued. "I had fulfilled my dream. I was there for over a decade, until the day I dreamed of the gate and Masa called me."

"Of course, the gate also appeared in your dreams . . ."

"Exactly, it's easy to forget that you and I share the same DNA. You, Mia, Murakami, and I are siblings! The four of us have been chosen to finish creating this world from within, just like the gods sent by Zeus from Mount Olympus to carry out earthly missions."

"Doesn't it bother you to think that our destiny has always been controlled by the samsara gene? By Masa's desires . . ."

"Cause and effect, destiny, what comes before or after . . ." murmured Akira. "You can twist it any way you want, but in the end it doesn't matter. Van Gogh said 'Normality is a paved road; it's comfortable to walk, but no flowers grow on it.' That's why it's advisable to add chaos to our lives."

He filled his sake cup again. "Let's celebrate our brotherhood," he shouted, banging the cup against mine. "Kanpai!"

"Kanpai!" The samurai sharing the place with us joined the toast, raising their wooden cups full of sake toward us.

One of them, overcome by alcohol, fell and hit his head on the tatami, to much laughter. I pretended to take a sip of my sake, as I was starting to feel drunk. Akira noticed.

"Don't be a coward. Drink more, Nathan. Here, we don't have real livers! Take advantage of the benefits of being in a simulation. You don't have to worry about your health!"

"But . . ."

Akira plunged my cup into the sake barrel and placed it back in front of me, full to overflowing.

"*Ikki*! Down in one!" he shouted, fixing his gaze on me.

"Ikki, ikki, ikki!" shouted the samurai. One of them stood up and began waving his katana while dancing to the rhythm of his words. "Ikki, ikki, ikki!"

Caught up in the atmosphere, I downed my sake in one gulp. Akira was leaning toward the sake barrel to refill his cup when a katana-wielding samurai grabbed him and dunked his head into the liquor. Delirious laughter followed, and then the barrel was passed around.

"It's time to go," said Akira, tugging at my sleeve. "There are only stinking samurai here, no women."

We stumbled out onto the street. Orange lanterns dimly illuminated the facades of the houses. The first stars twinkled in the evening sky. We passed shadows of drunken men until we turned a corner into a dark alley lit only by one lantern. I followed Akira, who was making a beeline for that point of light.

The lantern was hanging next to a door. He knocked on the door five times.

"This is an oiran house," said Akira, as we waited for someone to answer. "Oiran are courtesans who specialize in entertaining and pleasing men. Let's put it bluntly, they're high-end prostitutes."

"I don't want to go in. I've never wanted to . . ."

"Relax, Nathan," interrupted Akira. "Just enjoy. Remember, all of this is virtual. Think of it like having sex in virtual reality. You can't catch diseases, and they won't get pregnant. It's a freaking paradise."

Despite being completely drunk, I felt uncomfortable with that crude attitude.

"Don't feel guilty, Nathan. Remember that we are inside a simulation! It's like watching pornography on the Internet with a virtual reality headset, but better, much better!"

Akira's words, fueled by drunkenness, finally broke down my resistance. When the door opened, we were greeted by an elderly woman dressed in a bright red kimono printed with flowers. On each sleeve, the floral designs transformed into a yellow phoenix. On her head, golden hairpins gathered her dark hair into three buns, forming the shape of a clover. Her tiny feet, protected by white socks, rested on wooden geta clogs with soles several inches high, making the old woman almost as tall as me. Akira, on the other hand, looked like a forest sprite beside her.

The woman covered her red lips with her hand and exchanged some words with Akira in a low voice I couldn't hear. As she whispered, she looked me up and down suspiciously.

Akira turned toward me with a sly smile. "She says you're too big."

"What does she mean by 'big'?"

"Don't play dumb. She says he'll only let us in if you promise to be gentle with the girls."

My mind intoxicated and my decision-making ability impaired, I found myself surrounded by a dozen girls in colorful kimonos serving us cups of sake and keeping us company. There were so many of them it was difficult to focus on any one in particular.

"Do you have children?" asked one of them, sitting down next to me.

"No," I said, looking into her eyes.

"How is that possible, being so handsome?"

She was a woman of extraordinary beauty. The proportions of her eyes, nose and mouth were in perfect symmetry. My eyes traced the white skin of her neck down to the place where her shoulder disappeared beneath her kimono.

"I designed her face by processing data from the thousand most beautiful women in Japan," said Akira, loudly, snapping me out of my state of enchantment. "Do you like it? I also created the experience of this orgy." He smiled, his tongue almost hanging out. "Everyone will want to pay to live here. It's better than reality!"

His words reminded me that none of this was real. However, before I could dwell on it further, the perfect girl created by Akira collapsed onto the tatami. Her companions began to undress her, like a gift for me, first opening the top of her kimono to expose her breasts.

Stunned, I looked at all the young women around me, not knowing what to do. The perfect girl was offering herself to me naked. The others were also starting to undress, while they kissed and caressed each other. The kimonos piled up on the floor, covering the tatami with color, while the scent of sake mixed with the aroma of incense. In an unsettling chorus, some girls moaned, almost screamed, while others uttered deep, prolonged sounds.

On the other side of the room, Akira had fallen into a mountain of naked bodies, as if those women were a group of predators about to devour him.

Two girls pounced on me and undressed me with four hands, their eyes drinking in my naked body—which refused to respond. I was scared. Even though I was taking part in something that was every man's sexual fantasy, I only felt confusion. Something wasn't right.

The chorus of moans had lowered its tone but it maintained a sinister rhythm. I felt as though these women were dragging me into an abyss. Then, one of the folding screens adorned with flowers that concealed the entrance fell on top of the girls. Suddenly, the moans transformed into screams of terror. Three samurai appeared behind the folding screen and stood there threateningly.

"Akira, you're going to pay what you owe us," said one of them, who seemed to be the leader.

Akira emerged, naked and terrified, from among the girls who were on top of him.

"I don't owe you anything!" he protested.

"Prince Genji disagrees," said the leader. "By the way, who is your friend? We've never seen him around here before."

The three samurai started advancing toward us at a slow pace, careful not to step on the girls, whose bodies, paralyzed with fear, now resembled the dunes of a white desert.

I stood up, pulling on my *hakama* trousers to cover myself. "I'm Nathan."

"What a strange name. Are you a Taira, like your buddy Akira?" said one of the samurai.

"I don't know," I whispered softly.

"If you hang out with a Taira, you're a Taira," said another samurai.

I realized that in this world, I still didn't know who I was. All I knew was my name.

"Leave us alone, you brutes," I snapped.

"Are you trying to start a fight?"

As they drew closer, I instinctively executed a jujutsu move, sweeping the legs out from under one of them so that he collapsed onto the tatami.

The other two drew their katanas at lightning speed, their tips suddenly mere inches from our noses.

"It would be a shame to have to cut off your head when we've just met you," said one of them.

The last thing I remember was a sharp blow to the base of my neck.

23

THE IMPERIAL PALACE
Ψ

We woke up on a pile of straw, surrounded by cows grazing, unaware of our presence. We were both tied with ropes to a post.

With a stiff body and a head about to explode, I protested, "You said you designed the girls and the orgy . . . Are you also responsible for this?"

"Having problems is synonymous with being alive. Don't you like adventure?" said Akira.

"If you've also programmed this experience, you should know when they're going to set us free."

"The truth is, I don't," he admitted.

"What do you mean you don't?"

"There's a random component to what happens in Kyoto Mythos. We let the quantum computer decide much of what happens. Once the characters are created, they do as they please. Otherwise, it would be boring."

"And you've never tested this version of the story where they make us prisoners before?"

"No," he replied, looking away.

At that moment, the group of samurai from the previous night kicked open the stable door. Without a word, one of them cut the ropes with his katana, while another threw a couple of worn-out *jinbei* jackets over our naked bodies. Dressed in those rags, we were marched out of the stable at sword point to a gravel courtyard. In the center stood a huge tree, its trunk encircled by a thick rope.

"That rice straw rope is called a *shimenawa*," said Akira. "It's used to indicate that it's a sacred tree."

"Shut up, you filthy Taira!" one of the samurai ordered, giving him a shove.

Using the position of the sun, I quickly oriented myself. On the roof of the building that bordered one side of the courtyard, two golden horns pointed toward the sky. They were like the ones I had seen at the end of Suzaku Avenue the day before. I concluded that we had been brought to the Imperial Palace.

We were taken into a gigantic building. In the first rooms, the walls were adorned with landscapes of mountains, wooded groves, and temples with multistory pagodas. We went along a narrow corridor with paintings of tigers and phoenixes that looked at us with distrustful eyes. Some tigers bared their teeth, and others had their mouths open so wide you could see into their throats. We reached a door bearing a carving of dragon with a golden ball in its claws. One of the three samurai stopped in front of the door and opened it gently.

We entered a majestic hall with golden walls. The three samurai escorting us sheathed their katanas and knelt on the floor. We knelt too. After what seemed like a long time, another door at the back of the hall opened.

The samurai and Akira bowed their heads, their eyes fixed on the ground in a gesture of subordination. I understood that it was forbidden to look directly. I followed suit, but I couldn't help stealing a glance just before I lowered my head.

In the center of the hall I saw a young man advancing with such elegance that I immediately knew it was the Prince Genji that the samurai had mentioned before their attack on us yesterday. To his right was an old man with a long white beard. To his left, were three women dressed in plain kimonos.

When I noticed that one of them was Mia, my heart skipped a beat. I forced myself to look down at the tatami.

"You may raise your heads now," Prince Genji finally said.

When I did so, I saw that Mia and the other two girls were sitting now, with their hands on their knees. I turned my gaze to study the prince. His jawline was strong, and his gaze intense and seductive. He was an extremely handsome man. If he had lived in the future, he would have been a movie heartthrob, idolized by women worldwide.

"Welcome to the palace," said the prince.

"Thank you," Akira replied.

"I didn't give you permission to speak. Just listen. I have a proposal for settling our debt and making peace." Akira nodded silently.

I remembered the last thing Murakami had told me as we left his room in Cherry Blossom Villa: "She's at the Imperial Palace, with her fiancé." Seeing Mia's calm and strangely cold expression, I understood that she was accustomed to being near the prince. She gazed beyond us without acknowledging my presence.

"I want to take Mia as my third wife. Our marriage will serve as an alliance between the Taira and the Genji."

Without showing surprise, Akira turned to me. "According to *The Chronicles of Japan*," he whispered, "he was the most handsome prince in the country's history. A real ladies' man. If you've got your sights set on Mia, you don't stand a chance, buddy . . ."

I knew Prince Genji was a virtual character and that everything that happened in Kyoto Mythos was theater. Could this be a plotline created by Murakami to test me? Whatever the situation, I couldn't stop feelings of anger and jealousy rising up.

I remembered the warmth in my heart when I'd woken next to Mia in Cherry Blossom Villa. After the joy of reuniting with my platonic love, this handsome prince (virtual!) comes along and steals her away. Was I still a fool, like in my student days?

"Actually, it's already decided," said the prince. "The wedding will be tomorrow."

"I won't allow you to marry her unless she wants to," I bravely said. "Have you asked her?"

The prince let out an arrogant laugh, as if my words carried no weight. Then he turned to the elderly man with the long beard.

"Who is this poor fellow?" he asked.

"Your Majesty," the bearded man replied, "according to the scroll we received from the guards at the Rashomon gate, this man comes from a remote place and has been given the mission of erecting a tower with the most precise clock humanity has ever known."

"He's staying with us at Cherry Blossom Villa," added Akira, pleadingly.

There was a long pause.

"Let's make a deal," the prince said, finally. "I will postpone my wedding with Mia until you've built the most precise clock humanity has ever known—if you really can, of course. And, should you be able to complete the clock successfully, well then—" He broke off to laugh to himself, shaking his head in apparent disbelief. "Well then . . . Mia will be yours. If you're sure that's what you really want. Is it? Because you should know that if Mia becomes yours then war will inevitably break out and all my Genji soldiers will come after you . . ."

"War!" exclaimed Akira, as if the idea of armed conflict excited him.

Prince Genji stood up and, following a gesture of his hand, Mia and the other two women followed him as he withdrew from the room.

24

5-MeO-DMT

Masa stroked Reiko's thigh with the tips of his fingers as she sipped her tea. Both of them were attentively watching the dozens of screens in the control room. In isometric perspective, they observed the four carriers of the samsara gene in Kyoto Mythos. On the central screen, Akira and Nathan were kneeling, watching with resignation as Mia left the room with Prince Genji and his other concubines. On another screen, Murakami could be seen writing in his room on the second floor of Cherry Blossom Villa.

Reiko checked the monitor where Nathan's vital signs and DNA code were displayed.

"We have Nathan's complete sequence thanks to the latest generation of sequencing machines," she said, using a digital pencil to select a string of base pairs.

AGCTTCGTGATTACACTCTGCGTC . . .

"You know the sequence isn't important," said Masa. "What's important is the expression of the samsara gene. You failed in your mission to persuade Roku to give us the Kusanagi sword. We're in need of a new plan. Without the sword, the chances of Nathan's gene being expressed at 100 percent are very low."

Reiko sighed and shook her head. She moved to another terminal, where she confirmed Nathan's status:

Samsara gene expression in Nathan:
completed to 43.5382%

"Request a more thorough analysis to search for correlations of metabolites in Nathan's blood and hidden patterns in his DNA," Masa ordered.

Reiko messaged the head of biotechnology with Masa's orders, then they returned their attention to the central monitor. They could see that Akira and Nathan were talking with the bearded man.

"If we added more drama, that would make it a lot less boring," said Reiko.

"But that's not our job," replied Masa, shaking his head. "I trust Murakami's judgment; we need to leave everything in his hands. Remember, he's the one that's responsible for developing possible plotlines and deciding on the actions of the virtual characters."

"I would have one of the samurai kill Akira with the katana to terrify Nathan. Imagine the blood and intestines spilling out and staining the tatami red . . ."

"Do you like blood?"

"I like taking risks," Reiko said, pursing her lips. "I hate being a spectator of other people's adventures."

With that, Reiko turned away from the monitors. She pinned up her hair, revealing the tattoo of the infinite rope behind her ear, and leaned toward Masa, caressing his belly. Taking no notice of her, Masa began typing rapidly on a dark screen with green letters. He was accepting a merge request to refine the graphic engine that controlled Newtonian physics in Kyoto Mythos.

Reiko continued with her caresses, her hands moving down his belly.

"No sex in the office," said Masa. "How many times do I have to tell you?"

"But you're feeling good today," Reiko replied. "Let's make the most of it."

He continued typing, trying to ignore her caresses. When he finished executing the merge request, he placed his hands on her shoulders and gently pushed her away.

"Come on, we have work to do in the bathtubs."

Masa started his wheelchair, and Reiko followed after him. They passed in front of Van Gogh's *Sunflowers*, went out into the hallway and headed to the last room on the right. Once inside, they looked into the bathtub where Murakami and Nathan floated unconscious in this world, but fully present in Kyoto Mythos.

Reiko prepared a syringe while Masa monitored the vital signs of the two bodies on a tablet.

"Glucose levels dropping. Glycogen metabolism in the liver rising to normal ratios."

"Everything's fine," Reiko said with a focused expression, observing the tip of the syringe. "Time to feed these babies before they start bawling."

She leaned over Nathan's naked body, her eyes resting for a moment on his penis. Then she carefully examined the muscles of his arm. In the dim light that emanated from the bathtub, she could see the veins standing out. With total ease, as if this was something she had done hundreds of times she gave Nathan and Murakami three different injections each, then inserted two tubes into each of them, one extracting feces and the other urine.

"You should hire a nurse for this," Reiko commented as she pressed a button at the end of one of the tubes.

Masa seemed not to hear her, all his concentration seemingly focused on the screen of his tablet.

"Both are still endogenously producing incredibly high levels of 5-MeO-DMT, after the effects of the pill they used for the initial entry wore off."

"Yes. If you look at it from a biochemical standpoint, it's the common denominator of the four chosen ones," Reiko added. "Perhaps their naturally high levels of 5-MeO-DMT activated the dream of the Rashomon gate in them."

"I wish we could make anyone maintain those same levels. I'm convinced the samsara gene is responsible, working in harmony with other elements we still don't know about," said Masa thoughtfully.

Reiko gathered the instruments, and they left the dark room, where the two bodies floated, oblivious to the passage of time.

25
A CLOCK TO STOP TIME
Ψ

The samurai left, finally freeing us from the constant threat of their katanas. We remained with the old man with the long white beard.

"My name is Su Song," he said solemnly, sitting cross-legged on a cushion, stroking his beard with the tips of his fingers.

"Meeting Su Song" was what I had read in Akira's hut the day before. I assumed I was on the right track in the mission assigned to me.

"It's a pleasure to meet you," we both responded.

"Like you, I also come from distant lands. My dynasty belongs to one of the three kingdoms of China. Before my father passed away, he asked me to cross the seas to come here, to Heian. He entrusted me to await the arrival of the Master of Eternity. And finally, I have found him! It is truly an immense honor to meet you."

"The honor all is mine," I replied, surprised by the title just bestowed upon me, playing along with this virtual character.

"Time is relative in the palace. It slows down so much that sometimes minutes seem like years, but then there are years that can pass in a matter of seconds."

"That sounds like Einstein," I said, forgetting that many centuries were yet to pass before the German physicist's birth.

"My father was obsessed with time. He came to the conclusion that if we eliminated from the universe all instruments that measure hours and minutes, we would fall into an eternal present. He said that the past, the present, and the future were the same entity. The passage of time is an illusion. Don't you think so, Master?"

Akira observed our philosophical conversation as if watching a tennis match.

"Changes in the physical world make us feel that time is passing," I said, playing my role.

"Wise words, dear Master of Eternity. If the universe were to suddenly disappear and then reappear afterward, how much time would have passed?"

"If there's no space, matter or anything, time wouldn't have passed," I replied, thinking again of Einstein and his concept of space-time.

"We say that a day has passed because the sun has risen and then it has set again," said Su Song, fixing his sparkling eyes on mine. "We know that a season has passed because it gets warmer or colder. We calculate that ten years have passed because our dog dies. Or we measure hours by a candle that has burned down. But what would happen if the sun didn't move or the temperature didn't change?"

"Even if the sun stopped moving," I said, trying to follow his logic, "our hearts would still beat. It's another way of measuring time. The length of our lives can be approximated by counting the number of heartbeats from birth to death."

"My father believed that even that could be surpassed. He was so determined to stop the passage of time that he locked himself in the darkness of a cave. He stayed there for seven days and seven nights, without eating or drinking anything. When he came out of there, he was so emaciated and weak that he could barely crawl. I gave him some water, and after gulping it down, he said to me, 'I have finally seen eternity. It is the most beautiful and the most terrifying thing I have ever witnessed.

You must go to Heian and serve the Master of Eternity. He will help you build the most precise clock humanity has ever known.' And after he said these words, he collapsed and died. While he was lying lifeless on the ground, his hand opened, revealing a mark that had been carved with something sharp into the palm of his hand."

Su Song rummaged in the lapel of his emerald green *suikan* formal kimono and pulled out a tiny scroll. After unrolling it, he showed it to us.

"I copied the symbol on my father's hand onto this scroll."

"I know that symbol," I whispered, remembering Reiko's tattoo of the infinite knot behind her ear. "Why did he give you the task of building a clock to measure time with the greatest precision possible?"

"I have pondered this question many times. To find an answer, before setting out on my journey, I delved into my father's library. Most of his books were classics from ancient Greece." Su Song took a deep breath. "Reading these works, I learned that according to Zeno's paradoxes, if we were to divide each moment infinitely, it would take an eternity. In one of my father's notebooks, I found a design that suggested that if we built a clock that could measure time with infinite precision, time itself would stop."

"Let me see," I murmured, recalling what I had studied in quantum physics. "Even though time may seem continuous to us, and mathematically we can divide a second into infinite pieces, that second will not stretch into eternity, no matter how precise a clock we build, as your dear father suggested. The latest advances in this field, in the world that I come from, suggest that time is not continuous because there is a minimum unit of time."

"Clearly, your knowledge of the subject surpasses mine. My father was right! You are the Master of Eternity," he said, excitedly. "Can you build a clock that divides time down to that minimum unit you mentioned?"

"It is impossible to build such a clock."

I had considered atomic clocks, which measure the number of transitions between energy levels in cesium-133 atoms, dividing a second into nine billion parts. Theoretically, we could surpass the precision of these clocks until we collided with the limits imposed by the Planck distance. The formula 5.4×10^{-44} seconds is how long it takes light to travel this distance, the minimum division of space in our universe. That was one of the few constants I had memorized.

"Nothing is impossible, Master. There are only impossibilities whose possibility is yet to be discovered."

"Well . . ." I tried to set aside my rational calculations.

"Here are my father's notes on the passage of time," he said, pulling out a golden cylinder from the lapel of his suikan. "With this and the wisdom you carry, I have no doubt we can build the most precise clock humanity has ever known."

Su Song raised the object toward me, and I stood up to receive the offering. Akira watched as if he was witnessing some kind of sacred act. I grasped the golden tube to take it from him, but Su Song kept holding onto the other end tightly, as if he wasn't ready to let go yet. He looked at me anxiously before he spoke again.

"Let us remember, Master, that in this universe, everything is possible. There are no limits other than those imposed on us by our imagination."

I bowed my head in reverence, and Su Song released the cylinder, which was heavier than it looked. I tucked it under the lapel of my jinbei.

Su Song accompanied us to the palace exit. From there, we walked along Suzaku Avenue until we arrived back at Cherry Blossom Villa. Akira retired to his hut, and I crossed the stream to reach my room. I was beginning to feel that this was my home in Kyoto Mythos.

I felt the urge to play music before going to bed, but in the Japan of 1178, I had to settle for the frog chorus reverberating from every corner of the garden. I was extremely tired, but the events at the palace had filled me with a mysterious energy. I had a mission now—how could I sleep? I opened the cylindrical case, and dozens of scrolls with tiny notes and diagrams made by Su Song's father spilled out. I spread them out on the tatami and began to read.

To build the most precise clock in the world, it is necessary to recreate the cosmic egg from which this universe was born. Within it, yin and yang struggled in a state of chaos. Eternity, the future, the past, and the present were one and the same.

Pangu was the first living being to divide the egg in two. Yin transformed into the Sky. Yang created the Earth. But to maintain yin and yang in balance and in order to build the rest of this universe, even the all-powerful Pangu needed to seek help from the Four Legendary Beasts. The Tortoise came from the north, the Qilin came from the south, the Phoenix came from the east, and the Dragon came from the west. The Four Beasts descended to Earth and set to work creating a habitable world for us humans.

But, even with the help of the Four Beasts, the presence of chaos was so powerful that the task seemed impossible. After much deliberation, Pangu concluded that he must sacrifice himself. And so his body disintegrated and transformed into seas, winds, fire, rain, lightning, stars and trees.

Our Creator God sacrificed his original form so that he could build our universe. Pangu is now in everything that surrounds us. Pangu is in the air that we breathe and the water that we drink. Our universe is God, it is Pangu. Our bodies are Pangu. The stars are Pangu. The infinite is Pangu.

Beneath this was an image of the infinite knot. Coming across this symbol again made my head start to spin. That ancient myth of the universe's creation that I was reading aligned with our contemporary theoretical framework, where everything originates from a small egg pregnant with pure energy, and an event called the Big Bang—in other words what was referred to here as Pangu—initiates the creation of all matter, energy and time.

I glanced up at the blossoming cherry trees in the garden. I reached the logical conclusion that Taira Corporation's quantum computer, simulating both the cherry blossoms and my eyes, was the Pangu of Kyoto Mythos.

I continued reading Su Song's father's scrolls:

> When Pangu disappeared and the World became habitable, the Four Beasts took on tasks that had until then been carried out by the Creator. The most important of these was to control the passage of time.
>
> If time were to stop, chaos would once again engulf the universe, returning it to the primordial egg.
>
> The Four Beasts withdrew from the world, leaving behind the humans who populated it, and ascended to the firmament.
>
> The Tortoise rose to the northern constellations, the Qilin traveled to the southern constellations, the Phoenix to the eastern ones, and the Dragon inhabited the stars of the west.
>
> From the heavens, the Four Beasts now watch over the universe, ensuring that time continues to flow. Only in this way do we prevent chaos from surging up again.

The writing ended with a drawing of the Four Beasts against a starry sky, as if this document was an astrological fable rather than instructions for building a clock.

I turned to the next page.

In sacrificing himself, Pangu took with him the answer to the great question: what is the purpose of the existence of this universe?

And, by extension, what is the purpose of the existence of humans?

The answer remains hidden, but Pangu is everywhere, and his consciousness permeates every corner of the universe we live in. To unveil that answer, it will be necessary to build the most precise clock that has ever existed in the universe. That will allow us to transcend the infinite, recreating the primordial state of the cosmic egg. The prophecy says that the Clock Tower will be built as follows:

1. *First construct the most beautiful and prosperous city that any civilization has ever witnessed. Its layout must be rectangular, symmetrical and perfectly aligned with the cardinal points.*

2. *It will be called the City of Peace, in other words, Heian.*

3. *The city will be protected by a wall and will have a single entrance to the south called Rashomon, the Gate of Heaven.*

4. *At each cardinal point, it will be necessary to keep the time candles lit, each one illuminating one of the Four Legendary Beasts.*

5. *The Master of Eternity will arrive in the City of Peace from a parallel universe, entering through the Gate of Heaven, and will be the one who knows how and where to build the Clock Tower.*

6. *The prophecy says that Qilin, near the Rashomon gate in the south, will initiate discussions with the Master of Eternity.*

After I had read that mixture of mythology, poetry and prophecy, I knew that my next step would be to go and speak with Qilin.

26

THE KEYS OF A PIANO

When she had nothing to do, Reiko liked to be alone. Her father's death had marked a turning point in her life. Although she had stopped blaming herself for the tragic event, since he had died she had begun to believe more in superstitions and less in everything else. She was convinced that if a human being became obsessed with a dream, they could make that dream come true.

In company, she was seen as an outgoing woman. Sometimes she was even impulsive and uncontrollable, as if an inner force compelled her to overwhelm those around her with her emotions. This characteristic scared many, but it also made her very attractive to a certain type of man.

But when she was alone, she became a different person. She locked herself away to read philosophy books. She had already completed a degree and a doctorate, but still she voraciously read philosophical essays as if they were the medicine that would cure what ailed her heart.

She knew that, in some way, she loved Masa, but that feeling was a mixture of compassion and gratitude for what he had done for her and her mother to save them from misery. And another part of her affection stemmed from the pity she felt seeing that man—who had achieved everything in life—suffer from a terminal illness. She would have liked to have a cold and calculating heart to protect herself from all dangers, but she did not.

Reiko had taken the liberty of staying at Nathan's apartment, where his suitcase was still open. The scent of his clothes transported her to the night they had spent together. Two shirts, some underwear, and the jeans that had gotten stained during their escape from the sushi restaurant hung on a chair. The cleaning robot could take care of the laundry, but Reiko put the clothes in the washing machine herself.

Then she prepared a simple dinner and sat by the window overlooking Kyoto. As she ate, her gaze traced the pagodas peeking out through the forest, the twinkling lights of the city spreading out on both sides of the Kamogawa River, and finally, the Taira Corporation skyscraper. She visualized Nathan's naked body floating in the bathtub on the top floor of the building and couldn't help but wonder whether he was with Mia in Cherry Blossom Villa.

After dinner, she poured herself a glass of red wine and a plate of *kaki-no-tane*, peanuts mixed with rice crackers. She took out Erich Fromm's *The Art of Loving* from her bag. She liked to think that if she stayed alone reading, the rest of the world would reorder itself back into a state of calm, but she knew it was just an illusion.

Nothing was going to change.

According to that book, which had been influential in the past, true love needs four fundamental elements: care, responsibility, respect and knowledge.

Reiko took a sip of wine as she reflected on her father. That aggressive drunk had been the antithesis of love. A lump formed in her throat as she remembered how he shouted while cornering her mother in a corner of the kitchen.

Care, responsibility and respect had not existed in her home. Nor had knowledge, because Reiko had never understood why her father acted that way, nor why her mother had not fled from the monster that tortured her. Ten years after her father's death, Reiko still trembled every time she opened the door to her family home. She wondered if Nathan possessed the four ingredients of love. Until now, he had respected her and cared for her. Masa had too, in his own way.

The book also explained that nobody can truly love another person if they do not love everyone else, humanity, the world— but it all begins with self-love. She realized that her heart was still full of resentment and hatred toward others, and also toward herself.

She was snapped out of these thoughts by a kind of electric shock around her navel, followed by a slight tingling, as though someone was delicately touching the keys of a piano. The unfamiliar sensation lingered for a while then slowly faded as she fell asleep with the book resting on her belly.

27

THE CITY LIMITS
Ψ

After reading Su Song's scrolls, I went out into the garden. The sun was shining, and the cherry blossoms seemed a deeper pink than on previous days. Birds flew overhead, tracing invisible lines in the spring sky. My body still felt numb from the night I had spent sleeping tied to a post in the palace barn. Struggling to combat the hangover I had after drinking sake with Akira, I performed several stretches accompanied by my routine of squats and push-ups. I finished by practicing jujutsu katas. I missed my sensei, and wished he was there to guide me through the training.

After that, I went for a walk to explore the garden of Cherry Blossom Villa. I followed the course of the stream until it disappeared into the forest. There, in the shade of the trees, was a small wooden *torii* gate leading to a shrine guarded by two fox statues holding stone scrolls in their mouths. From there, I turned to stare back at the villa. I could see Murakami, still at the window, still apparently writing.

I need to talk to someone. I remembered the "Do Not Disturb" sign on Murakami's door, so I decided to visit Akira. I went over the bridge and followed the path through the forest until I reached his cabin. The door was open. Inside, I found that rascal typing away, surrounded by screens. He wore a helmet from which dozens of cables emerged, disappearing into the maze of machines that filled the cabin's interior. He typed as if possessed by the source code scrolling across the screens.

"Akira!" I called out. He didn't reply. I shouted his name again, louder, but he seemed completely unaware of my presence until I touched his shoulder. He gave a start and a brief flicker of annoyance crossed his face, but then he smiled as he removed the helmet.

"You've started strong, my friend. What an adventure we had together! How's the hangover?"

"You could remove it from the simulation," I grumbled, rubbing my forehead.

"You must be as hungry as I am. Let's go and have a good nabe hot pot at an inn on Suzaku Avenue."

We left the cabin and, following a paved path that forked near the bridge, we reached the gate that separated the grounds of Cherry Blossom Villa from the rest of the city. Merchants walked by with baskets slung over their shoulders. A few chickens pecked around a puddle. To the north of the avenue stood the Imperial Palace, where we had met Su Song. To the south was the Rashomon gate. We headed in that direction until Akira made a gesture, and we went into an inn where the scent of stew filled the air.

We sat on the tatami next to a fire pit surrounded by sand. The innkeeper put a broth-filled pot over the fire, then brought several baskets of vegetables along with a bowl of beef pieces. Akira grabbed a handful of vegetables and put them into the pot, which was beginning to steam. With copper tongs, I added the meat.

"How are you feeling?" Akira asked, breaking the silence. After the wild night he had inflicted on me and his crude attitude throughout, I was surprised he cared about my feelings.

"Disoriented."

"At first it's tough, but once you get used to life here, you won't want to go back."

"I'm starting to understand the theory, but I feel like everything that happens here is fake."

"It's the opposite. Outside the simulation, your body is floating in a bathtub, asleep. It's like you're dead. But what you do here will be in your memory. Your decisions are all that matters. This nabe," he said, sniffing the pot, "is the realest thing for you and me right now." He plunged a ladle into the boiling broth of vegetables and meat and served me a bowl. The first sip tasted heavenly.

"It's the umami from the kombu seaweed they use to flavor the broth," said Akira, at the expression of delight on my face.

By the time I finished, the hangover had gone. I felt reborn.

"I don't know you yet, but I already consider you a great friend and I feel I can speak frankly," Akira said. "You're a very passive guy, aren't you? You always wait for things to happen instead of taking action. You have to stop being a spectator of life and dare to be the protagonist. Are you going to just hang out at Cherry Blossom Villa and Suzaku Avenue, waiting for Mia to come to you when it suits her? You saw her this morning at the palace. She seems to be comfortable with Prince Genji . . ."

"Don't stress me out, Akira. You're not perfect yourself—"

"But I'm very clear about what I want: my mission is to be the biggest badass in the universe, and the best hacker at the same time. One thing doesn't exclude the other. Play hard, work hard. Yesterday was a party, today it's our turn to work. It's time for you to start building the Clock Tower." He pulled a piece of cloth from a small bag hanging from his obi sash. "You have to start moving on your own. This symbol," he said, pointing to the piece of cloth, "will identify you as one of us, as a Taira."

With a needle and thread that he just happened to have in one of his pockets, he fixed the cloth patch to my lapel. As we stepped out onto Suzaku Avenue, Akira bid me farewell and headed north, back to his cabin.

I walked south, toward the Rashomon gate. In front of the imposing structure, there was no trace of the samurai corpses

The Taira symbol

The Genji symbol

that had greeted me when I'd arrived at Kyoto Mythos on that stormy night. On either side of the gate extended the city wall that protected the city. It was patrolled by groups of samurai in uniforms bearing the symbol of the Genji, just like the one I'd seen Prince Genji wearing.

Above the wall at the side of the gate, I caught a glimpse of the heads of the two demons watching over the city. Two soldiers with *naginata* spears fixed me with a stern look. Defiantly, I climbed a set of wooden stairs to reach them, and when I made a move to open the Rashomon gate, they blocked my path by crossing their weapons just inches from my face.

"By the decree of Prince Genji, no Taira is allowed to leave the city until further notice," one of them declared. The other pointed the naginata spear toward my chest, where the patch with the Taira symbol that Akira had given me was displayed.

"I need to speak with the Qilin," I said.

"The only demons on the outside of the gate are the ones who keep watch. The Qilin is on this side," one of them replied.

They both pointed toward a statue at the bottom of the flight of stairs I had just climbed.

I went back down the stairs and inspected the stone statue, which was of an animal with a lion's face and deer horns, just like the depiction of the Qilin in Su Song's scrolls. Its eyes were large and bulging, its nose stubby, and its mouth was open, revealing powerful fangs.

Suddenly, a girl came running down Suzaku Avenue. She had a round face, and short, straight hair. With her wide eyes and tiny nose, she looked like an anime character. Her movements were quick, agile, and full of energy.

Ignoring my presence, the girl placed her bag next to a small pedestal beside the Qilin statue. On the pedestal was a candle in a glass box, burning down to its end. The girl greeted the statue with a bow. From her bag, she took out a candle, a telescope and a round bronze instrument that looked like an astrolabe, an ancient instrument for calculating the position of the stars—I'd seen a picture of one in a book. She pointed the astrolabe skyward, as though she was taking measurements. Next, she aimed the telescope toward the Imperial Palace, and made several adjustments. Then she replaced the candle that was about to burn out on the pedestal with a new one.

"What are you staring at, big nose?" the girl said to me. No one had ever called me that before, so I touched my nose to check if it had grown.

"Yes, you, big guy! Typical foreigner with that huge nose."

"What deity did you light that candle for?" I asked.

The girl looked at me like she couldn't believe my ignorance. "It's not for a god. Here in Heian, this candle is used to measure time. Every six hours, a candle burns out and needs to be replaced with a new one."

"Four candles a day . . ."

"Exactly, I take care of two candles: the one at six in the morning and the one at noon."

"You have an important job for someone so young."

"I'm not young," she said, glaring at me, "I'm five years old!"

After returning her things to her backpack, she closed the door of the glass box where the new candle burned. Finished with her work, she turned toward the Qilin statue and closed her eyes. She bowed while moving her fingers as though she was counting. Without opening her eyes, she shouted, "Pangu, Pangu, Panguuuu!"

At that moment, the mouth of the Qilin statue started to move, and a deep otherworldly voice emerged from it:

"What is it, dear Kaori?"

"I've lit the noon candle."

"You're always punctual. Thank you, dear."

The girl looked proud. "Do you have time to play today?" she asked, eagerly.

The Qilin took a step forward and lowered its head to her level, the long whiskers on either side of its chin swaying as they brushed the ground.

I felt as though I was at the cinema, watching a fantasy movie.

"I have to return to the mythological universe as soon as possible," announced the Qilin. "A war is about to break out and could affect the peace of Heian."

"When will you take me to that mythological universe you always talk about?"

"Someday, I promise," said the Qilin slowly, although it wasn't clear whether "someday" meant a week or a thousand years. "But now it's too dangerous for a girl like you."

Kaori's eyes widened. "What's more real, the mythological universe where the Four Beasts come from or Heian?" she asked.

The Qilin leaned closer to Kaori, almost touching her with its nose, observing her closely, as if examining a precious object.

"Reality is that which, when you stop believing in it, doesn't go away."

Recognizing that phrase from a novel by Philip K. Dick, I wondered if the consciousness of that beast was a tribute from the programmers of Kyoto Mythos to the science fiction author.

Upon hearing those words, Kaori seemed sunk in thought. The Qilin took a step back and turned to look at me for the first time.

"And who is this meddler?" it asked, with an arrogant laugh that revealed its fangs.

Kaori glanced at me out of the corner of her eye. "I don't know," she said. "Big nose here is a stranger I just met."

I decided it was time to introduce myself with the title given to me by Su Song at the palace.

"I am Nathan, the Master of Eternity. My mission is to build the new Clock Tower."

The Qilin stopped laughing immediately, closed its gigantic mouth, and lowered its head. With its gaze down at my feet, it said, "Forgive the disrespect, Master. We have been waiting for you for millennia."

With surprising dexterity, the Qilin lifted one of its claws, removed a chain from around its neck and passed it to me. The chain held a green, curved pendant.

The Qilin stared at me for a moment. "This is the Magatama pendant," it said, "one of the treasures of the imperial house. It is a sacred object that comes from another universe, and only you, the Master of Eternity, can possess it in this reality. As long as you wear it, any of the thousands of Taira living within the walls of this city will follow your orders. With this Magatama pendant, you can build the Clock Tower, but to set the clock in motion, you'll need to invoke Pangu."

After this speech, I placed the chain with its curved pendant around my neck. The Qilin gave a great roar, and then suddenly returned to its inanimate state, its petrified gaze fixed on Su-zaku Avenue.

"I can help you build the tower," Kaori said.

28

LETTERS TO ANOTHER DIMENSION

Before heading to the office, Reiko's routine always included a visit to Smart Coffee. She would sit at the same table and order coffee and pineapple cake, which she enjoyed while reading. This time she dedicated to herself every morning provided her with a feeling of well-being that helped her face the day. But that morning, instead of reading, she took out a notebook from her bag and began drafting two letters:

Dear Mia

How's everything at Cherry Blossom Villa?

Here, after a few days preparing Nathan's entry into Kyoto Mythos, I'm back in my usual routine. Now I'm having coffee before heading to the office to take care of our beloved patron. I'm pleased to inform you that Masa seems rejuvenated by the new hope that Nathan has brought us.

I confess it's a pleasure and an honor for me to work with you. Since the day I met you, here in reality, I've admired your courage and bravery. After your entry into Kyoto Mythos and your decision to leave your biological body forever, I don't mind telling you that I miss your company. I know you still exist, but even though I can see you through the screen and communicate with you, it's not the same as working side by side.

Don't you miss the life you left behind?

Today there's something I feel I have to tell you. It's about Nathan. The day before his entry into Kyoto Mythos, we spent the night together.

You know I like to play around, perhaps because I've always found it easy to forget; what I feel one night disappears at dawn. My feelings are like waves crashing on the beach, they appear and disappear, appear and disappear . . .

However, Nathan has stirred up a strange and unfamiliar wave in my heart. It doesn't disappear, it doesn't want to merge with the sand on the shore, and it just keeps growing.

From your friend and admirer,
Reiko

Reiko's hand trembled as she wrote the last few sentences. She set the pen aside, and finished her pineapple cake. The waiter refilled her empty cup with more hot coffee.

Dear Nathan

I'm writing this at Smart Coffee. Do you remember the pineapple cake they have here? It's the best in Japan, in my opinion! I just devoured a slice, and now I'm on my second coffee.

I wish you were here, sharing this breakfast . . .

There's something Masa didn't want to tell you before your entry into Kyoto Mythos, but it's something I think you should know. Your time is limited.

Even as a carrier of the samsara gene, your biological body can only remain connected to Kyoto Mythos for twelve months. After that year, you'll have to make a decision: leave Kyoto Mythos and come back to live in reality, or let your biological body die to live forever within the virtual world of Kyoto Mythos, just as Akira and Mia did.

The freckles behind your ear indicate the number of months you have left, counting from your first connection to Kyoto Mythos. After each month you spend in Kyoto Mythos, one freckle will disappear.

Murakami has six freckles left to make his decision, but you have over eleven months left. Still, time flies, and it's best that you know the consequences of your decisions from now on.

I want you to know that, whatever you decide, I'll be here, in reality, waiting for you. If you decide to come back, you can find me here at Smart Coffee, every morning at ten o'clock.

I miss you.

Reiko

As she finished, she closed her eyes and imagined a future with Nathan. They would start their mornings at Smart Coffee and then take long walks along the Kamogawa River.

At that moment, Kamyu entered the café and sat down in front of her, rubbing his bald head as if trying to summon an idea. The waiter poured him a coffee.

"What's wrong?" Kamyu asked.

"Nothing . . ." Reiko replied. She bit her lip.

After years of serving as Reiko's bodyguard, Kamyu could sense her mood swings. "You know I'm here to serve you whenever you need me," he said.

Reiko nodded as she closed the notebook.

Later that morning, she typed up the two letters she had written and sent them to one of the terminals in Akira's cabin in Kyoto Mythos.

29

WHAT WATER STEALS, TIME STEALS TOO

Ψ

Waking up as a new day dawned at Cherry Blossom Villa, I felt I was getting used to living in this virtual world. I rolled up the futon and put it away in a cupboard that had sliding doors adorned with paintings of mountains. Then I slid open the screen door with its washi paper panels and sat at the edge of the garden, gazing at the cherry blossoms and the birds fluttering by the stream.

Mia and Murakami arrived, and after good morning greetings, they led me to an adjoining room. Overlooking the garden was a low table bearing trays of freshly made food.

As we prepared to have breakfast, Akira arrived, crossing the garden from his cabin.

"Hey, champions!" he shouted, jumping from the garden onto the tatami.

"Champions? You guys are troublemakers. You really dropped Nathan in at the deep end," Mia said, laughing as she covered her mouth with her hand.

"Looks like Nathan can't handle sake and even managed to provoke a group of Genji samurai," said Akira. "The night in the barn wasn't very comfortable, was it?"

I shrugged, shaking my head.

Mia and Akira laughed knowingly, as if they were accustomed to dealing with armed men on a daily basis. Meanwhile, Murakami was ignoring our conversation and had already wolfed down a bowl of rice. He stood up, excused himself, and went back to his writing.

Akira took out two envelopes from the pocket of his jinbei.

"Here are some messages from Reiko that she just sent via RealPeople to a terminal in my cabin," he said, with a mischievous smile on his lips. "You can be sure that I didn't read a word of them." Still wearing that smile, he got up and left.

Mia shifted position, stretching her legs to one side while resting her head on my shoulder. The scent of her hair momentarily transported me back to adolescence. Her elegant fingers slowly stroked my forearm, seeming to caress every inch of my skin down to the palm of my hand.

"Thank you for being here," Mia said, not lifting her head from my shoulder. "One thing that helped me make the decision to leave my biological body was that I knew you would come eventually. My disappearance may have looked like a tragic suicide to everyone, but for me it meant eternal life. I knew that the freckles behind your ear would eventually bring you to my side. That gave me the courage to make the final decision when I only had one freckle left . . ."

The two envelopes with Reiko's letters lay on the edge of the table.

I ran my free hand down her arm until our fingers intertwined. Mia kissed me softly on the neck and then sat up, reaching for her envelope. I did the same, and we began reading Reiko's messages from the outside reality together.

When I finished my letter, I reread Reiko's explanation and understood what Mia meant when she told me about the final decision she had to make when she only had one freckle left. Kyoto Mythos wasn't the paradise Masa had made me believe.

As Mia finished reading, her expression changed. A crease

furrowed her brow, and she suddenly tore Reiko's letter into pieces that she dropped into a half-full bowl of miso soup.

"What's wrong?" I dared to ask.

"I'm going to the palace for a while, to see Prince Genji."

With that, she got up and jumped down into the garden.

"If you really love me, you know what you have to do!" she shouted over her shoulder as she walked away.

Was that some kind of ultimatum? Was she really considering marrying that prince who was just a character in a simulation? What had Reiko said in the letter?

Loneliness seemed to be my natural state wherever I was. Frustrated, I retreated to my room. I unrolled Su Song's father's scrolls on the tatami and began to think about how I would build the Clock Tower.

One of the scrolls had a detailed map of Heian, which showed that the roof of the Rashomon gate was the highest point in the city. In front of it was an open space without houses, before Suzaku Avenue began. I decided that was where I would erect the Clock Tower, so that when it surpassed the height of the Rashomon gate, it would stand out as the highest point in Heian.

Focused on my mission, I forgot all the problems of my new life.

In other scrolls were detailed diagrams of the clock that Su Song and his father wanted to build in China, but never had. It was a clock that ran on water. I had heard of such clocks in history books; the Greeks called them *clepsydra*—which literally means "water thief"—because they required a constant flow of liquid.

"It steals water and time," I thought.

The design featured a central armillary sphere and a wheel filled with water buckets that were filled at a constant rate. The liquid first accumulated at the highest point of the clock, in a container called the "Celestial Lake," from which a wooden canal emerged to feed the buckets that needed to be filled.

To adjust the clock, a rudimentary transmission chain was used. It looked like a bicycle chain, but after analyzing the design in detail, I realized that for the time, it was the most advanced thing in the world. Su Song had named it the "Celestial Chain."

It wasn't clear how it would connect to the central armillary sphere so that the hands of the clock would mark the passage of time, so I began to draw my own diagrams, using a calligraphy brush. Gradually, I drew the multiple sections that would make up the clock.

My concentration was interrupted by Kaori, the girl I had met in front of the Rashomon gate yesterday. She came running across the bridge, her arms stretched either side of her, like a tightrope walker.

"What's wrong?" she said, with a big smile on her face. "You look down."

"It's nothing . . ."

"I told you I'd help you . . . You've started without me!"

"I was just thinking about the design."

"Things aren't built by thinking about them. Come on!"

A few minutes later I found myself being guided by Kaori down Suzaku Avenue to a district near the Rashomon gate filled with workshops where staff wore the Taira symbol on their clothes. Some were cutting wood into planks and beams, while others were metalworkers.

When they saw the Magatama pendant around my neck, all the workers paused and knelt before us.

"Master! We are at your service!" said one of the workers.

"We will fight to the death for you, great Master!" said another one.

"What are you waiting for? You're the construction chief, Nathan!" exclaimed Kaori. "They're waiting for your orders to start building the Clock Tower."

I surveyed the devoted men who knelt before me. Akira's words floated into my head—"You have to stop being a spectator of life and dare to be the protagonist." My time had come.

Akira's words were never far from my mind as I set about accomplishing my mission, determined to be the best leader that I could. At last, since losing my job in the real world, I had a purpose again, and it felt good.

At first, organizing the tasks of each worker was challenging. But as the months passed, I got to know the team, assigning foremen and their groups of workmen with different responsibilities for each element of the tower, and the construction pace accelerated.

Every morning, when I woke up with the first rays of sunlight, Kaori arrived at Cherry Blossom Villa, always running and always with a cheerful smile on her lips. The four of us would have breakfast together: Akira, Murakami, Kaori, and me. It was the time of day when I missed Mia the most. I tortured myself wondering what she would be doing at the palace with the prince.

After breakfast, Akira retreated to his cabin to continue programming, and Murakami went to his room to write. Kaori and I walked down Suzaku Avenue to the Rashomon gate. We always arrived a little before six in the morning.

Kaori woke up the Qilin and changed the candle that would burn for six hours until the next change at noon. While she replaced the candle, all of our workers knelt to watch the ritual.

After she had replaced the candle, she shouted, "Kyo mo isshokenmei ganbarimasho."[1]

Then I would give the day's orders to the foremen, each one of whom was in charge of a team of ten men. Some teams were in charge of collecting the stones needed to build the tower, other teams were assigned to assemble the scaffolds and others were responsible for the clock mechanism.

Kaori was a child, but her intelligence surpassed that of all the workers combined. They lacked initiative and got lost as

---

1. "Kyo mo isshokenmei ganbarimasho" can be translated to English as "Let's do our best today and every day."

soon as something new was asked of them. This led me to wonder if my little friend was a simulated entity like the others, or a human being like us four chosen ones.

At the end of working hours Kaori would extract a bunch of *wadokaichin* silver coins from her bag to pay the construction employees. Where did she get them from? Then Akira would come down to oversee our work. He always started by praising the good, but ended up pointing out the flaws half in jest, half seriously. "Good job, Nathan, but are you sure your tower won't look like the Leaning Tower of Pisa when it's taller than the Rashomon gate?" he might ask.

Once he had looked everything over, Akira would take us to have dinner at one of the many taverns along the river. Afterward, Kaori always disappeared. Where did she live? When we were alone, Akira would try to tempt me with sake, but I had decided not to do anything that would make deviate from my mission until it was finished and I had Mia by my side again. Disappointed by my "dullness," as he called it, Akira would retire to his cabin hidden among the flowering cherry trees, and I would go back to my room facing the garden.

That routine repeated itself day after day, without variation. After a few months, I had about a thousand people working for me. I was fascinated and happy to see the construction progressing. Finally, I had a great goal in life. But was it the work that made me happy, or was I intoxicated by the power I had gained?

I had become the most powerful Taira in the city, and everyone knew me. Even Prince Genji's soldiers had started to respect me and stepped aside when I walked down the avenue every morning. I had never felt so powerful. Had I been living as a sad puppet before this? It was nice to finally be in charge and have control. I supposed that was how a powerful and wealthy man like Masa felt.

I was so committed to my task that I didn't have time to think about other things during the day. But as night fell, when I lay on my solitary futon, I forgot about the construction chores. That was when Reiko and Mia took center stage in my fantasies. I remembered the gentle way Mia had treated me when I arrived in Kyoto Mythos and could barely get up from the futon. The way she knelt on the tatami next to me, the way she looked at me patiently, focusing all her attention on me, as though she could see into my heart—these things had been a balm for me.

And then I would suddenly remember the day when Mia and I got those letters from Reiko, the day Mia went off to the palace to be with Prince Genji.

Next came an image of Reiko. Her gaze, unlike Mia's, was impatient, even aggressive, with the power to penetrate deep within me whether I wanted it to or not. Visualizing Reiko's eyes made me tremble, my breath catching in my throat.

I had only spent a couple of days with her, and we'd slept together just the once, but an irrational force pulled me toward her, as if she was a black hole, a vortex capable of swallowing me. But I had the feeling that if I got close to Reiko again, I would be trapped and would never be able to separate from her.

Mia and Reiko attracted me like two different gravitational fields. Which one would I fall into first?

That dilemma stirred me so much that sometimes I wished a demon would erase all my memories of both of them.

30

THE TOWER UNDER THE MOON

As the days went by, Reiko retreated into solitude. After assisting Masa at the office, she would get home at dusk. She would have dinner and a cup of green tea on a sofa overlooking the city. Then she would connect her tablet to Kyoto Mythos. At first, she only followed the construction of the tower, but gradually she succumbed to the temptation of spying on Mia in the palace.

Reiko had made a conscious decision to rid her life of jealousy, which was why her relationship with Masa and other men was so open. But with Nathan, something had gone wrong; jealousy had returned to her life. When she saw Mia radiantly smiling with Prince Genji, she couldn't help disliking her. But what ate away at Reiko most was knowing that Nathan was building the Clock Tower to win another woman. She often wished something horrible would go wrong with the construction of the tower.

One evening, after dinner, Reiko sat down, poured herself a glass of wine and turned on her tablet. Mia and the other women of the prince's court appeared on the screen, sitting on tatami mats, writing on scrolls with brushes. As she watched the scene, Reiko smiled. "So many years in Japan, but she has written the penultimate stroke of the character 玄 wrong. She will never be completely Japanese like me, no matter how hard she tries."

After an hour of practicing calligraphy, the women went out to the gardens for tea. Afterward, they dined in the banquet hall with the prince and the rest of the Genji family. Reiko touched her tablet, positioning the camera so that she could see the head of the table, where Prince Genji sat. Mia was beside him, and around them there were many other family members. Reiko adjusted the tablet's volume to listen to the conversation.

"Love to all," the prince said, raising his glass.

"Kanpai!" they exclaimed, responding to the toast.

They then eagerly began to eat all kinds of delicacies. The table was full of *ise ebi*, gigantic lobsters from the coast of Ise.

"Shall we go to see a Noh play after dinner?" Mia asked.

"Of course, my dear," the prince said.

Later, as the evening drew to a close, the prince chose Mia to be with him that night. Reiko knew that rumors were circulating that Mia had become his favorite. When Mia lay down on the prince's futon, Reiko felt ashamed to notice that the initial caresses between the couple excited her.

She directed the camera to Nathan's room and zoomed in to observe his face. He seemed to be sleeping peacefully. Her gaze lingered on his strong chin, his thick eyelashes. She imagined him waking up to stare at her. She remembered how it had felt when they made love that night, and she began to touch herself, with half-closed eyes. Then she fell asleep on the sofa with the remnants of her dinner on the tray and the lights of Kyoto piercing the darkness beyond the window.

Meanwhile, in Kyoto Mythos, Mia waited for the prince to fall asleep. Then, as always, she quietly went up to the fourth floor and sat at the window of her favorite room, the one that overlooked Heian. A pearly moon seemed to almost touch the top of the Clock Tower, which was rising higher every day. Mia's heart beat strongly at the thought of what would happen when Nathan finished building it. As she stared out of the window, her sleepy eyes began to close, her face bathed in moonlight.

31
FENG HUANG
Ψ

One afternoon, after finishing another day's work on the Clock Tower, I accompanied Kaori when she went to replace a candle at another location in the city. We strolled along the edge of the wall, protected by countless Genji soldiers who watched us suspiciously. A soldier stopped Kaori and questioned her. She told him we were going to change the western candle, and he let us continue.

"If you weren't wearing the Taira symbol on your lapel, it would be easier for us to move around the city," Kaori said, pointing to her own lapel, where she wore nothing. "A war could break out at any moment between the Taira and the Genji. It's better to be anonymous."

I thought of the ultimatum the prince had given me: when the Clock Tower's construction was complete, he would declare war on the Taira.

"I can't say the Genji have treated me well since I arrived in Heian," I said. "And my friends Akira, Murakami, and Mia are all Taira . . ."

"Mia isn't Taira, she's Genji," said Kaori, matter-of-factly.

"Do you know her?"

"I often catch sight of her when I go to the palace. She's going to be the third wife of Prince Genji."

I nodded silently, not bothering to explain my deal with the prince to get Mia back in exchange for building the Clock Tower. A group of soldiers on horseback with black armor passed us, forcing us to stick to the wall.

"Every woman's dream is to marry the prince," said Kaori, as we started walking again. "I hope when I grow up, I'll be as beautiful as Mia and can marry him, although I still don't know what love is."

We kept walking, over the late-afternoon shadows cast by the wall onto the gravel underfoot. She walked ahead and I followed behind, as if she was a tour guide to the Kyoto of the past.

"Do you know what love is, Nathan?" asked Kaori, suddenly.

For a moment, I was blank.

"Love is another force of the universe," I heard myself saying, without knowing where those words came from.

"What is a force?"

"Something that attracts or repels."

"I don't understand. How can I feel this force called love?"

"You have to be attentive. The more attention you pay to everything around you, the more love you'll feel."

"That seems easy. When I have the chance, I'll look at Prince Genji with all the attention I can, to see if I feel the force of love."

"It doesn't work like that," I said, unsure of how to explain something I didn't fully understand myself. "Also it's important to remember those you love, even if they're no longer with you. The opposite of love isn't hatred, but forgetfulness."

After these words, memories of those I loved came flooding into my mind. First, my father, who until his death in the accident had always inspired me to be more. I also thought of my sensei, with whom I had spent years training, as well as my mother, who had been with me during my loneliest years. Finally, I thought of Mia's gaze and Reiko's eyes.

Kaori stopped in front of a small altar, protected by the statue of a phoenix. On the altar burned a candle with engraved numbers. The candle had burned down to the number five, 五.

"It's still a while before we change the candle and awaken the phoenix, Feng Huang," said Kaori, placing her backpack next to the altar.

We sat on a step, and she took out two onigiri rice balls.

"Do you want the onigiri with umeboshi pickled plum or just with rice and salt?"

"With umeboshi, please."

I opened the bamboo-leaf wrapping of my onigiri. The first bite tasted like heaven. The candle continued to burn, marking the hours, slowly approaching the number six, 六. The sun was setting behind the distant mountains, tinting the tiles of the altar with purple hues.

"Although I'm too young to know what love is, I have a special power," said Kaori. "I'm the only one who can summon the Four Beasts."

"No one else can awaken them?" I asked, astonished.

"No. They say there was another girl before me who could do it, but she disappeared without a trace. Some say she was my older sister, but I'll never know because I've never met my parents."

I felt sorry for her, but I admired her too—she showed no hint of sadness whatsoever.

When the candle was about to burn out, Kaori took out the tools from her backpack to replace it. Carrying out the same ritual as for the Qilin, she took measurements with the astrolabe. Once the new candle was lit, she stood in front of the Phoenix statue and, with her eyes closed, said louder than usual: "Pangu, Pangu, Panguuuu!"

As she pronounced the third "Pangu," the Phoenix came to life.

"*Hisashiburi*!" the Phoenix exclaimed. "Long time, no see."

"It's only been a day," Kaori replied.

"Forgive me, my dear," said the Phoenix. "You know I struggle to feel the passage of time."

Kaori couldn't help but laugh, and she ran her hand over the

Phoenix's head, caressing its crest as if it was an affectionate puppy.

The beast glanced at me sideways. Sensing its reproachful expression, Kaori introduced me. "This is my new friend, the Master of Eternity."

"You can call me Nathan," I said.

"It's an honor. I am the Phoenix Feng Huang," said the Phoenix, lifting its neck to look closely at me. "According to legend, you are going to solve our problems with time."

This was said with a suspicious expression, perhaps because Feng Huang was unable to believe that I was the Master of Eternity. It came a little closer until it was so close that I could hear its breath as it spoke. "When the Four Beasts and Pangu created the universe from chaos, we had no choice but to introduce a third variable: time. That served to bring order to the chaos, giving rise to this universe. But Pangu abandoned us, leaving us here with the unresolved problem of time."

"If time is necessary for this universe to function, I don't see how it can be a problem . . ."

"Time destroys everything, no matter what we do. It's the opposite of love—a force that separates everything," said Feng Huang with a sad expression. "The gods granted me the power to transcend time and live eternally, something I appreciate every day of my existence, but seeing the rest of the universe perish before the relentless march of time consumes my soul."

After this speech, Feng Huang huddled on the ground seemingly overcome by exhaustion. I felt some pity seeing it suffer.

Kaori took an onigiri out of her backpack and offered it to the Phoenix.

"Thank you, my dear, but I have no appetite. Witnessing so much suffering and destruction due to the passage of time weighs heavily on my soul."

She turned to me. "Only Pangu's energy can set the clock in motion on the tower you're building to allow us to transcend the passage of time."

"That's what the Qilin said. But how do I summon Pangu?"

"The Three Sacred Treasures are necessary. In addition to the Magatama pendant you wear around your neck, you'll need the Kusanagi sword and the Yata mirror."

"And how do I get them?"

"To obtain the Yata mirror, you'll have to kill the Dragon that guards it. As for the Kusanagi sword, I only know it doesn't exist in this universe; to get it, you'll have to leave here and return to the world you came from."

I was amazed that this creature, programmed for this simulation, could comprehend the existence of a world beyond Kyoto Mythos. Kaori looked at me with curiosity, as if trying to imagine the world I had come from.

Without giving me the chance to ask further questions, the Phoenix closed its eyes and transformed back into a stone statue.

With the setting sun at our backs, we returned to Cherry Blossom Villa. I felt like paying a visit to Akira. When we went inside his cabin, we found him programming. His dark glasses reflected the hundreds of LED lights that filled the room as he typed away at full speed.

When he noticed us, he unplugged the cable connected to the back of his neck. "What are you doing bringing an artificial intelligence character into my cabin?" he said.

"Artificial intelligence?" Kaori repeated, confused.

Akira leaned in close to my ear and whispered, so that Kaori couldn't hear him. "Damn it, Nathan! The inside of this cabin is reserved for humans, the four chosen ones who know the real world. What would happen if the virtual characters found out they're living in a simulation and that there's a world beyond?"

"Sorry. Kaori is so intelligent, so human, that I often forget her artificial nature."

"What does artificial mean?" she said, grabbing my sleeve to pull me away from Akira.

"Artificial is something created by humans that does not exist in nature," I replied.

"I suppose my parents created me, even though I don't remember them. Does that make me artificial?" she asked.

"Not exactly . . ."

Akira gestured for me to stop giving explanations and looked suspiciously at Kaori, who was curiously observing the inside of the cabin. It was the first time she had seen electronic devices.

"Girl!" exclaimed Akira. "All of this is secret, don't you dare talk about this place with anyone. Not even with your friends, the Four Beasts."

"Understood," Kaori said with a mischievous smile.

"Do you promise?" Akira asked.

"Promise."

Kaori approached one of the screens, fascinated.

"What are those beautiful lights?"

"They show the code that is generating this world. I'm the only one who has access to this code in Heian," replied Akira, more relaxed.

"Are you a wizard or something like that?" asked Kaori.

"I guess so! I had never thought of it that way . . . ," said Akira, "I am an all-powerful wizard!"

Kaori laughed.

In Akira's smiling eyes, I could recognize his hacker pride. He cleared a bunch of cables from a table so that we could sit down. He brought out trays of grilled fish, white rice, and fresh vegetables.

As we ate, I told Akira about the conversation I had just had with the Phoenix and Kaori, and the need to find the two remaining sacred treasures, the sword and the mirror.

"And the reason we have this information is thanks to my power to awaken the Phoenix," said Kaori, proudly.

"Thank you, Kaori, you're the best," I said, like a proud father.

"We want the Kusanagi sword not just to summon Pangu as the Phoenix told you. Masa also has his own reasons for wanting the sword and obtaining it will be the next step of your mission," said Akira, who seemed to know more than me about the subject. "The problem is that we still don't have a detailed three-dimensional model of the sword. That's why you need to go back to the real world and steal the sword so we can use a 3D scanner to create a three-dimensional model. Reiko failed in trying to persuade Roku to give us the sword. Once you have it in your possession, Masa will scan it with the highest definition so that we can reproduce it here in Kyoto Mythos."

"I don't understand anything," interrupted Kaori, confused.

"It's better that you don't understand, and remember your promise—everything you see and hear in this cabin is secret," said Akira. With a smirk, he added, "Do you know Nathan is doing all this because he's in love with Mia?"

"Is that a secret too? You're in love and haven't told me?"

Without knowing what to say, I took a sip of my miso soup.

"They say Prince Genji is going to marry Mia," said Kaori.

Akira took a sip of his sake, and nudged me in the ribs, with a sideways glance. By the time we finished eating, he was already half drunk. Letting his guard down, he started showing Kaori how to type on his terminals. He also explained what a video game was.

"Are they better than regular games?" she asked excitedly.

"At first, video games were so limited that it was more fun to play ball with your friends. But now they immerse you in other worlds."

"I want to play a video game!"

"I'll let you try one of the ones I have here," said Akira, suddenly switching to a paternal tone.

Akira fired up an emulator and ran *The Legend of Zelda: Breath of the Wild*. Kaori knelt on the tatami with a controller and started playing. Within minutes, she was completely absorbed in the game.

Akira and I continued to drink sake while eating tsukemono pickles.

"Isn't Zelda too difficult for her first game?" I asked Akira.

"Not at all—it's a simple retro game. Keep in mind she's an

artificial intelligence character. What you're witnessing is a computer versus computer match."

"Wow, you're right," I said, realizing I was still thinking of the girl as a living being. "Here, in Kyoto Mythos, everything feels so real that I forget it's all fake."

"It depends on how you define real or fake."

"I'm too tired for metaphysical conversations. How will I get out of here to search for the Kusanagi sword? The Rashomon gate is guarded by the Genji, and they won't let me out."

"Another problem is that the elevator you used to get into Kyoto Mythos is only an entrance mechanism, not an exit. Returning to reality is more difficult . . ."

"It's more difficult? When I came in, I thought I was going to die!"

"Well actually, you were dead for a few moments, so that you could get in here, and then you were revived. In fact, only Mia, Murakami, you, and I managed to come back to life. The rest of the beta testers who were born with the samsara gene and tried to cross over into this virtual world died during the entry process."

"So, to leave . . ." I murmured anxiously, "do I have to die again?"

"No. It's worse."

32

GOD HAS RETURNED

Masa took the stage for his annual public appearance at the Tokyo International Forum conference center. Minutes before, in the wings, Reiko had helped him inject several chemical cocktails.

Fans from the most remote corners of the planet had traveled to the Japanese capital to hear Masa, who, it was said, would change the future of humanity. His staunch supporters claimed that the founder of Apple was nothing compared to him.

Masa hated traveling, but he made an exception occasionally and boarded the maglev train that connected Kyoto to Tokyo.

Every year, the same ritual was repeated at the beginning of each performance. It started with synchronized applause from the audience until the curtains opened onto an empty stage. Then, silence filled the room. The audience knew that Masa was there, hidden in the wings with Reiko, making them wait for a few seconds that seemed endless, before stepping into the light. Every year, journalists commented on Masa's dramatic pause and the psychological effect it had on his followers, who could barely contain their mounting excitement.

When he finally glided on stage in his wheelchair, trying to keep his neck upright, it seemed as if he was casually strolling into his living room, indifferent to the fact that thousands of people had their eyes fixed on him and hundreds of millions were watching him on live stream.

He always dressed the same, in a navy blue Italian-cut blazer, white T-shirt, jeans, and white sneakers. Once in the center of the stage, he looked out at the audience and broke the silence with his words, like a prophet with extraordinary knowledge.

As always he began his presentation with a question.

"What sets us, human beings, apart from the rest of the living beings on the planet?" he said. He took a deep breath and gently stroked his chin. "One of the most important differences is that we—*Homo sapiens*—are capable of creating technology. Almost two million years ago, we began developing rudimentary tools to control fire and that was when we transitioned from being hunted to being hunters. Thanks to increasingly sophisticated technology, we have become the dominant species on the planet. After thousands of years of development, we live in symbiosis with the technology we have developed. Can you imagine your lives without electricity or the Internet?"

The audience held their breath in the packed auditorium.

"Other living beings can live without technology," Masa continued, "but we depend on it. It is part of our ecosystem. Imagine for a moment that technology is not inert, but a living being like any other, subject to Darwin's laws of evolution. Only the most advanced and adaptable technologies survive in the harsh natural selection. The rest fall into oblivion, like dinosaurs. At Taira Corporation, we are aware that this harsh natural selection could render us obsolete at any moment, and turn us into prey for competing technological companies."

Everyone in the audience knew that when Masa spoke of competition, he was referring to Genji Corporation and his eternal enemy Roku. For Masa to name names was not only unnecessary, it was like giving his foes free publicity.

"That's why we gather here once a year, dear family, to show the ones who prey on us that they will be the ones to perish." He examined the palms of his hands for a moment then he raised his gaze to the audience.

"We will survive!" he exclaimed.

A thunderous ovation erupted. The large screen behind Masa showed the interior of a hangar with a huge metallic sphere in the center surrounded by cables and screens.

"What you see is our quantum supercomputer. Its computing power is greater than the combined power of all the computers that exist or have existed on our planet to this day. Continuing with the analogy of natural selection, it's as if a new living being has appeared and no other living beings can kill it. With this computer, we are invincible."

The audience rose from their seats, and jubilation once again filled every corner of Tokyo International Forum's auditorium.

"Our team of engineers has managed to make this the first general-purpose quantum computer, capable of solving problems of any kind. It's not like the quantum computers made by our rivals, which only solve specific problems."

The presentation continued, showing technical details of the quantum computer and images of the interiors of the facilities—endless corridors filled with blue-colored cables and LEDs, whose glow reached everywhere, and ceilings covered in cooling tubes.

Then the screen went blank. Everyone was waiting for something more from Masa; they knew he always kept an ace up his sleeve.

"And you must be wondering, what can we do with this computer? What's the point of so much computing power? Before I answer these questions, let me tell you something. The motivation that led human beings to control the planet was the insatiable explorer instinct. Our ancestors conquered every corner of the earth. Neil Armstrong was the first to set foot on the moon, and Elon Musk was the first to walk on the surface of Mars. But we can also travel and explore in other ways. Taira Corporation's quantum computer will allow us to travel to virtual universes never imagined. The first of these new universes, which is already in the beta testing phase, we have named . . ."

He gave another dramatic pause, and images of Heian—the

Rashomon gate, the palace of Prince Genji, and the Clock Tower—appeared on the projection.

" . . . Kyoto Mythos!"

The audience rose again in an ovation that lasted several minutes.

"Our teams are working on creating the simulated world of Kyoto Mythos, indistinguishable from what we consider reality but set in late twelfth-century Kyoto. Users of this simulation will feel like time travelers."

Masa continued explaining the details of the simulation, hinting that a genetic modification injection would be necessary for users before connecting. At no time did he mention the samsara gene, something he still considered secret, although Roku already knew about it thanks to the industrial espionage carried out by Genji Corporation. Of course, Masa also did not mention that all users would be limited to twelve months of connection, keeping their biological bodies floating in tubs before deciding whether to abandon reality or live eternally in the virtual world.

After finishing, Masa bowed from his wheelchair, and the applause lasted for several minutes.

As the audience filed out of the auditorium, news of Masa's latest presentation was already going viral:

> Taira Corporation, now the world's largest company, will open to the public an alternative universe called Kyoto Mythos simulated by a quantum computer. According to statements at the Tokyo International Forum by Masa, the Taira Corporation CEO, it will be set in late twelfth-century Kyoto, where we can take part in adventures indistinguishable from reality. Users will feel like time travelers. Masa has risen to the rank of God, creator of a new universe.

33

WAKING UP IN REALITY
$\Psi \rightarrow$ Reality

When the Clock Tower, still shrouded in bamboo scaffolding, surpassed the height of the Rashomon gate, I felt proud. Akira started coming out of his hut more often to lend us a hand. He helped us recruit masons and blacksmiths to speed up the construction. When the time came to assemble the clock mechanism, Su Song also visited us. He checked the gears, and we made sure everything followed his father's design.

The Clock Tower had become my passion and my obsession. If Masa's goal had been to activate my samsara gene 100 percent, he was succeeding. My fixation on the work was such that my feelings for Reiko and Mia took a back seat, as if they were solitary clouds floating in a clear sky, always present but not bothering me. Many evenings, when I returned to my room at Cherry Blossom Villa, I kept working on deciphering Su Song's father's scrolls until I fell asleep. I was trying to figure out how to feed the "Celestial Lake" at the top of the Clock Tower, ensuring that it was continuously supplied with water.

Su Song and I decided to build a canal from the Kamogawa River to the base of the tower. To make the water rise more than 150 feet to reach the Celestial Lake, we designed a system of gears and waterwheels we would install inside the tower.

"With endless water, we will mark time eternally," declared Su Song, as we worked together one afternoon.

"We need to find a power source to make the water rise," I said, thinking about how simple this would be in the real world.

"The easiest thing would be to have four strong men working in shifts to keep rotating the wheel at the base of the tower," Su Song said.

"Like Conan the Barbarian," Akira whispered, his eyes shining with pride. He had probably programmed the lines of code that would make the idea of using men as a power source emerge in Su Song's mind.

"What will happen to my job of changing the candles once we have the clock?" asked Kaori.

"Hmm," said Su Song, stroking his beard. "Your current job will no longer be necessary."

Kaori looked up at the tower with a worried expression. That day they were covering the top with black tiles.

"Don't worry, we'll find a new job for you," I said.

"If we stop changing the candles and one day the clock stops, will time cease to exist?" Kaori asked.

"No, the days would continue to progress, following the rhythm of the sun."

"And if the sun ceases to exist?"

"That won't happen," said Su Song. "Pangu is time, and its matter is also part of the sun, the heavens, the earth, and the waters."

"And if Pangu—"

"Pangu is the universe, and the universe is Pangu!" Su Song exclaimed, not allowing Kaori to finish her question.

"This clock, besides robbing us of water and time, is also going to steal my job," Kaori complained.

I gave her a reassuring pat on the shoulder. "Your new job can be to watch the tower and make sure the water always reaches the Celestial Lake at the top, and never stops," I said.

The worried look on Kaori's face vanished, and we got back

to work. That afternoon we were assembling the armillary sphere with the Celestial Chain, which would be the heart of the clock.

The Clock Tower stood imposingly, watching over the entire city. It was so tall that it even seemed to challenge the mountains surrounding Heian. I felt like this was the masterpiece of my life. Was it the culmination of my career as a clock designer? But at the same time, I realized that my greatest creation was just an illusion in a virtual world.

One evening, at the end of another day's work, I agreed to go with Akira to a tavern instead of returning to my room at Cherry Blossom Villa.

"Why are you walking with your head down?" asked Akira, as we went along the road.

"This always happens when I'm about to finish a project. I feel uncertain and empty, not knowing what will come next."

"Uncertain? When something ends, the next step is always to celebrate it big time," Akira said before taking a sip of his first glass of sake. "Think about everything you've achieved! Soon your samsara will be activated 100 percent, you'll save our dear Masa, and you'll also allow Taira Corporation to offer this world to the rest of humanity. When we open the connection to Kyoto Mythos, thousands of people will live here and admire the Clock Tower. They will know it was your work. You won't be forgotten, Nathan. You'll go down in history as one of the four chosen ones who participated in the creation of the first virtual world."

"Yes, but what will I do once everything is finished?"

"When the clock starts ticking, the prince will release Mia without marrying her, just as he promised you. Mia will be yours," Akira said. "And then, war will break out between the Taira and the Genji. How exciting! I'm forging several katanas to use in the fight!"

If there was one thing I'd learned from Akira in the short time I'd known him, it was that despite his craziness, he faced everything with enthusiasm.

"Mia . . ."

"You'll live happily ever after," said Akira.

"Forever?" I wondered if he was joking.

I couldn't help feeling confused. I knew I loved Mia, but I also wanted to show the Clock Tower to Reiko. The people we want to show our achievements to are usually the ones we love. And I wanted to show my father too. I had always wanted to achieve something he would be proud of, but he died too soon.

"A new era for humanity will soon begin, and all thanks to you!" Akira exclaimed, raising his wooden cup in a toast.

I stared silently at the sake cup as Akira's voice faded. I wondered how Mia was feeling about what would happen when the tower was successfully constructed.

The next day, after several hours watching our workers position the clock hands, which were so huge they were visible from any point in the city, I declared the construction finished. After this declaration, Su Song, Akira, Kaori, and I opened the gates of the canal that connected to the Kamogawa River. Four strong men began to turn the wheel that lifted the water up to the Celestial Lake at the top of the tower. But just as the Phoenix had predicted, the current failed to start the clock gears. Mysteriously, the laws of physics as I knew them were being violated.

"It's time for you to go get the Kusanagi sword," Akira said. "Without it, there's nothing more we can do here. Only by invoking Pangu will we get it moving."

Su Song set off for the prince's palace, and the three of us returned to Akira's hut. As soon as we arrived, Kaori started playing *The Legend of Zelda*. Since the afternoon I first brought her to Akira's, he and Kaori had hit it off, and Kaori came and went from there as if her own home.

Akira began typing into a terminal.

```
Nathan.current_mission();
```

On the screen appeared:

> MISSION > obtain the Kusanagi sword
> CURRENT STATUS > return to reality

He poured me a huge glass of sake.

"Drink it all, you're going to need it," he said in a strangely serious tone.

I downed the liquor to the last drop as Akira opened a black case engraved with the symbol of the Taira. Inside was a golden needle about two inches long. "To return to reality, you have to stick this needle in your eye," he said. "You need to feel enough panic and pain to wake up your body, which is floating in the bathtub."

Unaware of our conversation, Kaori continued playing *Zelda*. After pouring me another full glass of sake, Akira carried on typing source code:

```
if (character.type() == master_of_eternity) {
character.assign_mission(legendary_kusanagi_
sword);
    if (character.needle == true && character.pain_
threshold > EXIT_PAIN) {
character.exit_kyoto_mythos_virtual_machine
== true;
            _asm
            {
                    mov al, 13h
                    mov ah, 0h
                    int 10h
            }
            QuantumTaira.system.exit(character);
    }
}
```

"Isn't there an easier way to get out of this damn simulation?" I said. I took the needle from the case, my arm starting to tremble.

"Unfortunately, not right now. This method is a temporary hack of mine, the only one we can use. In the future, when we launch Kyoto Mythos on the market, there'll be a more harmless way to exit."

I lay down on the tatami, dizzy from all the sake I had drunk. Kaori continued playing her game in a corner of the room, completely absorbed in the *Zelda* universe.

Akira knelt beside me and said, "Remember, the pain here is just an interpretation by your brain. If you stop interpreting the situation, the pain ceases to exist."

I took a deep breath, my heart pounding, and managed to bring the needle within a millimeter of the cornea of my right eye. But my arm didn't respond to my will. I couldn't stop shaking, and although I had my eye open, everything was blurry, and I couldn't focus.

"Can't you do it for me?" I said, terrified.

"Coward. A hero has to fend for himself."

"Pangu, Pangu, Pangu," I told myself. "Mia, Mia, Mia . . ."

Repeating those words gave me the necessary courage to finally make a quick movement and stick the needle into my eye. Holding my breath, I felt the cold line of gold piercing through the vitreous fluid until it reached the macula, like a snake entering the entrails of a freshly deceased cow in search of its heart.

When the needle completely pierced my eyeball, the initial unbearable pain transformed into a freezing fire that seemed to consume my whole body. Then, my consciousness leaped into nothingness. I don't know how long the nothingness lasted but there came a point when I was able to feel my body again. My heart was beating strongly. I had the sensation that I was surrounded by warm water.

I tried to open my eyes and move, but I couldn't, which made me panic and my heart race even faster. I felt as though I was drowning, a great pressure crushing down on me as if I was deep underwater, although somehow, at the same time, I knew I was floating with my face above the water.

In a corner of my consciousness, the image of Mia dressed in a colorful kimono emerged. I saw her follow Prince Genji into a room in his palace. I had a strong urge to follow her. Then, suddenly, I was able to open my eyes and breathe easily again.

I was in the bathtub, a milky clarity beneath me, projecting my shadow onto the ceiling. My body was stiff and sore. I managed to move my fingers, and shortly after, I could tilt my neck. That's when I realized Masa and Reiko were there, watching me wake up.

"Welcome back to reality," said Reiko, in a sweet voice,

I tried to reply, but I still didn't have the strength to articulate words. Without losing her serene expression, Reiko prepared a syringe and proceeded to inject it into my shoulder. Moments later, I felt a surge of energy waking up every cell in my body.

Masa watched me from the wheelchair with a satisfied smile. "We are very proud of your work in Kyoto Mythos," he said. "It has been an honor to have you as our clock designer in our virtual world. It's been over eleven months since you and Murakami both entered, but Murakami only had six freckles left. When his last freckle disappeared, he had to make the decision. Of course, he chose to stay in Kyoto Mythos, and we had to discard his biological body."

I was struck by the coldness with which he pronounced the word "discard," making this sound like a routine procedure, like taking out the trash.

Instinctively, I touched the back of my ear. To my surprise, I found only one freckle remaining. That meant I had a month or less to remain connected to Kyoto Mythos and keep my biological body alive in the bathtub.

"I'll have to make the same decision soon. How much time do I have?" I asked.

"One week," Masa replied. "The most difficult part, which

was building the Clock Tower, you have already achieved. For the rest of your mission in Kyoto Mythos, that week will be enough. I am certain that the samsara gene will express itself 100 percent within you, and you will save me! Once you finish your work for me, the decision about whether you should stay in Kyoto Mythos will be yours and yours alone."

I clumsily stepped out of the bathtub.

"Cover yourself up, we can see everything," Reiko said, one hand over her mouth while her other hand passed me a towel.

PART THREE

The Master of Eternity

THE THREE SACRED TREASURES

At the conclusion of the Potsdam Conference in late July 1945, Emperor Hirohito's main concern was not the destruction of his country. Knowing that the end of the Second World War was near and defeat was inevitable, he ordered his personal advisor, Koichi Kido, to relocate the Three Sacred Treasures, which symbolize the legitimacy of the emperor, to ensure "at all costs" that they were not destroyed or did not fall into the hands of the Allied powers.

According to legend, the Three Sacred Treasures were brought to Japan from the heavens by the god Ninigi-no-Mikoto, who was sent by his grandmother, Amaterasu, the sun goddess, with the mission of bringing peace to the Japanese islands. Later, the Three Sacred Treasures ended up in the hands of Jimmu, the first emperor of Japan.

It is believed that from the seventh century to the present day, during the coronation ceremony of each new emperor, Shinto monks bring out the Three Sacred Treasures from the secret locations where they are kept and present them to the emperor who is to be crowned. This ceremony is held behind closed doors, and there are no photographs of these three objects; therefore their existence cannot be confirmed.

The Three Sacred Treasures comprise the following:

- The Magatama Pendant (Yasakani no Magatama): a jewel in the shape of a crescent moon with a hole for it to be worn as a pendant.
- The Kusanagi Sword (Kusanagi no Tsurugi): according to legend, it emerged from one of the eight tails of the serpent-dragon Yamata no Orochi.
- The Yata Mirror (Yata no Kagami): a sacred mirror in the shape of an octagonal shield. It represents honesty and truth, because it reflecting reality as it is.

Today, the Three Sacred Treasures are still considered the most important possessions of the Japanese people, and the location in which they are kept is a highly guarded secret. The Magatama Pendant is in the Imperial Palace in Tokyo; the Kusanagi Sword is allegedly kept at Atsuta Shrine in Nagoya; and the Yata Mirror is in the precincts of Ise Shrine. But none of them are on public display, and therefore it is difficult to confirm that they exist.

34
THE KUSANAGI SWORD

From the window of Masa's office, I took in the bird's eye view of Kyoto. I couldn't believe that I was a time traveler who had visited the past and was now returning to the present. The Kyoto that I looked down on now had no city walls, no Rashomon gate, no endless rows of traditional machiya houses. But like ancient Heian, modern Kyoto still retained its characteristic rectangular structure, sandwiched between the mountains to the east and west and straddling the Kamogawa River running from north to south.

From where I stood, I could see the Imperial Palace, unchanged since it had been built in the Heian era. It contrasted starkly with the ultramodern station with maglev trains coming and going every two or three minutes, located to the south, near where the Rashomon gate had stood in the past.

"It's one of the few cities in Japan whose structure has remained intact for centuries," said Masa behind me as he maneuvered his wheelchair to the table in the center of the room. "That's why it's ideal for modeling a historical virtual world without major headaches." His neck was straight, and his body was almost upright. He seemed rejuvenated since our last meeting. I moved away from the window and sat next to him.

"Do you understand now why I had trouble explaining your job to you?" said Masa. "Just to show you that I keep my promises, check your bank account."

I took out my phone and checked. My bank balance had multiplied.

"I hope you enjoyed my work of art," said Masa.

"Are you referring to Kyoto Mythos?"

"Yes, of course. You're lucky to have been inside it. I am the architect, but I still cannot be part of my work."

"It's been one of the best experiences of my life," I said.

"The best?"

Feeling as if I was responding to a survey, I pondered for a moment and replied, "The best, without a doubt."

"You've suffered more than ever, and the bottom line is it's just a simulation of a world based on medieval Kyoto, without any luxuries. What makes you rate it as the best experience of your life?"

"It's made me feel useful and valued. I have a mission."

Masa smiled. "Exactly! That's what I want to achieve with Kyoto Mythos. The more meaning we give to our daily lives, the more human we become. It's what the Japanese call *ikigai*—our life's purpose. My intention is that in Kyoto Mythos, everyone can live in harmony with their ikigai."

"But are we really human if we lose our biological bodies and end up connected to a large computer, living in a virtual world?"

"As long as you feel you have a purpose, you are human, regardless of whether you have a physical body or not. The figure of the hero is the epitome of the meaning of life. In our quantum computer, you are the Master of Eternity. Here, in reality, you are a single man approaching forty who doesn't know what to do with his life. Isn't it obvious which life you—or anyone—would choose?"

Masa suggested going out for a meal. Kamyu acted as a chauffeur and drove us to the old district of Pontocho, home to the geishas. He dropped us at a restaurant specializing in traditional Japanese kaiseki cuisine.

"Why can't you just design the Kusanagi sword in three dimensions and be done with it? In fact, I could do it with my watch design knowledge," I said, after the wait staff had brought us oshibori hand towels and oolong tea.

"We could do that. But there are several reasons why we need the original so that we can copy it exactly. First—you should never skimp on the details; we need to show our clients the great dedication we have put into building this universe. We can advertise: 'When you enter Kyoto Mythos, you'll be able to wield the legendary Kusanagi sword.' Second—any act of heroism on your part, both within Kyoto Mythos and here, in reality, helps increase the percentage of samsara gene expression in you."

He pointed to the screen attached to his wheelchair:

Samsara gene expression in Nathan:
completed to 94.9382%

"Good job, Nathan. As you can see, we're almost there! Soon we'll be able to extract the samsara from you, and you'll save me, but we need you to act like a hero until we reach 100 percent. And the third reason," he said, eyes sparkling, "is that it belongs to the Taira."

"Is it in a museum? You're a powerful man. Why not ask to borrow it for scanning?"

A waiter came over to our table carrying two trays bearing small dishes of vegetables, rice, beans, and meat, along with bowls of miso soup.

"The sword is not in a museum. It's hidden," said Masa. "The Kusanagi sword is possibly the most important object in Japan's history. Legend has it that the Ashinazuki family was being attacked by the serpent-dragon Yamata no Orochi, which had eight heads. It ate seven of the eight daughters, and when only one remained alive, Princess Kushinada, the god of storms and the sea came to rescue her."

"It sounds like a story from Greek mythology, but the Lernaean Hydra had nine heads, not eight."

"Exactly. Myths from around the world are similar because they originate from the same place."

"From the human psyche?"

"Not exactly," said Masa with a mysterious look on his face as he picked up a shiitake mushroom with his chopsticks. "Let me tell you what happened. Susanoo, the god of storms and the sea, made a deal with Ashinazuki. If he killed the serpent-dragon Yamata no Orochi, Ashinazuki would let him marry his last daughter. Susanoo faced the monster, whose body occupied the space of eight mountains and eight valleys. When he cut off its tail and ended its life, the Kusanagi sword was found inside the body of the dragon. This sword was used by several heroes in Japan's history until, in 1185, it was lost when it fell into the ocean during the battle of Dan-no-ura."

"So the legend that the sword is at the bottom of the ocean is true?" I asked, startled.

"Not anymore. In an expedition I funded ten years ago, we used state-of-the-art remotely operated submarines and managed to find the sword at the bottom of the sea off the coast of Kanazawa. It was big news in Japan, and it helped me establish a close relationship with the emperor. I donated the sword to the imperial house, and they kept it with the other sacred treasures, the Yasakani no Magatama pendant, which you know after months of wearing it in Kyoto Mythos, and the Yata no Kagami mirror. A year ago, Roku's henchmen broke into the facilities of the Imperial Palace in Tokyo and stole the sword."

"The same Genji Corporation employees who attacked Reiko and me at the sushi restaurant?" I asked.

"Yes. They're always meddling in our affairs. Damn them."

"How can someone steal the sacred treasures? Wasn't there any security?"

"In Japan, there is very little theft. This makes people complacent. Throughout the country, we have alarms and cameras that are said to work perfectly, but everything is full of security holes. Because of that, it's easy to commit robberies. Recently, some thieves broke into the home of the president of the largest security systems company in Japan."

"That's crazy!"

"Officially, no one knows where the sword is, but we have discovered where Genji Corporation is hiding it." Masa dropped his chopsticks onto the tray and clenched his fists. "We suspect that the Kusanagi sword is hidden inside the temple next to your house."

Masa pointed through the window, toward the mountainside to the east. Among the trees, I could see the temple pagoda I had looked out on when I woke up next to Reiko, the day before entering Kyoto Mythos.

"It's a private temple owned by Genji Corporation. It's heavily guarded, but we've been studying for months how to get the sword. Reiko will give you the details of the operation we've planned."

"And I have to be the one to steal the sword? I don't remember this type of work being in my contract conditions."

"You're not going to steal anything. You're going to recover something that belongs to Taira Corporation, the company you work for."

"Why not go to the authorities?" I asked.

"There are certain things in Japan that operate above the law and the authorities. Not even the emperor has the power to recover the sword. No one has conclusive evidence that Genji Corporation stole it, but I'm sure of it. That's why we must act outside the law."

"Still, I don't think I'm the right person," I said.

"I want you to be the hero of this operation. As I just explained, any heroic act helps increase the percentage of samsara gene expression within you. Also, it's not just about scanning an object in three dimensions to reproduce it in our simulation; this is one of the most important pieces of treasure in Japan's history, and it's in the hands of our enemy."

"I suspect that the operation is part of your vision of life where everything is mythology and art. Am I a character in your work, like I was in Kyoto Mythos?"

Masa smiled without answering, and I wondered why the richest man on the planet had chosen me as the protagonist of his exploits. Or perhaps it was my father who had made that initial choice before I was even born by convincing my mother to allow the samsara gene to be introduced into my embryo.

"Just as Susanoo passed into Japanese history as the hero who cut off the tail of the eight-headed serpent-dragon, if you manage to find and rescue the Kusanagi sword, you too will become a legend."

35

DREAMS AND DELIRIUM

Back at my home on the eastern slope, I stood at the open window. The setting sun tinged the rooftops of Kyoto with reddish hues. I glanced anxiously toward the temple. I noticed it was surrounded by a wall with cameras.

A gentle breeze caressed the trees surrounding the old structure, eliciting the song of the cicadas, a rhythmic and serene murmur that heralded the beginning of summer.

I should have been feeling nervous about the task ahead, but instead I lay down on the sofa and let a sense of lethargy enveloped me, reminiscent of the days when, in my years of solitude, I would spend weeks doing nothing in my study, awaiting a new commission.

Suddenly, I realized that I missed Akira and little Kaori, my adventure companions. I also longed for Mia, whom I imagined in the prince's palace, waiting for the Clock Tower to start ticking.

Filled with melancholy, I closed my eyes for a moment and wondered if everything I had experienced in the past months had been an induced dream. But when I opened them again, this luxurious house offered to me by Masa as part of my work at Taira Corporation seemed more unreal than Kyoto Mythos. I felt as though all of Japan was an ethereal world, set apart from the rest of the planet.

I went to the kitchen in search of something to eat. While I was making myself a sandwich, I noticed a bottle of Hibiki Ya-mazaki whiskey on top of the fridge. I didn't really like drinking alone, but I couldn't resist opening the bottle and pouring myself a glass.

I sat on the sofa, bathing in a bittersweet feeling of freedom mixed with loneliness. I ate the sandwich and started drinking. A starry sky blanketed the city. Drowsiness overcame me, and I fell asleep with the glass in my hand. I had a brief dream, set against a backdrop of rustling trees, and the sound of a piano. When I awoke from my doze, I could still hear the piano music, but it was inside the room. I recognized the tune—*Forbidden Colours*. Each note seemed to caress a hidden part of my consciousness, making me wonder whether I was still dreaming.

When I turned my head, I recognized Reiko's graceful back as she sat at the keyboard of the grand piano, several bulging paper bags on the floor next to her. She was completely absorbed in the subtle notes flowing from her fingers. Although I couldn't see her face, I was overwhelmed by her beauty. Sensing my gaze, she stopped playing and turned toward me.

"Hey. Are you OK?"

"I just had a weird dream. I was crossing a suspension bridge, swaying in the wind, but I never made it to the other side. I could see you playing the piano at the far side of the bridge. The music was guiding me toward you but you stayed in the distance, and I couldn't reach you . . ." I paused, trying to remember the end of the dream. "By the way, you play wonderfully."

Reiko blushed and, ignoring my words, picked up the bags next to her. As she placed them on the coffee table in front of the sofa, I let my eyes trace the curves of her body.

"What are you looking at?" she said.

"The night sky."

"You can touch me if you want."

With that, she moved away, as if to tempt me to follow her. Deciding not to play along for now, I stayed where I was and took the last sip of my drink.

From the bags, Reiko took out some packages of prepared food and poured herself a whiskey. I began to nibble on some edamame beans. She sat opposite me, blocking the view of Kyoto with her body.

She picked up a skewer of yakitori chicken from one of the trays. "What's wrong?" she said. "Aren't you interested in me any more? Have you become so accustomed to virtual women that you're afraid of a real one?"

"No . . . but I've noticed something between you and Masa."

"What Masa and I have is open and without commitments, different from what I feel for you."

At that outburst of frankness, I didn't know what to say.

"Masa is rotten with money, but he envies you. He's giving everything he has in exchange for your power to enter Kyoto Mythos. He's depending on you. I, on the other hand, am repulsed by the idea of living in a virtual world."

"Why? Inside Kyoto Mythos, everything feels exactly the same as here, but better. In fact, I'm having trouble adapting to reality. Everything is more exciting there."

"Without risk or sacrifice, life lacks meaning. In the simulation, you always know that no matter what you do, you won't die, like when you realize you're dreaming and decide to fly off the top of a mountain. There's no risk in any of your actions. That's why, in Kyoto Mythos, you appear to be a brave man, but here you're quite cowardly."

"Cowardly?"

"Masa says you're a hero, but in reality, you're nothing more than a daddy's boy."

I threw down the skewer of the yakitori I'd just eaten. "I had the courage to pierce my eye with a needle to return. I am the Master of Eternity! All the inhabitants of Heian respect me. Soon, I will succeed in summoning Pangu and setting the Clock Tower in motion."

"Do you realize you sound like someone who has completely lost their mind?"

"There's a difference: everything I just told you is real, at least for me."

"Are you sure—" She paused dramatically. "Are you sure Mia is real and waiting for you in the prince's palace?"

Confused and almost delirious, I took a sip of my second whiskey and took a deep breath to try to calm myself.

Reiko scanned me from head to toe with her seductive gaze.

"I am real," she said, caressing her leg. "You will never be half the man Masa is . . ."

I knew she was playing with me, but I couldn't control myself. Possessed by an unexpected impulse, I grabbed her with all my strength, lifting her up. I pressed her against the window, where I bit her neck and kissed her while her nails scratched my back.

The heat of our bodies fogged up the glass, causing the nocturnal view of Kyoto to blur like a dream fading in time.

36
KENJA MODE

I was woken up by the wet touch of Reiko's tongue. I kept my eyes closed, and surrendered to the pleasurable sensations, although suddenly, I found myself imagining that it was Mia between my legs. But as I reached the peak of pleasure, I opened my eyes. The woman between my thighs was Reiko, and my desire for Mia remained unconsummated. I fell back into a light sleep, bathed in the rays of the dawn sun.

"Did you miss me?" Reiko whispered in my ear, waking me up again, her naked body spooning mine from behind.

"Not anymore . . . ," I murmured sleepily, turning to kiss her. Her eyes reflected the green of the trees outside. The swaying net curtains cast light and shadows in her gaze.

"So . . . why do men always just fall asleep or turn away after orgasm? We call that attitude kenja mode in Japanese."

"Kenja mode?"

"Yes, it's those minutes after orgasm when men become completely lost in a world of their own."

"It's not that, it's more that I feel free from thoughts and worries. In that kenja mode you talk about, for a moment I think I'm so satisfied that I'll never need anything or anyone again."

"Is that why you turned away from me?" She began to kiss me while fondling my groin. She pressed her body against mine as she continued caressing me. I felt the cold, hard touch of her nipples against my skin. She kissed me with such intensity—

her tongue completely inside my mouth—that I couldn't think, couldn't breathe.

I pulled away. "I need to eat something. I'm hungry."

"Eat me for breakfast," Reiko replied, spreading her legs.

We spent the morning floating on waves of pleasure, under the watchful gaze of the trees and the temple pagoda beyond the window. I wished I could stay in that bed forever.

When we had both satisfied every last drop of desire, she started making scrambled eggs with spinach, while I sat on the sofa with a coffee. The summer sun had risen mercilessly over the city, and the cicadas sang with force. After putting the food on the table, Reiko took a sip of her coffee. "This is the second time you've fucked me without a condom," she said. "Aren't you afraid I'll get pregnant? This is reality, not a world full of virtual women. Your actions here have consequences."

"Aren't you on the pill?" I replied, surprised.

"I'd like to have a child with you," was her response. With that, as though the conversation was closed, she went to the piano. On top of it was a thin black briefcase. She opened it just enough to take out a folder, so I couldn't see what else was in there. She put the folder on the table and I read its title.

草薙の剣
The Kusanagi Sword
Confidential, Taira Corporation

"Masa has assigned us this mission," she said. "He wants us to work together. It's a great responsibility, but he trusts us."

I nodded.

"If we're going to do this together, I need you to promise me you won't be a coward."

"I promise."

She looked at me with seductive eyes, biting her lip. For a moment, I felt she could see the hidden fears in the depths of my soul.

37

THE TEMPLE WATCHER

We spent the morning reviewing the documents for Operation Kusanagi. Focused on analyzing those papers, Reiko seemed like a different person from the one who had possessed me in bed. The papers included several maps detailing the layout of the temple, as well as all details about the electrical installation, alarms and cameras. One diagram indicated the location where Masa's spies believed the sword was: a lacquered box on the altar of the *honden*, the main pavilion of the temple. I noticed that Reiko was chewing her lip more than usual.

"Are you nervous?" I asked.

"No, I've carried out many missions. I'm only worried about how to get past the Genji Corporation guards. Although, according to these documents, there's only three of them on night watch."

We were interrupted by the sound of the doorbell. It was Kamyu, carrying two black backpacks, one in each hand, as if they were supermarket bags.

"Hello, friends," he said, in his peculiar military monotone.

We sat around the temple maps, and Kamyu opened the backpacks. From them, he pulled out some black thermal suits, along with harnesses and two pistols.

I looked at the guns, alarmed.

"Don't worry, they're 9mm," he said. "If you aim for the

limbs, the wounds are not lethal." He took one of the pistols and aimed at my foot.

"How do you expect me not to worry? I don't even know how to shoot."

"You know jujutsu," said Kamyu.

Leaving the pistol on the table, he aimed a punch at my face, following the trajectory we had practiced in the dojo. Although I was unprepared, my reflexes kicked in and I was able to dodge it. Satisfied with my reaction, Kamyu's bionic eye blinked. "You're still in shape," he said.

"We'll only use the guns in case of emergency," said Reiko.

We spent hours reviewing every detail of the plans until night fell. It was time to set off. Reiko and I dressed in the thermal suits and we each placed a pistol in a holster hanging from our belts. We got into Kamyu's black car, and he drove us to the temple.

We parked among the zelkova trees surrounding the sacred grounds and got out of the car. The dim light of the moon cast an eerie halo on the damp mist that invaded every corner of the forest. A little bird flew out of a bush and landed on Kamyu's left shoulder. As he observed it with his bionic eye, he gave a slight smile, something I had never seen on the face of that always serious man.

We had planned to get inside the temple by climbing over a fence at the back monitored by only one camera, which was an old model and easy to disable.

Kamyu helped us adjust the harnesses over our thermal suits, and he threw two ropes over a bough of one of the zelkova trees that grew on the other side of the fence surrounding the temple. Reiko and I tied one end of each rope to hooks on our harnesses, and Kamyu proceeded to reel the other end into a pulley installed next to the car's bumper.

"Keep your spirits up and do your best," said Kamyu as he executed a bow.

He tapped the touchscreen of his watch, and the ropes began

to tighten until Reiko and I started to rise above the ground.

When we were high enough, we swung ourselves up to perch on top of the fence, just above the surveillance camera. Reiko pulled out a pair of pliers and wrenched open the padlock of a box next to the camera. With the circuitry in sight, she proceeded to cut two wires controlling the motion sensors. The next step was to disable the recording. I took a small camera from my backpack and Reiko plugged it into one of the free switches next to the surveillance camera she was operating. She then disabled a jumper on the PCB board so that only the first minute of recorded data would be shown, in a continuous loop. After a minute had passed, I opened an application on my phone that connected to the camera we had installed. I confirmed that our hack was consistently replaying the same minute.

We had a clear path to enter undetected.

Next, we slid down to land on the sacred ground. After unhooking the ropes from our harnesses, we found ourselves surrounded by graves. That confirmed we had entered through the cemetery, at the back of the temple. The humid summer mist wreathed the tombs like a veil. The six-story pagoda emerged through the thickness of the trees like part of the mountain's vegetation. Mist clung to the roof of the temple, giving it a ghostly aura.

A sudden rustling among the bushes surrounding the graves made every hair on my body stand on end. Reiko nudged me and whispered:

"Don't worry, it's a tanuki raccoon dog."

I looked through the bushes and could make out the outline of that strange animal. It looked like a giant, chubby weasel with tiny legs. Its eyes gleamed in the darkness as it moved slowly, sniffing the ground for fallen berries.

A crow perched on one of the graves seemed to give us a disapproving look.

Huddled behind a stone lantern, Reiko checked the maps loaded on her phone. According to the plan, to avoid triggering any motion sensors, we had to enter the main temple pavilion through a very narrow vent that only Reiko could fit into. We crept quickly and stealthily from one stone lantern to another, until we reached the back of the pavilion where the vent opening was. She slipped inside with feline agility.

Following the plan, I carried on alone, skirting the temple building until I reached a corner from where I could see the courtyard and the main entrance. The moon was high in the sky, illuminating the compound with its milky glow.

In the center of the garden, facing the temple's access stairs, a statue with a human silhouette stood out in the dim light. The crow cawed from the cemetery before flying to perch on the temple roof, directly above me. A slight gust of wind caused cedar leaves to fall. Some kind of big round seed also dropped from a tree, rolling down the stairs with a dry, rhythmic tapping.

Hidden under a low roof, I waited for Reiko to open a window from the inside. The air was so humid and thick it was hard to breathe. Sweat trickled down my forehead into my eyes, blurring my vision and making me feel that the statue was observing me.

The crow cawed again, as if warning me of something.

I took a step out of the shadow of the temple to get a better look at the statue watching over the courtyard. It seemed to me that one of the statue's arms had moved.

Was I still in Kyoto Mythos? I reached behind my ear and felt the small bump of the last remaining freckle.

Another gust of wind cleared the mist for a moment. It wasn't a statue, but one of Genji Corporation's guards. He was heading toward me. Several LEDs began to glow on his face, beneath his helmet. Without my thermal suit, he would have detected my presence earlier.

The crow cawed again several times, and the guard looked up at it.

I hid back in the shadow of the temple building. As I did so, I felt a hand on my shoulder and jumped in fright.

"Don't move," whispered Reiko's voice behind me, coming through an open window.

I reached for Reiko's hand, and despite the danger, her warm touch made me feel safe. With the other hand, I slid the window open wider and climbed through it to the temple interior.

We were in a tiny room barely the size of six tatami mats. The dim light of several candles revealed golden walls. Hanging on one wall was a painting of a phoenix flying toward the sky, escaping from a widespread fire below it. It made me think of my conversation with the phoenix Feng Huang in Kyoto Mythos about the power of time to destroy everything that has ever existed or will exist. I also remembered that Feng Huang had entrusted me with finding the Kusanagi sword.

With the dim candlelight at our backs, we cautiously advanced down a corridor with creaking floorboards. According to our maps, the door at the end of the corridor led to the main hall of the temple.

The door was locked with a padlock, something we had anticipated. Trying to control my nerves, I took bolt cutters from my backpack and, gritting my teeth, applied all my strength until the padlock broke. The noise reverberated inside the temple. When the echoes of the noise had died down, we opened the door cautiously. Just as our maps had shown us, a set of stairs led to a basement where the chest with the sword was located.

As we descended the stairs, we heard footsteps creaking on the wooden floor of the corridor we had just walked along. We wondered if the guard was coming to check the source of the unusual noises. We closed the door behind us, but it was impossible to put the padlock back in place from the inside.

Once in the basement, we made our way to the center of a room filled with bronze Buddhas. They all gazed toward a greenish chest resting on a small altar illuminated by candles. As I took a step toward the chest, I felt a chill. Irrational fear suddenly paralyzed me. The Buddhas seemed to be staring at me, judging what I was about to do, and even judging my entire life up to that moment. I found myself questioning was real and what was not.

I closed my eyes to escape those thoughts but then I was overwhelmed by a sense of panic and confusion that was almost physically painful. For a moment, I was tempted to collapse onto the tatami and give up. Then I felt Reiko's warm touch on my shoulder, her hand caressing the freckle behind my ear. I remembered her words: "Promise me you won't be a coward."

Gathering courage, I advanced toward the chest and opened it. There was the Kusanagi sword, lying on the velvet lining of the chest, covered in rust and imperfections after spending so much time at the bottom of the sea. At first glance, it didn't look like one of Japan's three most important treasures.

As I was about to grab it, I once again felt a mysterious force paralyzing me, maybe a kind of warning that I was about to desecrate something sacred, and that doing so would bring a terrible curse upon me. After a few seconds of hesitation, I pulled the sword out of the chest. With a triumphant gesture, I turned to show it to Reiko. To my surprise, she fell to her knees on the tatami like a dead weight, revealing the figure of the guard behind her. With one blow from his baton, he had knocked her out, and she lay unconscious on the tatami. The LEDs on his helmet pointed toward me.

Remembering Reiko's words—"We'll only use the guns in case of emergency"—I drew the 9mm with my free hand. But as soon as I did, the Genji guard struck my arm with the baton.

In pain, I dropped both the pistol and the sword, which fell onto the tatami beside Reiko's body.

I was left with only jujutsu to combat the adversary who was ready to subdue me, just as he had done with Reiko.

Without a second thought, I leaped to lift my legs in the air and executed a flying *juji gatame*. It was the first time I had used that hold in a real fight. It was a risky move, but it caught him by surprise. Wrapping my legs around him, I grabbed one of his arms and brought him down. I bent his arm, applying leverage until he began to scream in pain. Two more guards came running down the stairs. I left the first guard writhing on the floor, and crawled to retrieve my pistol.

Lying on the tatami, I shot at the foot of one of the two guards running toward me. The first shot missed, but the second hit its mark, causing him to fall to his knees.

Too late . . . The other one reached me and disarmed me with a blow.

With me on the ground and my enemy standing, I lost hope. The first guard I had taken down with the juji gatame had recovered and was also coming for me. On the stairs coming down to the basement, I saw the unmistakable light of Kamyu's bionic eye.

"Our savior," I thought.

Kamyu strangled one of the guards from behind. The other guard swung his baton toward Kamyu's ribs, but Kamyu managed to dodge it and counterattacked with a punch. The guard fell onto one of the statues.

After leaving the three of them practically incapacitated, I saw Kamyu swaying strangely. Moments later, he collapsed unconscious.

When I tried to get up, I realized it was impossible; my strength was leaving me, and I was short of breath. I realized too late that the guard I had shot had just thrown a gas bomb. They were protected by helmets, but we had no escape. With one last breath, my instinct led me to caress Reiko's arm with one hand, while gripping the Kusanagi sword with the other. I felt myself sinking with it into the depths of an abyss.

38
THE STORY OF THE SWORD
Ψ

I was awakened by a gentle nudge from Reiko. We were sitting on a leather sofa, and in front of us was a tray with green tea and a bowl of dried fruit. Through a glass window, dawn was breaking over Kyoto.

I was dizzy and still struggling to focus my vision due to the effects of the gas. A little beyond Reiko, sitting in a chair next to the sofa, I could see Kamyu.

I didn't know this room, but I knew we were on the west side of Kyoto because below us the Golden Pavilion glittered in the morning sun, which was beginning to rise behind the mountains where we had carried out our mission.

"Good job, guys," said a slim, middle-aged man behind us.

From Reiko's disdainful expression, I knew that this must be the person who had captured us after gassing us.

The man took a seat on the other side of the table with his back to the window. He wore a navy suit with a striped tie. On his wrist, I noticed a limited edition watch, designed years ago, that only a few millionaires had been able to afford.

"Dear Reiko, you'll never learn that Masa lacks style," he said, ignoring my presence.

"Well, maybe you have style, but you're an unscrupulous loudmouth."

"I find it ironic that you talk to me about scruples when you work for him. You broke into our temple to steal something that doesn't belong to you and you shot someone."

Our elegant captor lifted his teacup and, after the first sip, turned to me.

"Forgive me for not introducing myself, Nathan. I'm Roku, the CEO of Genji Corporation. My men offered you a job when you arrived in Kyoto, but you let that opportunity pass you by."

"I remember being attacked by your men and having to run out of the sushi restaurant," I replied. My mouth was dry and my eyes felt gritty.

"Sometimes we use unorthodox methods. Masa is allied with the government and the imperial house. We play at a disadvantage, so we have to resort to force and industrial espionage/ But it's you who started using guns." He smiled, making a playful gesture with his hands like a Wild West gunslinger. "Bang, bang!"

"We risked our lives to recover the Kusanagi sword, which belongs to Masa."

"Masa may have told you he rescued it from the bottom of the sea," he said, as one of his guards gave him a box. He opened it and extracted the sword with a theatrical gesture. "But it's a lie. Or a half-truth. That dog is always hiding information."

"I doubt you're an example of transparency. But tell me, what hasn't he told me?"

"He hasn't told you that the sword belonged to my family, the Genji, before it fell to the bottom of the sea. It all goes back to the same era that is simulated in Kyoto Mythos. This is where you will find the origins of what is now Taira Corporation and my company, Genji Corporation." Roku placed the sword on the table before continuing, with the calmness of someone who holds all the cards. "Japanese people don't make a huge effort to preserve buildings and monuments because of the frequency of earthquakes and tsunamis that destroy them—we have no choice but to rebuild them regularly. But we preserve history through family lineages, which are extremely important to us. In the past, Japan was divided into provinces controlled by feudal lords called daimyo. Each one protected their own province, and gradually they organized into clans that controlled several provinces. Over time, the daimyos have been replaced by private companies. The CEOs of the major corporations are the new daimyos of Japan."

"So you're saying that a Japanese company is an extension of the family?"

"Exactly, and you decided to sign with Taira Corporation. Whether you like it or not, you're now part of Masa's family."

"He pays me well."

Roku laughed scornfully.

"Do you also get paid well?" he asked, addressing Reiko and Kamyu.

"Go to hell," Reiko replied, sunk into the sofa, still looking sleepy.

"What a lovely mood your girlfriend is in," Roku said, turning to me.

Reiko leaned forward, fixing him with a firm stare, and said firmly, "I'm not his girlfriend."

I glanced at her out of the corner of my eye, and although it was true, I couldn't help but feel a pang.

Roku responded to Reiko with a slight smile, which I interpreted as a gesture of disdain.

"In 1180, an ancestor of Masa's, from the Taira family, became a government minister who was favored by the imperial family," he continued. "Using all his power and influence, he married his daughter to a member of the royal house, and managed to make his grandson, Antoku, the new emperor. As a result, the Taira family took control of the imperial treasury, including the Kusanagi sword," he said, pointing to the relic on the table. "As you can understand, my family, the Genji, didn't like this at all."

"Prince Genji! I know him," I said, feeling like a time traveler.

"It's because Masa is so obsessed with that era that he's created Kyoto Mythos. When your family took over the imperial house, the Genpei War began, in which the Genji fought against the Taira. This war marked a turning point in Japan's history, establishing the first *bakufu* military government in the city of Kamakura. This government had more power than the emperor. By the way, Kamakura is a beautiful place—you should visit. Anyway, in the naval battle of Dan-no-ura, which occurred in the last year of the Genpei War, your Taira family was defeated. Most of your family was on board one of the ships while the battle was taking place. Young Emperor Antoku, only six years old at the time, was taken in his grandmother's arms as she jumped overboard. They both drowned. This was preferable in the grandmother's eyes to facing the misfortune and dishonor that awaited them. The sword also sank, preventing it from being recovered by us, the Genji, the winners of the battle."

Roku leaned back in his chair, glancing sideways at Reiko, who was listening to us with a bored expression.

"The Genji sword spent centuries at the bottom of the sea until Masa came along, squandering his resources and exploiting his friendship with the current emperor to find and retrieve it. As you can understand, we had no choice but to take it back. Since we defeated you in the battle of Dan-no-ura, it belongs to us."

Definitely, something Masa and Roku shared was the tendency to tell endless stories. Moreover, they seemed to be obsessed with the same topics.

"So, to sum up, Masa lied to you. The Kusanagi sword originally belongs to us," Roku stated.

"It depends on how you define 'originally,'" I countered.

"At Genji Corporation, we've also launched our first general-purpose quantum computer," Roku said, ignoring my interjection. "Our own simulated world is in the testing phase. Of course, we also need the Kusanagi sword, and you, and the samsara gene you carry. If you work with us, we'll pay you twice as much as Masa does and give you shares in Genji Corporation. I can also offer you something more important than money," he said, standing up and coming to sit next to me on the sofa. "We have the technology to make your freckles grow back. I bet your greatest fear is that soon you'll have to decide whether to stay inside the virtual world and discard your biological body."

"He's lying," said Reiko. "Don't believe anything he says."

Roku put his hand on my head and pushed back the hair behind my ear. Kamyu made a move to stand up, as if to protect me, but one of the guards forced him to stay seated.

"You only have one freckle left, Nathan," Roku said.

"Don't listen to him, Nathan!" Reiko shouted.

The sword began to vibrate on the table, followed by a violent shaking of the room. Coffee cups fell to the floor, spilling liquid at our feet.

"Is it an earthquake?" I asked, frightened.

"No," Reiko said, smiling.

A rumble echoed through the building followed by several explosions. The door of the room crashed to the floor, and several men in military attire appeared. They wore the Taira Corporation logo on their uniforms. Roku stood up with a frustrated expression. He didn't seem scared. I had the feeling he might have experienced something similar before. Then came the characteristic faint squeak of Masa's wheelchair as he entered the room.

"We've come to reclaim what belongs to us," Masa announced. "The Genpei War is not over yet."

"You damned lying idealist," sneered Roku.

Amidst the confusion, Reiko grabbed the Kusanagi sword and brandished it in front of Roku's nose.

"You're not just a tramp, you're a rebel," Roku said, raising his hands and smiling sarcastically.

Kamyu lunged at one of Roku's guards, giving Reiko and me time to run over and position ourselves with Masa's men, where we were protected.

As we left the room following the wheelchair, several soldiers from Genji Corporation appeared through another door, ready to attack us.

"You're late, you useless good-for-nothings," Roku said.

"Kamyu!" I shouted as I watched him continue to struggle against the guard.

Several shots rang out, hitting Kamyu in the back. Blood stained his uniform red.

When Kamyu's bionic eye glanced at me one last time before he fell, it seemed like he was winking goodbye. I was filled with a sudden urge to kill the guards who had shot him. But before I could do anything, Reiko grabbed my sleeve.

"Damn it, don't let them escape!" Roku shouted. "We need Nathan alive. The rest, eliminate them!"

Masa's wheelchair rolled at full speed down the hallway, followed by me, by Reiko carrying the sword, and by all the Taira Corporation soldiers.

When we reached the end of the hallway, we exited through a hole in the wall that the Taira men had blown their way through, and jumped into a van with the Taira logo.

39
A TELEVISED TESTIMONY

I was back on the sofa, under Van Gogh's *Sunflowers*, in Masa's office. Sitting across from me, Reiko was absorbed in her phone, her legs stretched out casually, her heels brushing against the coffee table legs, suggesting she was completely relaxed, as if what had just happened hadn't affected her.

"Despite several setbacks, you did it, Nathan," said Masa. "The Kusanagi sword is already in the three-dimensional scanning room. Soon we'll have an exact replica in Kyoto Mythos."

"I couldn't have done it without Reiko and Kamyu," I pointed out, still not able to believe that Kamyu was no longer with us.

"Occupational hazards," said Masa, guessing from my sad expression what I was thinking. "Kamyu joins your father on the list of people who sacrificed their lives for a better future for humanity."

"I thought my father died in a fusion power plant accident."

"He did, and Kamyu's death was also an accident. We never want to lose lives. But when we do, I like to think their deaths aren't in vain." He caught his breath suddenly and clutched his chest in a gesture of pain. Seeing this, Reiko put her phone aside and got up to administer an injection into his arm.

Meanwhile, on the screen attached to his wheelchair, it read:

Expression of the samsara gene in Nathan: completed
to 97.4812 percent

"Your father would be proud of you," said Masa. "Many years have passed, but I still remember the day I promised him that you would be the first to reach a 100 percent expression of the samsara gene, and I have no intention of breaking that promise. Mia, Akira, and Murakami never surpassed 90 percent, but you're about to achieve it. Our masterpiece is almost complete."

I couldn't help but think that although he argued his work was for the future of humanity, maybe we were all disposable items whose sole purpose was to save Masa's life.

Next, we went out into the hallway, following the wheelchair, until we arrived at a room full of cameras, microphones, and green screens. Several employees who were bustling about paused when they saw us come in and bowed in our direction.

"We need to record your testimony, so that we can use it to promote Kyoto Mythos when it hits the market," said Masa.

"Damn it, Masa, I thought I was chief architect of Kyoto Mythos, not an actor in an advert," I grumbled, even though I had no choice but to do what he asked.

An assistant led me to a dressing room where a suit of samurai armor was waiting for me.

"Don't be nervous, we'll do as many takes as necessary," said the assistant as he wrapped me in tight white bands that seemed to serve as undergarments. "And, if you forget any words, we can digitally edit your voice and add whatever is missing." He pulled the underwear so tight it was hard for me to breathe.

Then the assistant proceeded to put each part of the armor on me: leg guards, breastplates, and giant shoulder pads with decorations on the edges. Finally, he fitted me with a helmet with crescent-shaped horns.

"I love reading history books," said the assistant. "I've always been curious about what it would be like to live in the past. I'm going to teach you a trick they used in ancient times." He adjusted a belt that secured the armor on the outside. "Look, the belt has slots to carry onigiri rice balls."

"Thank you, that will be useful when I walk the streets of

Heian," I said, nostalgically remembering the onigiri I had eaten with Kaori on the stairs in front of Feng Huang.

I left the dressing room walking with difficulty under the weight of forty pounds of armor. Facing the dazzling lights in the studio, I read the words that appeared on a teleprompter.

"I'm Nathan, one of the first users of Kyoto Mythos. After a little over eleven months living in that virtual world, I can assure you that it has undoubtedly been the best experience of my life. It's more than a virtual world. I would say it's a more powerful experience than real life. In Kyoto Mythos, I have felt more alive than ever. In less than a year, I have had adventures that I could never have dreamed of in the course of my boring earthly existence."

On several screens in front of me, I saw myself surrounded by locations from Kyoto Mythos. Some screens showed aerial views of the city; others showed close-ups of the prince's palace and Suzaku Avenue.

Next up was Masa, who had been silently observing me in front of another microphone. "At Taira Corporation, we believe in the power of artificial intelligence, but we're also aware of the great problem that companies like ours have created in society. Many of you are watching us from the comfort of your homes, which are equipped with the latest technology from Taira Corporation. Thanks to these advances, we have gained comfort and security, but to be happy, we need to feel useful. If we replace everything we do with robots and virtual characters, what will we dedicate our time to? We need to find meaning in life. To solve this major problem that affects us all, we have created Kyoto Mythos." At this point, Masa raised his voice to announce solemnly: "Welcome to a virtual world where you can have an eternal life that is full of purpose."

After Masa's thought-provoking words, my image appeared again on one of the screens, now next to the Rashomon gate and the two gigantic demon guardians. It was my turn again.

"In Kyoto Mythos, I am a time traveler. I have walked through the streets of ancient Kyoto, gazing upon the Rashomon gate, and I have even spoken with the demons that protect it. I have also met the legendary Prince Genji. In fact, his men captured me and held me prisoner in his palace. I have made friends and enemies. I have summoned the spirit of the phoenix, Feng Huang. I have a job: I am the architect of the Heian Clock Tower, something that has made me happy. I have understood deep within myself what it means to have a vital mission. Within Kyoto Mythos, I live in a wonderful house, the Cherry Blossom Villa, where I enjoy an eternal spring, waking up every morning to the sight of cherry blossoms in bloom. This virtual world has made me feel more alive than ever."

40
THE RETURN

hen we left the studio, we headed to the reception area on the top floor of the building. The ceiling rose in a dome shape and the glass walls let in the light of the setting sun, which tinted every corner with orange reflections. I felt as if I was flying over Kyoto. The clack clack of Reiko's heels signaled to the receptionist that we were passing by. We descended a few glass steps and Masa wheeled his chair down a ramp. We came to a door bearing a plaque that read:

Quantum Resolution 3D Scanning Room

Inside, we were greeted by a spherical-shaped scanning station large enough to fit a person inside. Next to this machine, several screens displayed the Kusanagi sword in different states. One showed only the three-dimensional mesh, and on other smaller screens, different parts were magnified. On another large screen separate from the others, you could see how the final appearance of the sword was being generated. On the bottom of the screen ran the text:

Kusanagi Sword - Scan and rendering: 97% complete

Reiko touched one of the screens and zoomed in on the hilt until a spiral with thousands of multicolored arms emerged.

"Do you see this fractal structure?" asked Reiko.

"It's beautiful," I said, amazed by what this seemingly simple sword concealed.

"I'm fascinated by geometric shapes that repeat infinitely," said Reiko, touching her tattoo of the infinity rope.

She let me touch the screen and zoom in on other areas. Hypnotized, I realized that I could enlarge the image practically infinitely. New patterns shaped like galaxies appeared again and again.

"When we finish scanning, the next step is for you to find the sword in Kyoto Mythos," Masa interrupted.

"Can't you tell me where it will appear in the simulation?" I asked. "That way, I could go straight for it and save time."

"It's not that we want to hide it from you," said Masa. "It's better if you find it yourself."

"It's done," Reiko said, pointing to the screen:

Kusanagi Sword - Scan and rendering: 100% complete

"Fabulous! We have all the pieces of the puzzle now," said Masa triumphantly. "Now, all that's left is for you to reenter Kyoto Mythos to put those final pieces together."

He made an effort to lift his head to look me in the eye. "Thank you, Nathan," he said, in an unfamiliar tone of sincerity. "See you soon."

Masa remained contemplating the Kusanagi sword, and Reiko and I headed toward the bathhouse.

As we approached, I remembered how hard it had been for me to enter Kyoto Mythos the first time. But I wasn't afraid anymore. On the contrary. For some reason, I longed to return to my life within the supposed unreality of ancient Heian. Perhaps it was because I simply wanted to evade my responsibilities in the real world, but whatever the reason, the world I was about to return to attracted me with the force of a lost paradise.

I wanted to complete my mission and see how the clock

hands moved, stroll with Kaori, and continue my adventures with Akira. And, of course, I longed for Mia to leave the prince's palace and return to Cherry Blossom Villa. Even if it was just to have tea together every morning while we listened to the birds chirping and the murmuring of the stream.

When we went into the room, illuminated by the spectral light of the bathtub, I saw Reiko biting her lip with a worried expression as she lowered her head. As I undressed, she averted her gaze.

"Are you crying?" I asked.

"No," she replied.

I caressed her cheek, feeling the dampness of her tears.

"Whatever you decide, I'll be waiting for you always," were her final words.

Without warning, she kissed me. It tasted like goodbye. It was the first time Reiko had kissed me without it being a prelude to ending up in bed. I stood there for a moment, trying to hold onto the sensation of her lips on mine.

I touched the last freckle behind my ear. Soon, I would have to make a decision.

I stepped into the bathtub, swallowing a 5-MeO-DMT pill. As I closed my eyes and floated on the fluorescent water, I felt the same prickling sensation as the first time, right next to the freckle. Seconds later, I lost all sense of my physical body. My consciousness emerged again in a shapeless universe.

Galaxy-shaped spirals began to surround me until vertigo made me fall through the center of one of them. This time, I didn't feel fear. I surrendered to that psychedelic journey, knowing that I couldn't control what was happening around me, but that in the end, everything would be fine.

41

THE TRUE NAME OF GOD
Ψ

My consciousness entered my naked body again. I found myself once more in the underground glass elevator. When I emerged above ground, it was night, and ominous clouds danced above the Rashomon gate, intermittently filtering the moonlight. I remembered that when I went through the gate for the first time, I had collapsed from exhaustion amidst the bloody corpses of several samurai. Now I felt stronger, familiar with the place and with the rules for survival. Yet, my legs still trembled as I climbed the stairs toward the gate—I couldn't tell if it was from excitement or fear.

As I approached, the two wooden demons stirred.

"You still haven't revealed the secret to us. Where do you come from?" said the one with the threatening, gaping mouth. They obviously hadn't forgotten me.

"There is no secret," I replied.

"Don't treat us like we're stupid, Nathan! We are demons," he said, making a grotesque gesture with his enormous mouth. "There are too many secrets weighing on your soul. If you tell us the one we want to hear, we will be helping you release some of the burden that is suffocating your happiness."

"I don't need you to help me be happy."

"Let me tell you a story." The voice came from the demon with the closed mouth, who had helped me go through the gate on my first arrival. He sat down, leaning against one of the gigantic columns on either side of the gate. Being naked in the middle of the night in front of those two beasts didn't feel great. I didn't want to listen to the story; I wanted to reach Cherry Blossom Villa as soon as possible. It was strange to have something resembling a home in that world of the past.

"Do you see those mounds?" said the beast, pointing to the base of one of the pillars supporting the gate's structure. I squinted in the dim light at what appeared to be piles of clothes. Just then, the clouds parted, allowing the ghostly moonlight to shine through.

"Those are corpses. Murderers come here to dump the bodies of their victims because they believe the Rashomon gate will absolve them of their guilt. Each wrongdoer comes with their own story: revenge, theft, betrayal . . . Each justifies their evil deed in a way, but all carry secrets in their hearts."

"Get on with it," the other demon muttered impatiently.

"Where was I? Ah, yes . . . An elderly woman worn down by life used to come here every day. She made a living by cutting the hair from corpses to make wigs. One day, a low-class man who had been expelled from his clan wandered through the wastelands you see behind you. He was so thin that when hunger allowed him to think, all he could think about was how to steal the things he needed to survive. The idea of stealing ate away at his soul every second, but his sense of honor kept him in check. He preferred to die of starvation than to commit a crime.

"Exhausted and on the verge of collapse, while wandering aimlessly through the southern wastelands, he saw the Rashomon gate on the horizon. As he approached, he saw the old woman cutting the hair from corpses and he was horrified. His disgust made him resolve more strongly that he would never be a thief. He confronted the old woman, but she told him she needed to do this job to feed herself. 'And,' the old woman said

241

looking at the corpse of the girl whose hair she was stealing, 'this particular girl hid a secret for most of her life. She deceived the inhabitants of Heian: she sold snake meat at a stall on Suzaku Avenue. She passed it off as fish.' The old woman remarked to the man that she didn't think badly of the girl who was doing what she needed to survive. But, following the wheel of karma, this allowed her, in turn, to cut off the girl's hair to avoid starving to death. Upon hearing that, the man lunged at the old woman and violently stripped her of her clothes, leaving her naked and trembling with cold. 'For the same reason,' he said, 'don't blame me for what I just did. Now I'll go and sell your clothes so I don't starve.'"

I looked toward the pile of corpses, imagining that terrifying scene, and I didn't know what to say.

"It's just one of the thousands of episodes my companion and I have witnessed while watching over this place. It shows that evil is transferred from heart to heart."

"It's human nature."

"When times become tough, people are capable of the greatest cruelty, even if it involves killing their friends."

"Come on, not everyone has it in them to behave like that."

"You're wrong, Nathan!" the beast exclaimed. "The hearts of human beings carry the seeds of evil. And when these seeds are fertilized by secrets, they keep growing and slowly corrupt our souls. How do you know if you're on the side of good or evil? Be careful. Masa is rotting your heart."

"Do you know Masa?" I asked, surprised.

"He has never been here. We can attest to that because we have guarded this gate since the beginning of time. Nevertheless, we know he exists somewhere."

I was plunged into thought. Theoretically, these demons were virtual characters. Could they be aware of Masa's existence without having met him? Maybe it was some kind of memory that Masa's ego had introduced into the demons' source code.

"Is this something you've known since birth?" I asked.

The other demon, who had been silent until then, let out a laugh that made the clouds in the night sky tremble.

Then he said, "Demons aren't born; we've existed since the beginning of time."

"We are the oldest beings in this place," the other interrupted. "That's why we know that the creator god believed in by all the inhabitants of Heian is not Pangu. His original name is Masa. I just revealed a secret that few know; meanwhile, you still haven't spilled a word."

"If all goes well, soon you will be able to meet your creator god Masa," I said, feeling close to those demons. "But I need you to let me into Heian."

The gesture of both abruptly changed. The more talkative demon stepped aside, while the other opened the large gate leading to the world where I was beginning to feel like a hero.

42
THE TITLE OF YOUR STORY
Ψ

I arrived at Cherry Blossom Villa when the moon had already dipped below the horizon and the first glow of dawn was carrying away the stars from the sky. I crossed the garden bridge and arrived at my ground floor room with the same relief I always felt when coming home after a long journey.

I went up to Murakami's room. I knocked on the door hesitantly, as the "Do not disturb" sign was still hanging. After a few seconds, he opened it with an expressionless face. He didn't seem pleased or displeased that I was visiting, as if my presence was the inevitable consequence of a divine plan. He was neatly groomed, fresh-faced, and dressed in the usual black attire.

A shaft of dawn light cast a warm glow over his desk with its piles of papers. The phoenix feather pen lay next to the inkwell.

"Sorry to bother you," I said.

"What do you want?"

"Do you ever leave this place?"

"I only leave when it's strictly necessary. If I stop writing, my ability to feel diminishes, along with my reason for existing. My body starts to become transparent. The only way for me to become solid again is by writing incessantly."

We sat on the tatami mat beside his desk.

"I just came back from the real world," I told him. "I was

aware that you were no longer next to me in the bathtub. I'm curious to know what it was like when you lost your physical body after your last freckle disappeared."

"I didn't even notice."

"I only have a few days left until my year is up, and I have to make the same decision that you did. Do you regret it? Do you miss reality?"

"This is my reality. Here I have everything I need to be happy. I haven't left anything or anyone behind." He lifted his face to watch a flock of birds flying across the dawn sky. "Actually, I was looking forward to the moment I could exist only in Kyoto Mythos. During that first year, it was difficult for me to exist in two realities at once. It's more comfortable to exist only in this one to focus on my mission: writing."

"But technically you're dead, like Mia and Akira."

"And are you alive, Nathan? Since when can the living talk to the dead?"

"For now, my physical body still exists in the real world." I spoke with confidence, but doubt suddenly gripped me. Had that last day in reality really happened as I remembered it? Now it felt like a dream: waking up in the bathtub, the night with Reiko in our house in the mountains east of Kyoto, the assault on the temple with Kamyu and Reiko to retrieve the Kusanagi sword, being captured by Roku's men, Masa's arrival to rescue us, Kamyu's death when he was shot, our escape and return to Taira Corporation offices to scan the sword, Reiko's last kiss before floating back in the bathtub, and then coming back to Kyoto Mythos, standing in front of the Rashomon gate.

"I guess I'm afraid that I'll miss the real world," I said.

"Will you miss the real world in general or will you miss something specific you'll leave behind? You've been in Kyoto Mythos for almost a year."

"There's someone I might miss," I said, thinking of Reiko.

"What you leave behind will stay with you as long as you don't forget. Uncertainty can rot even the bravest heart. Now you're like Schrödinger's cat," Murakami said. "You're straddling two realities, neither alive nor dead. Since my last freckle disappeared, I'm alive here and dead there. It's a release."

Looking toward his desk, I saw a scroll bearing the title:

The Master of Eternity and the Kusanagi Sword

"Have you changed the title of my story?" I asked.

"Choosing titles is the hardest part for me. What title would you give to your life? I had to keep changing and adapting the story as you made the decisions that would help you fulfill your mission."

"Is what I do here determined by what you've written? Did you know I would knock on your door today?"

"In part, yes. Remember, the plot lines I write are only possibilities—and I have to adapt what I write based on what you decide. It's like those *Choose Your Own Adventure* books. Plus, the quantum computer that simulates all this also influences what I write and what you decide."

"If you have the power to write what will happen in this reality, you're a kind of screenwriter for the gods."

"Don't give me so much importance," he said, flashing a sad smile. "In the strict sense of the word, it's not me who's writing. Haven't you ever heard what novelists say about their characters? Once created, they do as they please. My mission is to simply sit at the desk and let the stories be written through me. I'm a vessel. So, ultimately, I don't decide anything." He lifted his gaze to the blue sky, where a couple of solitary clouds drifted.

"I suppose I shouldn't read it," I said, as I traced a finger over the scroll.

"You're free to do as you please. But if you do, probabilities will turn into certainties, just as if you shot Schrödinger's cat. Do you really want to know what might happen in your future?"

"No, I guess I don't. For now, I just need to know where the Kusanagi sword is."

Murakami made a strange grimace, making me suspect he knew where the sword was but couldn't tell me to avoid altering the course of destiny.

"If you feel lonely, you know I'm downstairs, on the ground floor," I said, out of courtesy.

"Ah, loneliness . . . ," he said, with a sigh.

"I'll leave you to write the stories of this world. I hope they bring me a good future."

"You can only live through these stories if you stay with us. You don't have just one future, but many," he said, pointing to the scroll. "As Shakespeare said, 'Fate is the one that shuffles the cards, but we are the ones who play.'"

With that said, Murakami rose from the tatami and escorted me to the door. Before closing the door, he looked me in the eye.

"What exists and acts in the universe is alive and real. The cards are shuffled, now it's up to you to play them."

43

THE THREE SACRED TREASURES

The bullet train stopped in Tokyo early in the morning. Reiko stepped out of the carriage wearing a beige dress perfect for the occasion. Masa wore his best suit and was carrying an elongated briefcase. On the platform, a group of bodyguards was waiting, and escorted them through the station to the parking lot, where they got into a limousine. Masa and Reiko settled inside without speaking, each looking out of their own window, where the glass skyscrapers of the Marunouchi business district reflected on the tinted glass, as the car made its way through the streets of the capital.

The limousine entered a traffic-free tunnel. It moved slowly until it had to stop at a security checkpoint, marked by a guardhouse decorated with the chrysanthemum symbol of the imperial house.

After showing their faces to several cameras and being allowed through the checkpoint, they found themselves surrounded by a forest. They were at the Tokyo Imperial Palace. It no longer seemed like the center of the capital. The limousine advanced to a clearing where the forest gave way to gardens with pine trees whose foliage had been pruned to look like clouds.

They parked next to a modestly designed house displaying

none of the trappings of wealth or power, except for the imperial chrysanthemum symbol on the door. Some men in black suits opened the car doors and guided them inside the house. In the foyer, they parted ways: Reiko was escorted to the garden to have tea with the empress, and Masa was accompanied down another hallway. At this point, the entourage left him alone. He walked through a tunnel until he reached another building. Once there, he opened a door he was well acquainted with. There, in his study, was the emperor, sitting at a desk cluttered with papers, apparently absorbed in a book.

"Your Highness, the moment has come," said Masa.

"Did you manage to recover the sword stolen by our enemies, the Genji?" asked the emperor, abruptly, as he looked up, taking off his glasses.

"Of course. Everything is ready to create the new world."

"Thank you," he said, his voice trembling.

"As a loyal member of the Taira clan, it has always been a great honor to serve you."

The emperor stood up, opened a small door behind his desk, and they went into a windowless room with golden walls. The emperor tapped a light switch and three display cases lit up. The display case on the left held the Yata mirror; the one on the right, the Magatama pendant. The display case in the center was empty.

"We once again possess the three relics that have belonged to us for millennia," said the emperor solemnly.

With that, he proceeded to open the two display cases and carefully took out the relics for Masa to store in the elongated briefcase that housed the sword.

A couple of tears fell from Masa's eyes as he sealed the briefcase containing the three sacred treasures.

44

I WANT YOU TO BE MY PARENTS

Ψ

Back in my room, I slid open the screen doors to let the garden view adorn the morning. Gazing out at the cherry blossoms, I stretched on the tatami, and after warming up with push-ups and squats, I practiced jujutsu katas.

After the exercise, I lit a fire in the hearth, heated some water, and made myself some green tea. I drank my tea looking out over the garden, remembering the tea Mia had prepared for me the first morning I'd woken up here. I missed her, but I had the strange feeling she would soon return to be with me forever.

Contemplating the sun beginning to filter through the trees, I wondered if I was merely a vehicle for someone else's grand plan. After half a lifetime designing watches in my studio, a genetic modification made by Masa with my parents' permission had led me to this virtual world. I was about to set in motion the hands of the Clock Tower, which I had spent months building.

You can only live through these stories if you stay with us—
You don't have just one future, but many—
That which exists in the universe is alive and real—
The cards are shuffled, now it's up to you to play them—

Murakami's words echoed within me as I gazed at the cherry blossoms. Then suddenly I saw two figures emerging from the shadows of the forest where Akira's cabin was hidden. It was Kaori and Akira, and they were coming toward me. Even though I had only been away from that world for twenty-four hours, I felt like I had missed them. Kaori started to run, crossing the bridge and jumping into my arms to give me a hug.

"Where were you yesterday?" the little one asked. "You had me worried."

"On a journey. I went to find the sword," I replied.

"Where did you go?"

"To another reality."

"I want to travel too. I know every inch of this walled city, and I'm bored."

"When you're older."

"I'm already older!"

"Not old enough. There are many dangers outside Heian,"

"The real reason Nathan left us yesterday was to go and see one of his girlfriends," Akira said teasingly.

"I thought you were in love with Mia," said Kaori.

Akira pulled out two scrolls from the lapel of his jinbei. "You've got mail," he said. "It's from Su Song."

"Can I read it too?" Kaori asked excitedly.

After untying the ribbon of the first scroll, I spread it out on the tatami and we read it together:

Dear Master of Eternity

Thanks to you, the Clock Tower is now taller than the Rashomon gate and more beautiful than the emperor's palace. We are getting closer to fulfilling the prophecy. When the hands begin to move, the Clock Tower will mark time for the inhabitants of Heian. But for that, we still need to invoke Pangu.

Yesterday, I had a revealing dream.

In it, my late father appeared. He was so real that I thought he had come back to life. These are some of the words I managed to remember upon waking:

"Dear son, I miss you here, in the world of the dead. I had a vision in which I witnessed the Master of Eternity inside the prince's palace. He unsheathed a katana and aimed it at the Dragon's eyes. This act of defiance woke him up!

"Only by eliminating the Dragon will the Master of Eternity be able to obtain the Kusanagi sword and the Yata mirror.

"When he obtains the sacred sword, the Master of Eternity will have to use it along with the Magatama pendant and the Yata mirror to invoke our creator god, Pangu.

"If the Master of Eternity does not fulfill his mission, the Dragon will devour everything."

This is all I can remember from the dream.

Dear Master of Eternity, it is urgent that you come to the palace as soon as possible. The Dragon could appear at any moment.

Su Song

"The Dragon!" said Kaori, when she'd finished reading.
"I can't wait to see Nathan fighting the Dragon," Akira said.
"Nor can I!" Kaori chimed in.
I untied the ribbon of the second scroll.

Dear Nathan

Forgive my silence. I didn't consider it appropriate to intrude into your life while you were building the Clock Tower. Furthermore, after reading the letter Reiko sent me, I realized that your heart is in limbo. As I'm sure you understand, I don't take kindly to being a second choice.

Nevertheless, I can't help but think of you. My life in the palace goes on in peace and tranquility, but I must confess I miss you.

I have fond memories of when we read Mishima's The Sound of Waves *together as teenagers. Do you remember the ending, when Shinji saves the ship? It was only then that he became a true man.*

Even after all these years, I'm still waiting for your heroic act.

Mia

"Who is Reiko?" Kaori asked in her innocent tone.

"A girl," I replied.

"Can I meet her? Is she in love with you too?"

Akira smirked as he listened. He seemed to be enjoying the love interrogation.

"I don't know," I answered.

"Since you talked to me about love, I've seen Prince Genji several times in the palace. I've focused my gaze on him to see if I feel that force," said Kaori.

"And have you felt attracted to him?" I asked.

"Nothing at all," she replied disappointedly. "But I'll keep trying until I discover what love is."

I set the empty teacup on the wooden floor of the veranda and sighed. "I don't think I've ever fallen in love with someone I chose," I confessed. "I've always been attracted to girls who appeared in my life at the most unexpected moments."

"And you didn't choose Mia?" Kaori asked.

"No."

"Did she choose you?" she asked, surprised.

I tried to remember the moment I had opened the box that held Mia's photo. Had I chosen to lift the lid? And even before that, had I already decided on Mia? It was difficult for me to remember a chain of events that happened so long ago. When we were teenagers, we were good friends. We had fun reading novels, playing video games, and studying, but I couldn't remember the first time I felt attracted to her. Perhaps that's what love is, feeling comfortable with another person without knowing the reason.

"Is she in love with you?" Kaori insisted. "How do you know when someone truly loves you?"

"You never know. That's the mystery of love."

"Maybe you'll know when you're older," she said with a mischievous smile, standing up to get a teapot, which she placed over the fire in the hearth. Once it was hot enough I removed it from the heat and added a handful of green tea leaves from a lacquered jar. After a few minutes, the water turned green, and Akira served for the three of us.

"Kaori, you have to help us get into the prince's palace so Nathan can challenge the Dragon," Akira said.

"Of course!"

"But first, let's have a nice bowl of soba noodles," Akira said.

After finishing our tea, we walked across the garden and left the grounds of Cherry Blossom Villa. We headed north along Suzaku Avenue, which was crowded with people. Even after spending months in Kyoto Mythos, I was still fascinated by the thought that they were all virtual characters programmed to behave like inhabitants of Heian from the late twelfth century.

We turned down one of the alleys that led off the avenue and entered a tiny tavern. Several samurai with the Genji symbol on their uniforms were huddled in a corner over their steaming bowls of soba.

"Thank you for always coming here," said a cook dressed in rags, not taking his eyes off the long knife with which he was working. He moved the knife horizontally, a few millimeters each time, and then lowered it with quick and perfectly synchronized strokes that split the dough into noodles. Each cut resonated with a sharp and resounding "clack" on the wood.

"Give us the usual," said Akira.

Kaori and I followed him to a low table next to the only window in the place. Through it, at the end of the alley, we could see a vermilion bridge crossing the Kamogawa River.

When the bowls arrived, we began to slurp the noodles. They were delicious. The hot broth and the stuffiness of the place made beads of sweat appear on our foreheads.

"I want you to be my parents," said Kaori suddenly, looking up from her noodles.

I was speechless. She dropped the chopsticks on the table and stared at me, then at Akira, looking as if she was about to burst with joy.

"We're not serious enough people to—" Akira began jokingly.

Kaori grabbed him by the sleeve.

"Okay . . . but promise to be a good daughter and behave,"

"I promise!"

"Well, if that's what you want, we're officially nominated as your parents," I said.

"I finally have parents! Thank you, Dad and Dad!" Kaori jumped out of her seat and hugged us. Then she started dancing with joy on the tatami.

Seeing so much excitement over such a simple act brought a tear to my eye. Kaori was acting with more humanity than many people I had met in reality.

After finishing our bowls of soba, Akira ordered a large jar of plum liquor and poured a glass for each of us.

"We have to celebrate that we're family. A little won't hurt you," Akira said to Kaori.

After a timid sip, our officially adopted daughter made a disgusted face and rinsed her mouth with water. Then she started tucking into the plate of edamame beans we'd ordered. The liquor tasted excellent to me, so I quickly finished a second glass, although Akira, as usual, was ahead of me. By the time we left the place, Akira was staggering from drunkenness.

"What an example for your daughter," I joked.

"Yeeehaaaa!" said Akira, hanging onto my shoulder to steady

himself. It was amazing to me that such a drunkard could be the programmer of this virtual world. Kaori walked happily ahead of us, occasionally turning around to make sure we were following her.

After going down several deserted alleyways, we arrived at a dimly lit street that led to the north wall of Prince Genji's palace. There was an entrance guarded by two soldiers with the Genji symbol on their uniforms. Leaning against the door, they were chatting and drinking sake.

Kaori quickened her pace, leaving us behind, and started talking to them. As I dragged Akira's along, I saw Kaori take out a small flask from her backpack and pour drinks for the soldiers, who happily accepted the gift. After a couple of sips, the heads of those two faithful soldiers of Prince Genji started to nod. Seconds later, they slumped to the ground, fast asleep.

"Where did you learn that?" I asked Kaori, admiringly, as I reached the door.

"Playing video games in Akira's cabin," she proudly replied. "It's a sleeping potion."

Assuming my role as a father, I thought about lecturing her with a sermon along the lines that life was not like a video game, but I realized how absurd it would be to say that in a world whose rules were governed by a quantum computer.

I shook Akira, trying to get him to compose himself.

"Sharpen up, drunken Dad, we're going into the palace!" said Kaori.

"Thank you, daughter," said Akira. "As you can see, Nathan, I've raised her well."

Akira and I put on the armor of the two soldiers with the Genji insignia on the lapel and stored our clothes in Kaori's backpack. Then, we dragged the two unconscious bodies behind some bushes. Next, Kaori rummaged in her backpack and pulled out a bunch of keys. She tried them one by one until she opened the door.

The small door opened onto spacious gardens. Several paths

descended to converge in the center, where there were three ponds with lotus flowers. Passing the ponds, we went through deserted courtyards until we reached a pavilion supported by gigantic pillars. At first glance, there was no entrance door, but Kaori guided us through a small gap between the pavilion and another large wooden building.

We arrived at a doorway where the robed figure of a man emerged from the shadows and came toward us. Nervously, I adjusted the helmet of the uniform to hide my face. But thanks to our Genji armor, the man merely bowed when we crossed paths and continued on his way. We went inside the building and went stealthily down a hallway until we reached a set of sliding wooden doors. Kaori opened them just a crack, enough to peek at what was on the other side.

It was the gigantic tatami-covered hall where we had our audience with Prince Genji and Su Song the day Akira and I were captured by the Genji. Now it was empty.

"I'm going to tell the prince that you're here so he can get ready to receive you," Kaori said.

"Wait . . . we need katanas," said Akira, who finally seemed to have sobered up.

"Go down those stairs," Kaori whispered, pointing to a shadowy area of the hallway we had come from. "When you reach the bottom, turn right and enter the first door. I'll wait here."

In almost complete darkness, we began to grope our way down the stairs, feeling the walls with our hands. After going through the first door and closing it behind us, we were still in darkness. There was a damp smell and the air around us felt cool, giving the feeling of being in some kind of underground cave. After what felt like an endless time in the darkness, the flickering light of a candle became visible in the distance, like a beacon on a starless night.

45

THE UNDERWATER PALACE
Ψ

The candle flame seemed to float in the air toward us. As it came closer, we saw three figures behind it. First, the round and innocent face of Mia, then the bearded face of Su Song, and finally the small silhouette of Kaori.

"About time," Mia said.

"Well, that's rich, from someone who's just been sitting here in the palace while we were building the tower," said Akira.

Mia frowned. "You know what my role has been in this world so far."

"Making sure Nathan is in love with you without ever being able to see you?" Akira shot back.

With the flickering candle reflected in her pupils, Mia drew close to me. She stood on tiptoe and lifted her chin. When my lips brushed against hers, a shiver ran through my entire body.

She stepped back. "You're now ready for the final act, Nathan. Dying in reality isn't so bad. You will live here with me forever."

Faced with the unreality of the situation, with Akira and Su Song watching me, I couldn't process what was happening. Perhaps it was all part of the grand plan to activate my samsara gene at 100 percent. I didn't know what to say or how to react.

Su Song broke in. "At this point in the prophecy," he said, stroking his beard, "it is necessary for you to understand the nature of the passage of time. Have you understood what time is?"

"No."

"Time is the ether that is part of you and me. It is also the current that drags our existence toward its demise. But you are the Master of Eternity and, so, you are time and time is you."

"I still haven't finished understanding what it means to be the Master of Eternity," I admitted.

"When you leave behind the fear of life that has lingered since your father's death, you won't need to understand it. You will feel it. The great secret of existence is to live without fear."

Su Song always seemed to be much less human than Kaori. He seemed to be a simple automaton with little imagination who uttered preprogrammed phrases of apparent great wisdom. It was clear that Masa had instructed Akira to program this conversation to refer to the death of my father.

"When there is no fear left in your heart, Pangu will return to our world, invoked within you, and you will be able to manipulate space-time at will for all eternity. Nothing and no one will be more powerful than you. Pangu is everything, and everything is Pangu. The universe is Pangu and Pangu is the universe . . ."

Next, Su Song handed three katanas to Mia, Akira, and me. After securing them to our belts, we followed Mia through the cave illuminated by her candle. She led us through the lower levels of the palace, seeming to know them like the back of her hand. The scarce light made each corridor seem identical to the last. Finally, we began to see a glimmer of light that came closer and closer until we emerged into a garden. From there, we proceeded to climb some stairs that led to the tatami-matted chamber where Prince Genji held his audiences. The sliding screens that protected it from the outside were now fully open.

We went in. Prince Genji was seated on gold-embroidered cushions on a dais at the back of the chamber. Two lines of Genji samurai formed a pathway toward the dais, which we followed.

As we walked through the room I noticed the wall paintings adorned with gold details. Most were landscapes of rugged mountains and depictions of animals. Among them, I could identify two legendary beasts: the Phoenix and the Qilin.

I hadn't forgotten the prince's elegance, but I was once again impressed by how extremely handsome he was. Tall and strong, he had straight, shiny, chestnut hair. His intense gaze radiated light throughout the room.

When she reached the dais, Mia put the candle down and took my hand. Prince Genji stared at us, visibly offended.

"Hello, parents!" said Kaori in a casual tone to ease the tension as she descended from the dais.

"Parents?" said Mia, puzzled. "I didn't know you were a father, Nathan."

"Not technically . . ."

"But, yes, we are parents!" said Akira, proudly.

"Enough of this nonsense!" exclaimed Prince Genji. "You enter the palace without permission, intending to steal my future wife, and you don't even show respect?"

I bowed, and an arrogant smile lit up the prince's face. "I recognize your bravery, Nathan. Congratulations on building the tower. But remember our deal. Mia is still not yours. She remains my betrothed until the clock hands start moving."

I kept hold of Mia's hand. "Don't worry, we're about to activate the clock. But honestly, I'm tired of waiting and following orders."

"Separate them!" ordered the prince.

One of the samurai that had guided us through the room advanced toward us brandishing a katana. I stood in front of Mia to protect her. Seeing that I had no intention of letting ourselves be separated, the prince smiled disdainfully.

Then I drew my katana. The samurai backed away.

"How dare you defy me?" exclaimed Prince Genji. "Mia will stay by my side until you fulfill your part of the deal. Maybe then I'll forgive you for this little slip-up."

He gestured with his hand. "Guards!"

Immediately, the entire retinue of samurai broke ranks, making the floor tremble as they surrounded us. With no hope of defending myself, I sheathed my katana and surrendered. First they grabbed Mia, forcing her to climb onto the dais to sit on a cushion next to the prince. Next, they took the rest of my beloved companions in adventure to the side of the room and held them there, and I was left alone in the center of the chamber.

With a triumphant smile at having Mia by his side and me defenseless in front of him, the prince began to speak. "Let me tell you something . . ."

That way of starting a story, at the most inopportune moment, was surely the algorithm inside Prince Genji, the work of Masa.

"Do you see the Dragon?" he continued.

When I'd entered the room, I'd noticed the paintings of the Phoenix and the Qilin on the walls. When I looked at them again, I noticed that both sacred beasts were gazing up at the ceiling. I lifted my head and saw the Dragon staring at me with bulging eyes and threatening fangs. Its body was so elongated that it stretched across the entire ceiling of the room, coiling in spirals. It reminded me of the dragon adorning the dojo where I had trained with my sensei. I remembered my first encounter with Masa under Van Gogh's *Sunflowers*, when he spoke to me about the importance of art. The prince's personality, his way of speaking and acting, were undoubtedly Masa's.

The prince pointed at the giant fanged mouth of the Dragon. "That Dragon is the god Ryujin, one of the deities responsible for the creation of Japan, as well as the guardian of the seas. Ryujin was the great-grandfather of the first emperor, Jimmu. Therefore, I am one of his descendants. The blood of that Dragon runs through my veins. Ryujin had the power to transform into a human or a dragon at will. He could also live under the sea, so he decided to build an underwater palace called Ryu-gu-jo, where he lived with all his relatives and servants as well as with the sea creatures. Once upon a time, a man named Urashima Taro climbed onto the back of a sea turtle and it took him to the underwater palace. He spent three days there, eating and drinking surrounded by mermaids. Before leaving, the Dragon Ryujin gave Urashima Taro a tiny black box that fitted into the palm of his hand, telling him that he could never open it. Urashima Taro returned to the land with the help of the turtle, but when he arrived home, his family was gone, and everything had aged. When he asked the villagers, he realized horrified that during the three days he had been in the underwater palace, a hundred years had passed on the land. When Urashima Taro looked in the mirror, he was still a young man of twenty. Ignoring the Dragon's instructions, he opened the mysterious little box. When he looked in the mirror again, suddenly his face seemed to have aged eons. He was an old man, about to die."

The prince paused. "What do you think the moral of the story is, Nathan?"

I remained silent, as my thoughts raced through my head. What if Masa had planned everything that had happened to me since the moment I opened the box with Mia's photo? Or was the story of the Dragon Ryujin and the box that must never be opened just a coincidence?

The prince stepped down from the dais and walked solemnly toward where the guards were holding Su Song, Akira, and Kaori. With a swift movement, he pulled out a dagger hidden in his obi sash and plunged it into Kaori's abdomen.

Seeing her fall to the ground, I screamed in horror. "She was an innocent girl!" Kaori's blood formed a red puddle on the tatami. I felt faint with grief and fury.

The prince simply smiled.

46
THE CLIMACTIC MOMENT
Ψ

Masa decided that as part of the Kyoto Mythos advertising campaign, he would show the confrontation between Nathan and the Dragon by live streaming it on RealPeople.

In just a few minutes, after beginning with live images of Nathan talking to Prince Genji, it became the most-watched live stream in history. Millions of people glued to their screens from their sofas, watching this virtual recreation of Japan's past—a world to which they would soon have access.

Occasionally, a banner would appear at the bottom of the screen announcing a lottery to select the first thousand travelers to Kyoto Mythos:

Do you find your life in reality boring?
Do you want to be a hero in Japan's Heian era?
Would you like to live forever?

If you want to embark on adventures like Nathan's, we invite you to be one of the first thousand travelers to Kyoto Mythos. Participate in the draw by visiting *www.kyotomythos.com*

Anyone visiting kyotomythos.com would find this message on the home screen.

> Notice: To enter Kyoto Mythos, a medical procedure is required, which will be available at any Taira Corporation facility worldwide. You will be injected with a gene that will allow you to connect to Kyoto Mythos. Due to the technical limitations of the system, you can only connect and disconnect from Kyoto Mythos for twelve months. After the time limit, you will have to choose if you want to die in the real world but continue living in Kyoto Mythos. For more information, please contact our customer service.

Masa relished in his successful launch of Kyoto Mythos as he prepared for his own entry into this virtual world he had created. He was eager to free himself from a body that was being consumed by degenerative disease. Reiko, Masa, the director of quantum computing, the director of biotechnology, and several technicians gathered in the control room of Taira Corporation, eagerly awaiting the peak moment of Nathan's samsara gene expression.

The live stream being shown on the main screen in the room was no longer just about an internal project; this was something that was now open to the entire world. Nathan was taking a defiant step toward Prince Genji.

"Once you connect, the twelve freckles will appear behind your ear," said the director of quantum computing to Masa. "Technically, we could keep your body alive for a year, it all depends on how your condition evolves . . ."

Masa checked the screen on his wheelchair, looking at the indicator of the probability of dying in the next year, based on his health condition. The marker showed that the probability was higher than ever.

"Why bother? The chances of my heart continuing to beat

are extremely low. This disease has consumed every minute of my existence. Finally, I'll be able to escape. I don't want to come back here."

"Is it your wish, then, that we should remove your body immediately?" said the director, hesitantly.

"Of course," replied Masa. "I've been preparing for this moment for decades; I have no intention of leaving anything behind in this world."

"And so what do you want us to do with your body?" asked Reiko.

"I want a Buddhist funeral, of course. Make sure you invite the emperor and all the international media. I want the funeral not to be a celebration of my death, but of my rebirth in Kyoto Mythos. I want to be remembered as the creator of a new world whose inhabitants can live forever. People can laugh and celebrate at my funeral because I'm going to an infinitely better place. And many will follow me . . . Dying will cease to be something sad!"

A technician typed on a command line, and several strings of DNA illuminated the screen in different colors. On another monitor, a message flashed up:

Samsara gene expression:
Completed to 99.7391%

"We are very close," said the director of biotechnology, as he studied the monitor carefully. "We just need to identify a few thousand more interactions within Nathan's body with the samsara gene to understand its expression at 100 percent and insert it into your body along with the appropriate chemical cocktails."

"Perfect!" said Masa.

"Just one last heroic act from Nathan."

They returned their attention to what the Master of Eternity was doing in Kyoto Mythos. The number of people watching the live stream through RealPeople continued to rise, surpassing one hundred million.

Nathan took another step forward, ready to draw his katana. "You've finally stopped being a coward," Reiko thought, her heart pounding.

A smile appeared on Masa's face.

47

THE BATTLE AGAINST THE DRAGON

Ψ

The prince had no scruples. He had just killed Kaori and now took a step forward toward Su Song and Akira, clasping the bloody dagger in his hand. With an expression of complete terror on her face, Mia watched the scene from the dais.

"Remember what my father told me when I dreamed of him." Su Song shouted.

"A katana pointing at the Dragon's eyes," I said to myself, remembering the words of Su Song's letter that I had read that same morning.

I unsheathed the katana and brandished it above my head, aiming it in the direction of the painting of the Dragon on the ceiling. This act caused everything around me to suddenly freeze. Prince Genji became a statue. The soldiers, Su Song, Akira, and Mia were also paralyzed, as if they had been transformed into figures of clay. The flame of the candle Mia had been carrying had also stopped moving. Through the windows, the sun was now more than a round, flat orb, while several lonely clouds and a few birds seemed to be painted elements of the landscape. The execution of Kyoto Mythos on the quantum computer seemed to be on pause, and I was the only conscious being in that place.

I felt a strange liberation, as though the thousands of pieces that had composed my life up to that moment had agreed to fit perfectly. Suddenly, I wasn't so concerned about my past as I was about my future. The chains that bound my existence to time seemed to have been broken.

All the same, I didn't want to be trapped in that eternal moment. What would life be like in solitude, where the past and future lost their meaning, existing only in a never-ending present moment?

I noticed a tear running down my cheek.

Although the soldiers were unable to move, I couldn't shake the feeling that they were still watching me. I took a step past the frozen figure of Genji toward the dais where Mia was sitting, paralyzed.

As I passed the prince, it seemed as though he was starting to emerge from his frozen state. His eyes were beginning to grow, his face was quivering, and strange lumps and bumps were appearing on his cheeks. Moving as fast as I could, I climbed onto the dais where I took Mia in my arms and carried her to a corner of the room as far away as possible from the threat of the mutant prince. I lay her on a tatami mat.

Meanwhile, the prince's arms swelled like clogged hoses, making his sleeves rip. He opened his mouth to free the long fangs that had suddenly grown there. Thick, pulsating veins now covered his chest and belly, visible through the shreds of his clothes, while his bloodshot eyes were so large and bulging that it seemed as though they would pop out of their sockets at any moment. His nostrils flared, bull-like. A roar shook the columns of the building, as a long tail emerged from his back, and his limbs turned into claws. His head was now larger than a horse's.

Fully transformed into a giant Dragon, the creature's limbs could no longer be contained inside the room and they crashed through the windows into the garden, while its body still stood in the room, tail thrashing.

Tightly gripping the hilt of my katana, I brandished it to provoke the Dragon. Faced with this threat, it stopped to observe me with curiosity, like a child reveling in the fragility of an ant before crushing it. I was about to fulfill my mission. Surely, after finishing the three-dimensional scan of the Kusanagi Sword and introducing the model into the simulation, Masa would have hidden it in the Dragon's tail. The letter Su Song had read to me that morning also fueled my suspicions. Once I had the sword in my possession, I would recreate the legend of Susanoo that had been told to me.

The only problem left to solve was how to bring down that immense creature.

The Dragon stretched its neck and, with a quick movement, advanced until its snout was three feet away from me. It continued to watch me as if deciding how best to deal with me. I took a deep breath and raised my katana again. The beast opened its mouth and roared, displaying its fangs, as though ready to devour me. It lunged toward me, but I dropped with a *mai mawari ukemi* forward roll—a technique I had practiced in jujutsu—and ran to hide behind a column for protection.

It charged against the column I was hiding behind, smashing it and causing the structure of the building to tremble. As shards of splintered wood rained down on me, I jumped on to the Dragon's tail, ran along it until I reached one of the pointed scales on his back, then grabbing the scale, swung myself out of the window into the garden.

The Dragon's tail crashed through the window behind me, extending to reach a pond covered with lotus flowers like a Monet painting. A thunderous noise behind me made me turn, and I saw that the colossal head of the beast had smashed through the wooden wall, while its claws tore open a hole large enough for its whole body to exit. It swung its tail, ready to crush me like an insect. I jumped out of its path and rolled toward the tip of its tail, jumped up again and raised my sword. Before I knew what was happening, a giant claw descended toward me and I felt a piercing pain in my side. I fell to my knees, blood pouring onto the ground around me.

There was so much adrenaline inside me that, rather than pain, I only felt dizziness and confusion. This was followed by an explosion of energy. I managed to crawl toward the tip of the tail and plunged the sword into the flesh of that mythological creature. The Dragon fell, writhing in pain with serpentine movements. Using all of my remaining strength, I staggered toward the Dragon's head, raised the katana with both hands and thrust the blade into its throat.

The Dragon's body gave a great shudder, and its eyelids gradually closed. Like bubbles emerging from the bottom of a lake, three objects stained with blood were visible beneath the wounds to the Dragon's tail: a sword, a mirror, and a strange spherical object.

First, I grabbed the sword—the Kusanagi sword—the most important thing of all.

Second, I took the mysterious pulsating sphere with my hands, and in the pond, I cleaned the blood covering it. It was dark, yet transparent, and inside it, shapes shifted and mutated as I moved it. In the center, I thought I saw an eye that grew until it filled the entire sphere.

I realized it was my father's eye.

"Good job, I'm very proud of you," I seemed to hear him say. "My son, to complete our liberation, you only need to pierce through me . . ."

I left the sphere on the ground and wielded the katana again. As I pierced through the sphere containing my father's gaze, I felt the same terrible pain as when I had stabbed the needle in my eye to leave Kyoto Mythos. The broken sphere rolled away in fits and starts until it sank into the darkness of the pond.

Third, I took the Yata mirror, and last, I confirmed with my fingers that the Magatama pendant still hung around my neck.

I now possessed the Three Sacred Treasures. I was overcome by sudden dizziness. As my vision began to blur, I looked toward the Clock Tower and saw the hands beginning to move. Blood continued to gush from my side, and my adrenaline rush subsided, until I lost consciousness beside the Dragon's inert body.

48

SAMSARA GENE EXPRESSION: COMPLETED TO 100 PERCENT

Millions of people watched the live stream of events in Kyoto Mythos from the comfort of their homes. They had just witnessed the exciting climax where the Master of Eternity had defeated the Dragon. When Nathan fell, they fell silent, wondering if he was dead.

Then suddenly, the world of Kyoto Mythos ceased to be frozen. Birds began to fly, and clouds started to move. Mia appeared on screen, running to the garden to help Nathan.

Meanwhile, the monitors in the Taira Corporation control room read:

Samsara gene expression:
completed at 100%

Masa felt so much joy that he could almost feel himself rising from his wheelchair. "The time has come to leave the world of mortals!" Masa declared, his voice trembling with emotion. "I will no longer have to suffer any more pain, trapped in this body that is so close to death." Reiko stroked his hand, and Masa looked into her eyes. "It's a shame you don't want to come with us. I leave you in charge of this world."

She bit her lip.

Next, several assistants helped Masa undress and enter a bathtub filled with Epsom salts, just like the one Nathan had used.

Now that they had all the information they needed about the samsara gene, the director of biotechnology sent her technicians to prepare the final recipe for the maximum expression of samsara, so that this could be injected into Masa. Robotic arms sprang into action, hastily manipulating test tubes. Once finished, a technician injected the mixture into Masa's arm. The reaction was so rapid that the circle of twelve freckles appeared immediately behind his ear, indicating that he could enter Kyoto Mythos.

"Remember my wish: dispose of my body as soon as I enter my world." Those were Masa's final words.

Reiko leaned over the bathtub one last time and placed a 5-MeO-DMT pill on the lips of the person she had loved.

The director of quantum computing typed:

```
assert(imperialtreasure.magatama);
assert(imperialtreasure.kusanagi);
assert(imperialtreasure.yata);
assert(clocktower.running);
assert(herooftime.samsara);
kyotoMythos.betaVersion.terminate();
kyotoMythos.firstVersion.initialize(imperial treasure,clocktower, herooftime);
kyotoMythos.firstVersion.start(«The Age of Eternity»);
```

On the screens of all live stream viewers, a final message was displayed:

The beta version of Kyoto Mythos, previously available only to a select few, has ended. Nathan has sacrificed himself for us. Masa, our founder, the CEO of Taira Corporation, and the creator of this new world, has just entered Kyoto Mythos. Kyoto Mythos 1.0 is now active and is available to everyone. Welcome to the Era of Eternity. More information on leaving the present reality and living in the world of eternity is available at: *www.kyotomythos.com*

49

THE VITAL CHOICE
Ψ

During my state of collapse after my victory over the Dragon I had the sense that my consciousness freed itself from my body, allowing me to observe myself. My consciousness drifted away toward the sky, floating like a hot air balloon. My body lay on the ground, next to the sacred treasures and the Dragon, growing more distant. Next, I saw the palace from my bird's eye view and the city enclosed within the rectangular walls.

From there, I watched Mia run toward my lifeless body. Seeing her move reassured me; time had returned to Kyoto Mythos. Far below me, on the southern wall, stood the majestic Rashomon gate. In front of it was the Clock Tower, whose hands, I knew, were marking the passage of time.

Gradually, everything faded from view and I was suspended in darkness for seconds, minutes, or hours. I had no way of knowing. All I knew was that after a long time, or maybe a short time, I felt my eyelids slowly open. I found myself in a leather armchair in a room with marble floors. In front of me were Masa and Murakami.

"Consciousness is what emerges from the struggle between chaos and order," said Murakami.

"Let's leave the philosophy for another time," said Masa,

smiling. "Everything has gone according to plan, Nathan. Thank you for your services."

"I don't like dragons," Murakami said. "They seem childish. It was Masa's idea."

"The Dragon was necessary for the expression of the samsara gene to reach 100 percent," Masa replied.

"Oh, science . . ." said Murakami dryly.

I sat up. My mouth was parched and my body numb. I reached with a trembling hand for a glass of water from a near-by table and drank it in a couple of gulps.

Then I managed to utter my first words. "Are we in reality?"

"Of course not! Murakami is here with us, and look at me, I can walk!" Masa exclaimed, jumping from his chair. "Thanks to you, son, I'm finally here, with you!"

"Where are we?" I said. "This doesn't seem like Heian."

"I designed this modern house for myself. Even though I love the world of the past, I didn't want to give up the comforts of the future. From this house, I will oversee this universe."

Masa smiled and, using his new ability to walk, went to open the curtains hiding a large window. Seeing trees outside, I deduced that we were in a building hidden in the forest, on top of a mountain. Through the vegetation, I could glimpse the walled city of Heian, the Rashomon gate, and beyond it, my creation, the Clock Tower, whose hands continued to turn.

"And me . . . how much time do I have left? Is my body still floating in the bathtub?" I asked.

"Are you still undecided? Are you afraid of death? Or rather, of removing your biological body?" he said. "You are the Master of Eternity, the only one who could kill the Dragon to open the doors to samsara. You have saved humanity! Thank you for freeing me from my decaying and mortal body! But, of course, the decision is yours."

"How much time do I have left?" I reiterated.

"I'm afraid there's barely an hour left until your last freckle disappears."

I was relieved to know that even though time was short, I still had a body, that I was still alive floating in the bathtub, and that I could choose.

Murakami sat up from his seat. "How do you want to end this story?"

"My dear son, seldom does a character have the opportunity to meet his creators and decide his fate," Masa intervened.

"What options do I have?"

"Your first option is to return to reality and continue with your boring life as a watch designer. Once your last freckle is gone, you can never come back here; your body will no longer accept samsara. For some reason unknown to us, it is not possible to repeat the process once those first twelve freckles disappear."

"In my last encounter with Roku," I said, "he told me that Genji Corporation had the necessary technology to create an indefinite extension of connection time, without being forced to discard our bodies in reality."

A contemptuous smile crossed Masa's lips. "Do you still believe Roku's lies at this stage? Genji Corporation is a company full of spies who only copy what we do and lack original technology. Believe me, we have been researching this for decades. The limit imposed by the twelve freckles is unchangeable."

He lowered his voice to a whisper. "I suspect Reiko is waiting for you in reality."

At that moment, Akira entered the room and exclaimed, "You're a genius, Nathan, a damn hero. You killed the Dragon. It's time to celebrate the victory!"

He held a bottle of sake in his hands and a black case bearing the Taira symbol. He opened it in front of me, revealing the gold needle I had used to stab myself in the eye so that I could leave Kyoto Mythos.

"If you stab yourself again with this needle, you know what will happen," said Masa. "Your other option is to stay. If you wish, you can continue working with our team to build this world. I have big plans to recreate other cities from the past, and your experience in erecting the Clock Tower will be of great help. Your biological heart, which still beats in the body floating in the bathtub, will stop. But your virtual heart will beat here eternally. You will live with me, with Murakami, Akira, Mia, and Kaori, forever."

"Kaori . . . ?"

"Of course, we have resurrected Kaori," said Masa. You didn't think she had really died, did you?"

I gave a sigh, letting relief course through my body.

"Where are Mia and Kaori?" I asked.

"They're waiting for you at Cherry Blossom Villa," said Akira, Masa, and Murakami in unison.

I looked away from the black case with the gold needle to gaze at Heian through the window. I followed the line of Suzaku Avenue until I spotted the green strip of the Cherry Blossom Villa garden. I thought about Mia, waiting for me there. I remembered her kiss in the darkness of the caves beneath the palace.

"The choice is yours," said Masa.

50
REIKO'S LETTER

Reiko sat by the window overlooking Kyoto in the house that was now hers. Nathan had been with her in that house only briefly, but the place was filled with the memories of their time together.

Although she knew she shouldn't, she couldn't resist the temptation to pour herself a glass of wine. Without any desire to look at a screen, she grabbed a piece of paper and began to write a letter. She intended to scan it and send it via RealPeople to Nathan in Kyoto Mythos.

Dear Nathan

I've always been clear that when the time comes for me to die, I will accept it. Having a finite life seems the most human thing to me. But I must confess that you made me doubt this belief. Not having you in this world is painful for me, and I even seriously considered a life with you in Kyoto Mythos forever.

When I saw that you chose her, my doubt faded away, and I accepted that you had made the decision that was right for you.

My mother sacrificed her life and suffered a lot because of my father; her departure was a relief. Perhaps that's why I've always been afraid to open my heart until

*you came along. The irony is that, like my mother, I am
left alone, but not because I wanted to be.*

I am alone with our child, who will be born soon.

*I am pregnant by you, Nathan. That last time we
made love . . .*

What name do you want to give our son?

*We barely spent time together, but I feel like you are
the person I know best.*

I miss you.

Reiko

After finishing the letter, she took a sip of wine and let the
warmth of the alcohol spread through her. She would never
send the letter. She didn't want Nathan to suffer knowing that
he had left a child behind. It would be her secret.

As a tear slid down her cheek, she took another sip of wine
and tore the letter into little pieces.

51
THE GARDEN OF ETERNITY
Ψ

T he only thing marking the passage of time was the Clock Tower. But what sense did it make if the seasons didn't change? Living in eternal spring was strange, but little by little, I got used to it.

Mia and I didn't age, and the passage of hours blurred into days, months and years.

Beyond the confines of Cherry Blossom Villa, the city had filled with humans in whom the samsara gene had been inserted, and now they lived in Kyoto Mythos. That simulated Heian was no longer the same as when Akira, Murakami, Mia, and I had been the only humans, and the others were virtual characters. It had become a medieval amusement park where many had the chance to have a second life.

Although now that we had the Clock Tower, candles were no longer needed to measure time, Kaori and I still carried out the candle-changing ritual every day and the greeting of the legendary beasts. Our life in the villa was pure happiness. At the end of each day, Kaori enjoyed playing retro video games in Akira's cabin. Meanwhile, Mia and I made love in the light of the sunset until Kaori and Akira returned, and then we all had dinner by candlelight.

As she had done with Akira and me, Kaori expressed her

desire for Mia to officially be her mother, and she accepted. We were an unconventional but happy family.

Not long after I'd made the vital choice to stay in Kyoto Mythos forever, Mia and I were drinking green tea under the cherry trees, surrounded by blackbirds pecking at the grass at our feet.

"Why did you choose me?" Mia suddenly asked.

"I suppose I wanted to know what happened in the end. Can you stop watching a good movie when you're only halfway through?"

"Was it because you love me?"

"Yes. I love you."

Mia fell silent as she scanned the garden in its endless spring.

"Are those tears?"

"No . . ."

She turned away for a moment, and, once composed, she looked at me with shining eyes.

"Forgive me, Nathan, there's something I want to confess to you. A secret we've hidden from you until now. Something I was always afraid to tell you, and never dared to . . ."

I stroked her hands.

She swallowed, took a breath. "Even if you hate me for all eternity, I need you to know . . ."

"I could never hate you."

"You and I never met in reality."

"What? What about our adventures in high school, when we studied for exams, the novels we read together . . . ?" I suddenly found it hard to breathe. Mia took my hand and squeezed it gently.

"It was an illusion—memories implanted in you, like dreams. I never went to class with you, never helped you study, nor were we friends. All those memories were made up by Masa. With your father's permission, they implanted those memories in your mind through the circle of twelve freckles. You know they were the reason you dreamed of the Rashomon gate. All your memories of me are nothing more than dreams that were used to create your past reality."

"Are you telling me you're just a dream made real in a virtual world . . . ? What about that photograph of us sitting together on the sofa that I found in the box when I was cleaning my studio?"

"When you found that photo, what you thought was a memory was just a snapshot that had been digitally generated by Taira Corporation's computers. It served to initiate the entire sequence of events that brought you here, to my side."

"And who put the fake photograph in the box? Did someone from Taira Corporation break into my studio?"

"I don't know. Masa didn't tell me the details."

I felt both betrayed and confused.

"Can you forgive me?" asked Mia. "Everything has been for the good of humanity, and as a result, we also have this happy life."

"I forgive you," I managed to say, before lying back on the grass, still in shock. I closed my eyes, wondering for a moment if I'd find myself somewhere else when I opened them. But I knew that wouldn't happen. I didn't have another world to wake up to anymore.

"Do you think now that you know all this, you'll be able to carry on being with me?" Mia's voice trembled as she spoke. "Can someone love a dream eternally?"

I opened my eyes. A gust of wind shook the trees, causing a cloud of cherry blossom petals to fall on us.

"Of course I'll always be with you. You're a dream come true. For me, you're the realest thing there is."

EPILOGUE

Since Murakami moved to live with Masa in the modern house hidden in the mountains, I have inherited his desk on the second floor of Cherry Blossom Villa.

All stories have protagonists and readers.

Yes, I mean you, reading me from whichever universe and moment you exist in.

Who is writing your story?

Who will tell it in the future?

Who are you really?

Are you sure you are human?

As I'm writing this, I stop now and then to lift my gaze from my desk and contemplate the view of the garden through the window in front of me. I can see birds flying across a background of blue sky and cherry trees in full bloom.

What's your view like?

When I observe the sky reflected in the stream that runs through this garden, I feel that this garden is the universe that contains my family and my happiness. If I admire the beauty of the landscape with enough attention, I can hold eternity in the present.

Like me, you have the power to decide the storyline of your existence.

What do you want to be?

What adventure do you want to turn your life into?

When you close this book, you will have to decide if you want to continue living in the same reality or if you dare to make your dream come true.

To see a World in a Grain of Sand
And a Heaven in a Wild Flower
Hold Infinity in the palm of your hand
And Eternity in an hour.

—William Blake

"Books to Span the East and West"

Tuttle Publishing was founded in 1832 in the small New England town of Rutland, Vermont [USA]. Our core values remain as strong today as they were then—to publish best-in-class books which bring people together one page at a time. In 1948, we established a publishing outpost in Japan—and Tuttle is now a leader in publishing English-language books about the arts, languages and cultures of Asia. The world has become a much smaller place today and Asia's economic and cultural influence has grown. Yet the need for meaningful dialogue and information about this diverse region has never been greater. Over the past seven decades, Tuttle has published thousands of books on subjects ranging from martial arts and paper crafts to language learning and literature—and our talented authors, illustrators, designers and photographers have won many prestigious awards. We welcome you to explore the wealth of information available on Asia at **www.tuttlepublishing.com.**

Published by Tuttle Publishing, an imprint of Periplus Editions (HK) Ltd.
www.tuttlepublishing.com

LA ERA DE LA ETERNIDAD © 2021 Héctor García and Francesc Miralles. Translation rights arranged by Sandra Bruna Agencia Literaria, SL.

English translation ©2025 Héctor García

Interior illustrations from Shutterstock, Free PNG and Wikimedia Commons.

ISBN 978-4-8053-1910-9

28 27 26 25   4 3 2 1   2504TP
Printed in Singapore

TUTTLE PUBLISHING® is a registered trademark of Tuttle Publishing, a division of Periplus Editions (HK) Ltd.

Distributed by:

North America, Latin America & Europe
Tuttle Publishing
364 Innovation Drive
North Clarendon
VT 05759-9436 U.S.A.
Tel: 1 (802) 773-8930
Fax: 1 (802) 773-6993
info@tuttlepublishing.com
www.tuttlepublishing.com

Asia Pacific
Berkeley Books Pte. Ltd.
3 Kallang Sector #04-01
Singapore 349278
Tel: (65) 6741 2178
Fax: (65) 6741 2179
inquiries@periplus.com.sg
www.tuttlepublishing.com

Japan
Tuttle Publishing
Yaekari Building, 3rd Floor
5-4-12 Osaki Shinagawa-ku
Tokyo 141 0032
Tel: (81) 3 5437-0171
Fax: (81) 3 5437-0755
sales@tuttle.co.jp; www.tuttle.co.jp